THE TERRORS

Brian K. Morris

RISING TIDE Publications

Editor: Cookie Morris
Production/Interior Formatting: RT Editorial Services
Cover: Jeffrey Hayes of Plasmafire Graphics (www.plasmafiregraphics.com)

Loosely based on characters created by Richard E. Hughes, Don Gabrielson, Will Eisner, Charles Nicholas Wojtkowski, and Norman A. Daniels, along with Kellie Austin, Clyde Hall, Jeffrey Hayes, Cindy Koepp, and Brian K. Morris.

Special thanks to Karl Witsman for cigar consultation.

Rising Tide Publications
Lafayette, Indiana
www.RisingTide.pub

Please consider leaving us an honest review on Amazon and other platforms when you finish this book. It helps us immensely and we appreciate each and every one.

The Terrors/ Brian K. Morris. -- 1st ed.
ISBN 978-1-7330696-2-5

To Brian Hawkins (1975 – 2021)
I think you would have liked this one.

Special Note:

While this is a work of fiction, the negative attitudes toward persons of color and women during this era were all too real. This book mirrors a time when prejudices, whether consciously, unconsciously, or systematically, played a larger part in society.

In this work, we convey some of those attitudes as story flavor, but not as anything admirable or worthy of emulation. Instead, we present them as a reminder that we all must do better towards those around us and to consciously reject hatred, racism, and sexism in all its forms.

We at Rising Tide Publications offer this story with no intention to offend. Instead, we hope to show how far we've come...

...And to remind us all how far we have yet to go.

CONTENTS

CHAPTER ONE

"You're Closed for the Day."

A weekday in early January 1940

As if rehearsed, the brown-haired man locked the pharmacy's front door and turned the CLOSED sign to face the evening's foot traffic. He exuded the calm that came with feeling in command of his surroundings and being able to enforce that control through applied force. Before the CLICK ceased to echo throughout the empty pharmacy, he relocated to a spot six feet behind an older man who stood next to a rack of various bandages.

Dr. Bob Benton emerged from behind his counter at the rear of the building. He silently sized up the two well-dressed Caucasian men. They wore matching black suits and ties. Their hair was close-cropped, although one had gray hair that showed early signs of retreating from the top of his forehead. Also, the way each man stood reminded Benton of his uncles who served in The Great War, although also being of African American extraction, they didn't get to fight and die alongside their white brothers in arms.

"Can I help you?" Benton asked, concealing his trepidation.

"Indeed, you can." The gray-haired man practically marched to meet Benton. He didn't extend his hand but reached inside his jacket to remove a leather case. With a flip of his well-tanned hand that denoted many hours of practice, the man revealed a government-issued I.D.

"Colonel Travis Clay," Benton read aloud. "And just what does the United States Army want with me? I'm not sure I'm healthy enough to serve, even if you still had conscription."

The Colonel studied Benton through slitted eyes. The African American stood straight; his shoulders pulled back naturally with his hands at his side. Although Benton wore glasses, Clay saw none of the distortion that prescription glass would possess. The Colonel dropped his Identification back into his pocket. "Don't give me any lip, Benton. I'm not here to trade jokes or become your friend." Clay tilted his head and listened for a second. "I want to talk to both of you."

Benton thought for a moment before he said softly, "Tim, please join me."

Tim Rowling emerged from the next aisle. Although he barely reached Benton's shoulder, the twelve-year-old carried himself proudly. Colonel Clay waited for the slender young man to stand beside Benton.

Clay opened his mouth to speak when Benton looked past him. The military man held up his hand for silence. "Someone coming?" Clay asked his assistant.

Without a single glance over his shoulder to verify, Sgt. Ray Harding said, "Sir, Pfc. DeBurle has it covered, sir."

Clay nodded once while he watched the two black men's faces as they looked towards the entrance to their business.

Outside, an elderly woman approached the front door of Benton's Pharmacy. She looked at the CLOSED sign, pulled back her sleeve to confirm the time, then walked towards the front door.

Before she reached her destination, another Caucasian in a black suit practically leaped from around the corner of the store. He looked through the plate glass door, took a deep breath, then slammed his fist against its metal frame again and again. "Hey!" Pfc. Jack DeBurle shouted in mock fury. "Open this damn door up! It ain't five o'clock yet!"

"Young man," the older woman said, "you don't have to do that. I wasn't sure if Dr. Benton would stay late a few minutes. He's been known to do that for us."

DeBurle pointed into the building. "Well, your so-called doctor is standing there, jawing with some guys. I wonder what crimes the pharmacist pulled. They must be cops." He turned towards the door to shout, "To hell with you! I'm taking my business elsewhere."

With that, Pfc. DeBurle disappeared around the corner of the pharmacy once more and listened carefully for the woman's footsteps to become a part of the evening's traffic noise. DeBurle's scowl dropped instantly, replaced with a stern look that would have sent the elderly woman running for cover.

DeBurle picked up a large leather valise from the sidewalk and slung the strap over his right shoulder before he quietly resumed his study of the evening traffic.

Inside the pharmacy, Colonel Clay smiled coldly. "Now, back to business, Benton." He held out his hand. Harding reached into his own suit jacket pocket and withdrew two folded sheets of stationery. "Thank you, Sergeant."

Clay unfolded the ivory sheets as he spoke. "The three of us represent Operation Whitemask. It's a government initiative that's so classified that if you tell anyone about it, I get to murder you both in front of the boy's mother in the town square and no court would convict me."

Tim stepped forward; fury written across his unlined face. "You leave my mom out of this."

"QUIET!" Colonel Clay's voice erupted like a rifle shot in the enclosed space. He allowed the echo to decay before speaking again. "This is not a conversation, young man. This is a monolog."

Benton rested his hand on Tim's shoulder. "Relax, okay?" He leveled his sternest gaze at Clay. "If you've got a point, Colonel, kindly get to it."

Clay cleared his throat, which did little to soften his naturally gravelly voice. "I hold in my hand two documents, signed by a number of names you'll probably not recognize. But trust me when I say their John Hancocks turn these sheets of paper into something akin to what Moses brought down from the mountain." Clay extended his hands, each of them holding one of the letters to the pharmacist and Tim.

Benton read his, stopping several times to emotionally translate its contents. Tim gasped and looked to his friend for guidance. "Just what does this mean?" Benton asked, his voice shaking with barely repressed anger. "And just what is this 'Terror?'"

"Don't give me that," Clay spat as he took a step back from Benton, followed by a deep breath. "What I am about to say will not leave this room." He paused as Benton nodded in reluctant agreement. "If you've had someone read a newspaper to you, gentlemen, you'd know that former-Chancellor Hitler and his cronies are pushing the world towards another Great War."

"I've been reading about Lend-Lease," Benton admitted.

"And military conscription is as good as back," Clay continued. "Uncle Sam needs as many soldiers as he can get. He also requires heroes that those brave young men can identify with." Travis paused. "And since most of those soldiers are going to be as white as the first snowfall—"

Benton interrupted, "What does this have to do with Tim and myself?"

"Propaganda," Clay stated matter-of-factly, placing his hands behind his back. "And the best formats to reach our young men are radio, no surprise, film, and comic books."

Tim grinned. "I love funnybooks."

Without taking his eyes from Benton, Col. Clay continued, "Comic books are aimed primarily at children, or adults with stunted reading comprehension. They have no intrinsic value, nor will they in the future, aside from being a momentary distraction and entertainment." Clay glanced at Tim. "To prove my point, there are a lot of kids tying a bath towel around their necks and jumping out their bedroom windows to emulate their favorite long underwear types."

Benton stroked his chin, unhappy with the thoughts filling his head. "So, you're looking at creating pro-war indoctrination to boost the enlistment numbers, should America be attacked?"

"Not only that, Benton, they're to boost morale once our boys are overseas."

At this moment, Sgt. Harding moved his hands closer to his outside jacket pockets. The motion's significance didn't escape Benton or Tim's attention as the Colonel continued, "And our boys will mostly be white. That's just how the military works."

"I know," Benton said before letting out a sigh. "And you need role models for them."

"Exactly." Colonel Clay's tone resembled that of a teacher whose slowest student finally grasped the basics of trigonometry.

"Yes, each hero white as a lily. Well done, Benton."

Tim ran his thumb over the silk-woven paper as he reread it. "So, you're asking us to... take a break?"

"No, boy." Clay ground his teeth before speaking again. "Your government is demanding you retire. For good." He turned his gaze towards Benton again. "You've both been under observation for months. Our people have learned everything about you and others of your kind. You'll be debriefed and your adventures will be retold in graphic form to benefit the goals of Operation Whitemask." Clay grinned coldly at Tim. "You love those funnybooks, boy? Now, you'll get to be part of one."

Benton opened his mouth to protest, but Clay stepped forward until the pharmacist could smell the Sen-Sen on the soldier's breath. "You even think about defying the wishes of your government, there will be consequences. For one thing, we know neither of you are bulletproof." Clay leered. "Also, we might not be able to hurt you directly under certain conditions." He turned his gaze towards Tim. "However, your mother Velma is quite defenseless, isn't she?"

Tim's words stuck in his throat as Benton's eyes widened. "You wouldn't!"

"Yes," Clay stated, "I would. And if you retaliated, you might find yourself outgunned at your own game, if you know what I mean." The colonel narrowed his eyes and waited until the only noise in the room was the hum of the electric clock over the entryway, interrupted only by the occasional honk of a car horn outside.

"Everyone will know who we are," Tim stated. "We'll never have normal lives."

"You don't anyway," Colonel Clay replied. "No one with your abilities can claim a 'normal' life, so don't fool yourself." He allowed the tone of his voice to be less threatening, if only slightly so. "We will make efforts to ensure your so-called 'secret identities' can be maintained." Cole stared, unblinking, at Tim. "Or revealed if you get uppity. So, what do you say, pharmacist?"

Without even a glance at Tim, Benton whispered, "We'll do it."

Clay snapped his fingers, cueing Sgt. Harding to practically trot to the front door. The man unlocked it long enough to allow Pfc. DeBurle to enter. The latter soldier carried his shoulder bag to the pharmacist's office without even a sideways glance. De-Burle then placed the valise on Benton's desk.

"One of my men is explaining to Mrs. Rowling right now why young Timothy will be home late on a school night." Colonel Clay watched DeBurle pull out a wire recorder and microphone from the bag. As the Sergeant looked for an outlet to plug in the device, Clay continued, "You will dictate the events of your ex-tracurricular activities for the good Sergeant. After that, we all go home and if you behave, you'll never see us again."

Sgt. Harding motioned for Benton and Tim to relocate to the office, which they did slowly. Inside, DeBurle pulled the padded chair away from the desk for Benton to sit. DeBurle then moved a wooden stool beside the table and snapped his fingers before he motioned for Tim to sit beside the microphone. The private moved the mic to the edge of the desk as Tim took a seat. "Just talk here. Don't bother with your life histories. No one cares about that. Just tell us about Kid Terror and his adventures."

Harding's grin reminded Benton of a Conrad Veidt film he'd seen when he wasn't much older than his young assistant. Benton and Tim looked at each other, each silently regarding their lim-ited options. They sighed simultaneously, stymied by the odds against them. Tim sat down and set his fists on top of the desk.

"You ready?" Colonel Clay asked the youth. After a few sec-onds, he added, "Your mommy's an attractive woman, even though I don't favor her kind."

"Don't hurt my Momma," Tim growled as he drew his fore-arm across his eyes. "I know I'm just a kid, but I'll spend the rest of my life making you, all of you, pay if you harm her."

"Nicely said. Good spirit. Waste of time." Clay whispered as he locked his eyes with Benton's. "Operation Whitemask has a local representative who will reach out to you tomorrow. He has the files on you and the boy there. Any questions you have, he will answer. Any orders he gives, you consider them coming from my lips. You understand?"

Benton nodded slowly. "I understand, completely."

Clay turned to DeBurle, "Start the tape."

With a nod, DeBurle turned a switch on the recorder and motioned towards the microphone. Tim took a deep breath and stated with a quiver in his voice, "It began the day I saw Bob Benton getting knocked to the sidewalk by some local mobsters…"

As Tim related his history to the wire recorder, Benton leaned forward and whispered to the Colonel, "Allow me to correct you on one matter, Colonel. I will cooperate for now, but you and I will meet each other again someday. On that day, you will get to see the Terror firsthand." He added, "You have my most solemn vow on that.

Colonel Clay's sudden intake of breath almost made Benton smile with satisfaction.

CHAPTER TWO

"Repeat Customers are Overrated, Anyway."

Sunday, February 4th, 1942

If everyone's life could be turned into a motion picture, Charlie Cronin's final reel would likely never pass the Hays Commission. "Too violent," they'd say. But violence and villainy had never been strangers since his early teens when he beat up other newsboys for their paper money, through Prohibition and the illicit activities that made the Great Depression survivable for the weak.

Cronin had brushes with the law but never saw a day inside a jail cell. If he lived in Chicago, New York, or Los Angeles, he'd either be inside several different trashcans around the city or wearing cement galoshes at the bottom of the closest river.

But most Raceway City cops played by a set of unspoken rules, Cronin was glad to say. The town took care of its own. Being born and raised in the city, Cronin got as close to favored nation status as he hoped to receive. His out-of-town competitors who lived to either rewrite those rules of engagement or to burn them down completely and then spit on the ashes often wound up riding the rails out of town or they'd disappear.

It was good to have even the flimsy protection Charlie Cronin enjoyed that kept him out of the slammer. But not even he could sway the weather.

As predicted, the winter of 1942 proved to be the coldest on record in Raceway City. Cronin vigorously begged businessman Ray Maxley to reschedule their biweekly meeting. "Pushing my car out of the snow is a pain in the butt, Ray. You gonna help me do it?"

"For the money I'm paying you," Maxley stated slowly into

the telephone and with an often-practiced tone of menace, "you can buy a new set of wheels and leave the old one in the alley when the ashtray fills up." Thus, Charlie Cronin parked his Studebaker behind the Peterson Pharmacy Supply building in the earliest hours of that Sunday. It wasn't like he'd be going to church later in the morning, anyway.

The freak snowstorm from the previous afternoon coated the Raceway City landscape in white long before dusk. By now, most of the streets in town were a slippery mess. Only the fact that this was a business where employees needed to earn their paychecks, and the boss' city connections, guaranteed above-average snow removal attention.

Cronin exited his vehicle. He hiked up his collar in a futile act of defiance against the wet, thick flakes slamming against his neck. His slender frame rarely generated enough heat to keep him warm once he pulled the October page from his calendar. A thick layer of light brown hair, as well as a generous slathering of Pomade, protected his scalp from the cold and moisture.

As Cronin trudged towards the rear of his car, the warehouse door flew open. Ray Maxley stood in the doorway, glaring at Cronin. "You're on time," the mobster stated in a way that rang in Cronin's ears like criticism. Maxley stepped into the alley, one hand pulling a fedora onto his head as he clutched the collar of his waistcoat tightly with the other. "You could catch your death, not wearing a hat like that, you know."

"Never took good advice before." Cronin waited for his shivering to exhaust itself. "Why start now?"

Maxley glared at the dark skies briefly, as if challenging them to empty their ivory contents on him. He left the door of the warehouse open, not intending to be outside and uncomfortable any longer than he needed to be. "You bring it?"

Cronin's cold-numbed fingers groped for the trunk key in his pants pocket. His hands shook as he carefully slid the ridged metal into the lock. One twist of the wrist later, the trunk lid flew upwards and Maxley stepped forward to inspect the contents of a well-worn wooden crate.

"As promised, fresh off the railcar." Cronin's teeth chattered.

"I weighed each jar myself. Six times."

Maxley nodded as he inspected the contents of the wooden enclosure. He pulled up a glass jar filled to the brim with fine ivory powder, kept inside by a thick black rubber stopper. The entrepreneur stared at the uncut heroin like a chess champion would study the board. "The last batch count was off. Did it wind up in your arm or your nose?"

Cronin swallowed hard. He didn't like it when the crime boss addressed him without looking his way. "I don't play with horse, sir. Whiskey's my downfall. Anyway, you'll find some extra later in the week." Cronin pulled his shoulders back, proud of the quality of this product and the names he could drop. "My Singapore guy said the purity of his product will amaze you."

Deep laughter filled the alley. Maxley turned towards Cronin, the twinkle in his eye offsetting the sinister leer on his lips. "Purer horse? The last batch killed nine people, Cronin. That's after I stepped on it a few times too, you know what I mean? This 'purity' cost me some serious scratch to keep the D.A. off my back." Maxley laughed once more. "Ah, well. Repeat customers are overrated, anyway."

"There's always more where those guys came from." Cronin knew he should shut up and keep his so-called "humor" to himself, but he couldn't resist adding, "It isn't like the world couldn't spin a little lighter with those kinds of people on a slab." Cronin's heartbeat slowed down when he heard Maxwell's laughter join his own.

"You really think that's funny?" came a whisper from the darkness.

Both men turned towards the mouth of the alley. A still-thickening amount of snow fell more rapidly which obliterated the Studebaker's tracks. A single streetlamp glowed a sickly amber from around the corner of the warehouse.

And at the end of the alleyway stood an athletic figure in black. An icy northern wind lifted the crimson cloak up and away from the man's chiseled form. He ignored the frigid winds and freezing temperatures as one black boot after the other sank into the snow as he strode towards the men. With his back to the streetlight, the stranger's brown flesh merged with the shadows on his face, but both criminals could have sworn this guy wore a mask.

Charlie Cronin barely registered the yellow-white piping at the ends of the stranger's boots, gloves, and around his midsection. He risked a quick glance at Ray Maxley whose reputation for brutality, as he worked his way up the Midwestern criminal ranks, could turn the strongest stomach. Even the Chicago and New York mobs grudgingly respected Raymond Maxley.

The faux business executive's face turned pale, and his eyes widened in fear at the sight of this man in black. "No, not you again."

Cronin turned once again towards the cloaked stranger. The chilly winds now seemed to pick up in speed to dramatically lift the man's cape like the sail of a majestic schooner. It flapped gently, stretching out in scarlet on the underside and blue on the outward surface. A grimace flowered on the stranger's face, angry and terrifying. But what truly drew Cronin's attention, and fueled his fear, was the image of an ivory skull across the intruder's chest. That, and the speed at which it now approached as the mystery man broke into a run.

Maxley reached into his coat with practiced speed. Less than a heartbeat later, the mobster pulled out a snub-nosed .38. It wasn't much for range, but the mysterious caped interloper would soon be close enough to take a bullet to the heart.

To Cronin's astonishment, the costumed man launched himself from two dozen feet away towards Maxley. The stranger practically flew through the air with the speed of an arrow, his arms extended, and his hands stretched like claws.

Startled, Maxley pulled off one shot, but it flew past the ebony clad figure. Cronin spun on his heel, intending to drive away from this madman. His lack of a prison record wasn't because of his exemplary behavior so much as he knew when to vacate the crime scene.

However, his speed worked against him as he lost his footing in the snow. He dropped onto one knee as his ear slammed against the edge of the trunk lid.

Cronin pushed himself to his feet, vaguely aware of Maxley

being punched once, twice, then tossed back into the darkness of the warehouse as if the man's overweight frame weighed no more than a child's doll. Cronin also registered the warmth of his own blood as it trickled from a gash at the top of his ear.

Now in full panic, Cronin pulled himself along the side of his car. He clawed at the shiny black finish like a panther attempting to pull itself up the bark of a tree as he moved closer to the driver's door. The howling winds paused for one magical instant, just long enough for Cronin to hear the sound of a fist crisply striking flesh and a body dropping to the cement floor of the warehouse.

Instinct told Cronin to not look into the doorway of the warehouse, to not see the bizarre stranger standing over the stunned criminal entrepreneur, and from the pained groaning, not to expect Maxley to be calling his name any time soon. Fighting down his fright, as well as the urge to vomit, Cronin willed his legs to move faster as he struggled with his footing on the snow. As he reached for the automobile's door handle, the winds picked up again, threatening to turn the sweat on his face and neck into solid ice.

Then Cronin heard a loud THUMP behind him, followed by a menacing baritone. "Going somewhere?"

Adrenalin poured through Cronin's body like a flood of fresh, hot joe in his veins. He slowly rose to his full height, average as it was, lifted his hands into the air, and slowly turned to see the stranger in black.

The white of the man's eyes bored through Cronin like a drill through a cheap safe. He couldn't tear his gaze from the other man's furious stare. The winds picked up in speed, blowing snow into Cronin's sight, but he dared not blink. For several long, torturous seconds, he stared into the stranger's unblinking gaze, transfixed and wanting desperately to flee.

"I-I'm just a m-middle man." Cronin's stutter held no origin in his chattering teeth. "I get p-paid by Maxley to duh-drop off the oh-orders. Th-that's all."

Without a word, the stranger stepped back to the still-open trunk. He leaned forward to brush the snow off the contents of the crate.

Somehow, Cronin found the courage to approach the stranger

who held one of the jars in his gloved hand, rolling the bottle to check out its contents. A frown crossed the man's face. Then it turned into a grimace.

Cronin studied the open doorway on the other side of his vehicle. He saw the unmoving soles of Ray Maxley's shoes and was mildly surprised to not see a pool of blood under them. Then the drug runner calculated the location of the stranger's head to the proximity of the uplifted trunk lid and saw a great opportunity before him.

With adrenalin-fueled speed, Cronin placed both hands on the metal and pushed downward with all his might. The trunk lid raced towards the man in black's skull.

Seeing Cronin's action from the corner of his eye, the dark intruder dropped the glass jar into the crate as he pulled himself backward. The trunk lid just missed his head but landed hard enough to lock itself once again, trapping the costumed intruder's fingers in its adamantine clutches.

Cronin saw the lid biting down deep into the dark man's digits. He let out a short laugh of relief.

However, Cronin's cruel chuckle died in his throat as he saw a grin light up the stranger's face. It was then Cronin glanced down to where the man's fingers lay trapped under the trunk lid…and there was no blood.

A second later, the man in black braced his knees and back. Without even a mild grunt of exertion, he pulled upwards. The steel trunk lid folded upon itself like an accordion before another pull of those mighty arms yanked the metal free of its hinges.

Snarling, the stranger folded the trunk lid on itself again and again and again with no more effort than a normal man would fold a sheet of paper. He fixed his gaze on Charlie Cronin, who slipped in the snow to fall onto his backside. As the dark intruder stepped closer, closer with the metal square still in his hand, Cronin frantically pushed his hands and feet against the now-compacted snow to make so little headway.

The stranger soon stood over Cronin, raising the lump of metal high over his head. But all Cronin could see was the fury on the man's face.

Cronin wanted to plead for mercy, but his voice refused to work. He stared at the white skull that rested on the front of the stranger's uniform. Certain that his death would arrive in the next few seconds, Cronin's mind flashed to a recent family dinner where his adolescent nephew busied himself reading the latest batch of comic books from the local pharmacy. One suddenly flashed in his mind.

"P-please d-don't kill me. I-I'm just a middleman," Charlie Cronin begged, unable to avert his gaze from that skull. "Don't kill me, Mister Black Terror."

The stranger shuddered as his fury diffused. The wadded metal dropped from his fingers, back onto the thick carpet of snow behind him. He took a deep breath and drew the back of his gauntlet across the chocolate-brown skin of his face.

Instead of striking the criminal, the man seized a fistful of Charlie Cronin's coat and pulled the man up to a kneeling position. The black-garbed stranger leaned forward, his own brown eyes meeting Cronin's through the white lens of his mask.

Feeling the heat from his captor's breath, Cronin shuddered as the dark-skinned stranger in the ebony costume reared back his fist.

The last thing Charlie Cronin heard was, "I'm *not* the Black Terror." He barely felt the force of the blow that rendered him unconscious.

Later, Cronin awoke to more pain in his jaw than he'd felt in his lifetime of beatings at home or in the course of his profession. The snow stopped an hour ago, and the first rays of morning tickled the edge of the skies through parted clouds.

Cronin brushed the frozen precipitation from his eyes as he struggled to his feet. He circled the car, noting the foot-sized wounds in the sidewalls of each flattened tire. He stepped over what used to be his trunk lid and groaned at the empty space where the box used to rest. A chill swept through Cronin that made any Arctic winds feel like a breeze over the Sahara Desert by comparison.

On the other side of the doorway, Ray Maxley groaned as he pushed himself up to a sitting position. His eyes focused on Cronin and then the empty trunk.

"Nuts," he whispered fearfully, "The Terror is back."

CHAPTER THREE

"Very Unconvincing, Doctor."

"Gimme those drugs, mister!" The woman's mouth and eyes narrowed ominously. "Don't make me rough you up, pal."

Dr. Bob Benton looked over the top of his wire-rimmed glasses. "Really, Mrs. Cavanaugh? You'd hurt a poor, innocent pharmacist like me?"

The octogenarian's last reserves gave way, and she laughed hard enough to make her rotund body wobble like gelatin dessert. Her jaw dropped and her dentures followed a half second later. She closed her mouth to quickly press her gums against the upper and lower plates. "So much for becoming the local crime lord, huh?" Mrs. Cavanaugh's expression turned serious, but only for a moment. "And you can call me 'Amy,' all right? Not 'Amelia.' 'Amy' and nothing else will do."

Benton gently placed a brown glass bottle inside a paper bag, taking care to bend the top closed. He ran his pinched fingers over the fold again to seal the sack crisply. Handing it to Mrs. Cavanaugh, Benton smiled warmly. "Here's your vitamins, ma'am. Now be sure to use your powers for good."

"It's gonna be rough, but I'll do my best." The elderly woman eyed the wooden rack at the end of the aisle where a red-haired man stood with his back to the pharmacy counter. He held a magazine from the wooden rack, glancing up occasionally to look at the pharmacist from under the brim of his cap. "That reminds me. You got some of those new funnybooks in this week? My grandkids love them."

Swallowing hard, Benton pushed his glasses upwards with his index finger. "I think they're due tomorrow. With the war going on, deliveries can be hit or miss." The pharmacist declined to remind his customer that she didn't have any grandkids, but why steal the old woman's fantasies? "Anyway, I've put this on your tab. Use them in good health." Benton added with a smile,

"Amy."

Mrs. Cavanaugh blew her benefactor a dry kiss. "You are such a joy to this community, Dr. Benton. See you after the first of the month." Benton couldn't help but smile as he watched the woman walk towards the front door.

Before Mrs. Cavanaugh could reach the exit, the red-haired man returned his magazine to the stand and practically leaped towards the door. "Allow me, ma'am," he said. "Better button up. The wind's howling pretty badly." He pulled the door open with a boyish grin.

Mrs. Cavanaugh appeared startled by this act of courtesy. "Why, thank you, young man. How very kind of you." A smile grew across her lips as she gripped the top of her coat tightly with her free hand before exiting the pharmacy. "God bless you, sir."

"And you, ma'am," the stranger countered as he guided the door back to a closed position. Once Mrs. Cavanaugh reached the end of the block, the man turned around sharply. His eyes swept the store. Satisfied that only the pharmacist remained in the building, he shoved his hands in his pockets and walked with purpose towards the rear counter.

Dr. Benton watched the visitor approach and tried to take in as many details for the police as he could, in case this man had ulterior motives for being here. But the man's cap was pulled down to obscure the upper half of his face. His build appeared to be average, leaning towards being athletic. But his loose jacket might conceal some serious muscles, not that it mattered much to Benton. He'd never met a person who came close to his physical level, even this side of the Olympics.

"Can I help you, sir?" Dr. Benton asked. He saw the Caucasian's close-cropped red hair around his ears and guessed the man possessed either a military or police background from the severe cut.

Stopping a yard from the pharmacist, the stranger raised his head and tilted his cap back with his right thumb. His blue eyes twinkled in the glow of the florescent lights above. "I'm hoping so." He crooked the same thumb back towards the wooden magazine rack, towards the entrance to the establishment. "I see you don't carry many of those long-underwear comic book titles."

"I'm afraid not, sir." Benton's fists clenched instinctively. "I don't think they're healthy for children. Those comic magazines keep the kids busy while their parents shop." Benton narrowed his eyes, annoyed with his visitor's lack of verbal or physical reaction. "I don't sell that many, anyway. The few I stock are mostly cartoon characters and Sunday funnies."

The man nodded. "The sign outside said, 'Benton's Drugs,' not 'Benton's Library.' You probably make more, selling drugs than magazines or comic books." He smirked, satisfied with the edge in his tone.

"Might I ask what you're insinuating?" All civility left Benton's voice. "I'm a legitimate pharmacist and I worked hard to build this business. I don't take to—"

"Whoa!" The stranger raised his palms as if to ward off Benton's potential complaint. "I know you're legit, Dr. Benton." His voice dropped in volume to a whisper. "I read the reports on you."

Benton's blood froze. "I don't know what you're talking about."

"Very unconvincing, Doctor." The stranger balled his hands into fists and let them drop to his sides. "There's a lot happening on the east side, and I know you're trying to keep the peace around here on the west. It's quite admirable, truth to tell."

"I keep people healthy," Dr. Benton stated, his voice now a low growl. "The most powerful thing I dispense are vitamins and I challenge you to prove me wrong."

The stranger cleared his throat as he quickly glanced around the sales floor to reassure himself they were alone. "What you sell in here is not the most powerful thing in this building, and you damn well know it." He lifted his head suddenly, listening intently. "Someone's coming."

Dr. Benton took a step back and tightened his fists. Before he could ask what the visitor was talking about, the man pulled up his collar and lowered the brim of his cap to cover his eyes again.

"We will talk again soon," the red-haired man said, backing towards the door. "Until then, I suggest you curtail your vigilante activities." With the speed of a rattlesnake, the intruder crossed the sales floor, seized the front door handle, and pulled it gently. The bell overhead rang just as an elderly man crossed the threshold.

Touching the edge of his cap and nodding to the new arrival, the red-haired stranger stepped out into the cold as he closed the front door behind him. Benton stepped forward, moving quickly around his visitor. However, the red-haired man could no longer be seen from the doorway. Benton moved towards the curb, eyeing the rest of the block in either direction. But he couldn't see where the stranger could have ducked inside one of them to evade Benton's further inquiry.

Benton squinted, focusing his gaze on the sidewalk. He showed up early to clean the ice from his own section of the concrete, but not everyone shared his sense of industry. Just the same, Benton felt the lens in his eyes moving, refocusing, and pulling the imagery at his feet even closer for his consideration.

A set of footprints rested inside the unshoveled snow to Benton's left. He willed his eyes to sharpen. The space between footprints increased with every step the man made until each stride measured twenty feet apart. When the prints reached the curb at the corner, they vanished.

"Hmm," the pharmacist said. Benton took a deep breath. He briefly considered racing after the stranger, but suspected the man was long gone, judging from the speed of the guy's exit. Besides, the streets filled with early morning traffic and Benton held no desire to show off his considerable speed to the locals. Instead, Benton re-entered his apothecary.

Another one of Benton's regular customers, Davie Clanton, entered the building, which meant Dr. Benton now had a paying client. He forced a smile onto his face, ready to take on the rest of the workday.

But Benton promised himself time to consider this new development, the red-haired stranger, once he locked his door for the night.

Around two corners and deep into the next alleyway, the red-haired man dropped feet-first onto a pile of untouched snow, halfway down the path, far from any observers. Like a lot of economically disadvantaged neighborhoods, the trash would pile up along the sides of the buildings until the snow melted. From here, the trash of Raceway City's poorest found itself picked up by the wind to travel to God knew where.

He glanced back towards the street, expecting Bob Benton to be standing at the edge of the alley. Almost disappointed, the man looked up at the buildings on either side of him. In this neighborhood, many landlords filled their ground floors with retail operations because so many tenants couldn't be relied upon to remain from month-to-month. Often, the property owners for the west side lived in the more affluent parts of the city, if not in another part of the state, and their expensive tastes required a steady flow of other's income.

"Enough social inequity for one day," the man muttered. He eyed the edge of a rooftop six stories above him and noted the fire escape only reached up to the fifth. "Let's fix just what's within our power."

"Hope no one smokes in bed on the top floor," the man whispered as he bent his knees slightly and moved his hands behind him. His form resembled an Olympic swimmer, ready to launch himself from a diving plank. But from the aim of his stare, a witness might deduce quickly that this person's goal wasn't deep below, but way above.

Without a grunt of exertion, the man pushed himself upwards swiftly, throwing his arms to the skies. Immediately, his feet left the ground and just kept going up without slowing down. At the two-story mark, he stretched out his left arm and right leg. By the time he reached the third, he switched the position of his limbs rapidly as if running on the very air itself.

Barely touching the metal on the topmost railing of the fire escape, the man continued to defy gravity. He cleared the roof by another two stories before dropping soundlessly onto the snow-covered tar paper. Without a glance below, he resumed running, immediately reaching an impossible speed that carried him effortlessly from one building to the next until the west side was well behind him.

* * * * *

A half hour after Dr. Bob Benton exposed the CLOSED sign to the public, he strolled toward the small office at the rear of his shop to eat the last of his dinner and stare at the telephone.

The doctor's reverie ended when a knock sounded at the back door to the building. Benton rose quickly, his senses afire, closing the gap between his desk and the solidly locked oak door. He pressed his ear to the thick wood, his eyes narrowed.

After a few seconds, a young male voice sounded, "Bob? You in? It's Tim."

Benton didn't realize he'd stopped breathing until he unlocked the deadbolts, freeing the door to move inward. "Get in here, Tim."

Tim Roland jumped into the room. No matter how many indulgent customers or bigotries crossed his path on any given day, Tim's youthful energy often made Benton smile. But today, the mystery of the red-haired man dampened the doctor's mood.

"Mom told me you called." Tim closed the door behind him. "She's keeping my dinner warm so I can't stay long. So, what's cooking that I should come here instead of phoning you?"

"Has anyone unusual approached you recently?" Benton leaned on the door, just in case someone followed the boy. "Anyone at all?"

Tim's usually cheerful expression turned dark. "No, Bob. Not since…well, you know."

Nodding, Benton bit his lip as he thought. "Yeah. Same here." He quickly weighed the pros and cons of sharing what little he knew. "I had a queer encounter today." Benton sighed. "You're gonna need to know." He quickly related the encounter with the red-haired man.

Once the pharmacist concluded his story, Tim scratched his head. "Gosh, Bob. That's crazy. You don't think that he's—"

"I don't know," Benton admitted. "But you watch your mom, okay? And if anything strange happens, no matter what, you tell me."

Tim grimaced in a way that made Benton forget this was a kid, not an adult with all the weight of the world on his shoulders.

"Okay, I will." The young man studied the tops of his snow-covered shoes for a few seconds. "They said they'd leave us alone. They promised." Tim looked up, meeting his mentor's gaze. "We've done what they told us. We disappeared; we kept quiet."

Benton averted his gaze. "I know you have." He affected a small smile. "You better get home. Dinner's waiting."

"Okay." Tim opened the door. He stood in the doorway to look back at Dr. Benton. "If I see anything, I'll let you know." With that, the youth disappeared into the night.

A thousand ideas rolled through Benton's mind as he secured the door again. His own dinner sat heavy in his gut as he contemplated his next move.

CHAPTER FOUR

"Thanks For the Loan of Your Job."

"How can a new building have a squeak in the damn floor?"

Ben Pickern, born Benolito Picerni, carried his 325-pound bulk around the highly polished desk towards the specially cushioned chair behind it. As he did, the businessman stepped on a plank beneath the carpeting that always made a sound like the front door of a haunted house. Pickern lowered himself onto the chair with a strange soundlessness that belied his bulk.

Already seated at the visitor's side of the desk, local attorney Tony Quinn stared straight ahead through his shaded eyeglasses and waited for his employer to get comfortable. Quinn understood the value of patience and of not allowing his emotions to show. He crossed his dark hands, right over left, and awaited the reason for his summoning.

"Did you read the—damn!" Pickern sighed. "How many years has it been, and I still do that, blind man?"

Quinn purposely moved his lips into the smallest of smiles. "Perfectly understandable, Mr. Pickern. There are days when I wake up, expecting to see the sunrise again. Imagine how foolish I feel." Quinn's smile slowly vanished as he spoke. "However, this morning's radio news told of a warehouse robbery on the west side. As that was the only local news worth reporting, and your secretary called me into your office at nine o'clock because I'm your attorney, I assume the warehouse was yours?"

Pickern cleared his throat. "Yes." The man straightened his silk tie, a nervous habit from the days when he couldn't afford any outward sign of affluence. "I have an interest in a pharmaceutical distribution center there. We've invested quite a lot, getting our product into your neighborhood."

"That's very industrious of you." Quinn placed his well-worn briefcase and white cane on the floor beside his chair. "Getting helpful products into Raceway City speaks well of your benevolence, Mr. Pickern."

As usual, irony and thinly veiled sarcasm dropped from Pickern's notice like rainwater from a duck's back. The heavy-set man pulled a Cuban cigar from a highly polished cherrywood case resting at the corner of his desk. "Let's be honest with each other, a lot of people don't like driving deliveries into your section of town, Quinn. I'm glad to help all I can." He drew the cigar across his upper lip, savoring the tobacco's tangy aroma. "I admit I make a dollar or two in the process."

"Opportunity brings its own rewards in many ways, I'm sure," Quinn stated. "So why am I here, sir?"

Pickern's expression turned dark. "How insulated are we from the contents of that automobile?"

Quinn remained stoic. "As your attorney, I'd advise you to consider the limits of our professional relationship before I answer." He allowed the words to linger in the air before speaking again, "Were the contents of that vehicle…of dubious origin?"

"Allegedly." Pickern placed the cigar on the blotter of his desk. "We do research there too, you know. We're finding ways to remove the addictive aspects of the coca leaves, leaving only their therapeutic effects."

"Ah, cocaine," Quinn crossed his legs. "It's been quite the problem among my people."

Pickern studied Quinn's even expression through narrowed eyes. "It's because of that 'problem' that I don't want the shipment traced back to me." Pickern rested his elbows on the edge of his desk. "Yeah, it was an illegal delivery. But I'll risk it to make an omelet, you know what I'm saying?"

Quinn lifted his chin in a moment's thought. "You are concerned for your reputation, to not impede the social progress you create in Raceway City."

"Especially on the east side," Pickern reminded Quinn. "You've got new streetlamps down there and businesses are opening up there all the time. That means jobs and jobs mean prosperity."

"True," Quinn admitted. "It's a shame, however, that crime doesn't seem to have abated in recent years in my neighborhood.

I would guess they seek their own prosperity by non-conventional means."

Pickern inhaled sharply. "That community's prosperity also attracts the wrong element, sorry to say." He picked up his cigar again. "Funny how that doesn't happen on the north side."

That's because you can afford more police up there, Quinn mentally countered. *Also, you can pay to have them become even more "blind" to your illicit activities than I'm supposed to be.* Instead, the attorney remained silent as he waited for Pickern to speak.

As if prompted, Pickern said, "Now about that shipment."

"My office stands ready to defend your sterling reputation, Mr. Pickern." Quinn uncrossed his legs and smiled at the businessman. "And you don't have to wait until I leave to smoke your cigar."

"How?" Pickern's eyes narrowed with suspicion. "How'd you know, blind man?"

If Quinn took offense at the spotlight on his disability, he didn't let on. "My mother had a chest made of cedarwood at the foot of her bed. She kept her best clothing inside it. I grew up loving that aroma, so it brings back many dear memories. I take it the interior of your humidor is made from that?"

"Yeah, just the inside," Pickern said with a little bit of surprise as he sat back in his chair. "It's like burning the inside of a wine barrel to bring out the wood's flavor."

Quinn gave his subtle smile once again. "I never acquired a taste for strong drinks, so my information is simply anecdotal. It sounds as if I'm missing out."

"Probably not." Pickern took another appreciative whiff of his cigar. "It's good to have a clear head, at least during business hours." He gave a brief chuckle. "I forget your other senses are keener because of your condition."

"The darker the cloud, the brighter the silver lining." Quinn uncrossed his legs. "I'll be on standby and listening to the radio. If something comes up to challenge your standing in the community, I'll be ready with a libel suit. In fact, why don't I write some press releases to head off any challenges to your civic standing?"

Pickern bit off a tiny hole at the tip of his cigar. "Excellent. I can pass those on to the *Daily Guardian*. Good thinking, Quinn. Why buy a newspaper if you aren't going to use it, right?"

"That's why I helped with the purchase contracts, sir." Quinn picked up his briefcase. "If there's nothing else to discuss?"

Rising from behind his desk, Pickern announced, "Time is money. I like that about you, Quinn. You're no nonsense."

Quinn rose and held out his hand to shake. As he seized Pickern's meaty flesh, the attorney said, "Too many things to accomplish for mere fol-de-rol. I'll be in touch, Mister Pickern. Have a good day. I can let myself out." Quinn reached down towards the base of his chair, making certain to "search" for the white wooden cane that lay there. Two minutes later, the attorney found himself inside the elevator.

Upon entering the cage, Quinn made his way to the rear and casually pressed his back against the wall. "You're not the regular operator, are you?" Quinn congratulated himself for keeping the suspicion from his voice.

The man in question aimed a grim smile at his passenger before he closed the accordioned metal gate. "Otis is on break, sir." He smiled at his passenger. "Ground floor?"

"Please." Quinn allowed himself a glance at the elevator operation from the corner of his eye as the elevator descended. An unfamiliar person in this part of the city always merited Quinn's study and that orange-red hair made the stranger stand out even more. Quinn noticed the square-jawed operator stared back at him with a slight smile.

Soon enough, the elevator came to a stop on the ground floor. The operator opened the front gate, then stepped back towards the controls.

After a couple of seconds, Quinn tapped his white cane on the elevator floor. "Aren't you going to tell me to watch my step?"

The man chuckled. "I figure you don't need that warning, Mr. Quinn." He stepped outside ahead of his passenger, turning only to say, "We'll be talking. Good day, Quinn," before passing through the line that awaited the other elevator.

Quinn narrowed his gaze. Aside from a handful of local associates, who knew Tony Quinn wasn't truly blind? When the line

of men and women filled the other elevator, Quinn walked towards the exit. His cane tapped from left to right and back again
in a perfect rhythm of fake helplessness.

By the time Quinn reached the street, the red-haired stranger
had already entered the diner two blocks away on the opposite
side. Once he crossed the eatery's threshold, the man took inventory of the room out of habit.

Otis sat in a booth at the far end of the restaurant. Only a pile
of crumbs from his apple pie left any clue about his early lunch.
Otis' eyes brightened upon seeing the man slide into the seat opposite him. "Thanks for lunch, man."

"Cheap at twice the price, my friend." The stranger reached
into his pocket before extending his hand across the table.
"Thanks for the loan of your job."

Sliding his own hand to meet the stranger's, Otis felt something move into his folded palm. His brow furrowed with
confusion; the elevator operator pulled back his hand to inspect
the contents. "What?" Otis whispered. "A fifty? Mister, you
made of money or something?"

The stranger chuckled. "That's to guarantee you never saw
me, okay?"

"Saw who?" Otis dropped the bill into his pants pocket. "So,
this might be a bad time to ask, but am I going to get in trouble
for this?"

"Not at all." The stranger rose to his feet. "The guy in the next
car's taking care of his own business. As far as he knows, you're
taking a bathroom break with a newspaper, just like you always
do."

"Hmmph! You caught me." Otis rose to his feet. "Am I gonna
see you again?"

"You never saw me to begin with, remember?" The stranger
quickly moved from the booth without a farewell and walked towards the rear exit so quickly, Otis thought the guy sprinted like
Jesse Owens.

Patting his pants pocket, Otis decided against paying attention
to his curiosity in favor of retaining his employment. He waved at
the counter girl for his check just as the bell above the back door
announced the stranger's exit.

Outside, in the alley behind the diner, the red-haired man pulled his jacket collar up around the back of his neck, but only for appearances. He no more felt the cold than a statue would.

He looked to one end of the backstreet and then the other. Satisfied that no one could see him, the man leaped upwards,. He easily gripped the iron fire escape railing with one hand to swing himself upwards and flip onto the roof, landing feet first. Without hesitation, the man sprinted across the tar paper towards the front of the building.

From atop the apartment building that rested over the diner, the red-haired man surveyed Raceway City. Despite the racket of traffic and pedestrians below, all challenging the snow and ice to reach their destinations, the municipality appeared almost serene under its blanket of white. For a fleeting moment, the stranger thought of New York City, hoping to return one day.

"Soon," he promised himself. "But first, I think I need to take care of a very special headache."

CHAPTER FIVE

"So, How's the Drug-Selling Business These Days?"

"I swear I could have paid some brat a quarter to clean the snow off my driveway instead of hiring you." Carlton Brant grunted as he shifted his bulk in his leather chair. He reached across the mahogany desk in front of him to pull a thick Havana cigar from his host's humidor.

Ray Maxley smiled politely and nodded once. *You'd know all about keeping everyone in their place, wouldn't you?* he thought.

As Brant closed the cedar lid, he drew in an appreciative breath as he moved the hand-rolled brown cylinder under his nose. "But you did the sidewalks too, which I appreciate."

For a moment, Ray Maxley imagined living in a world where his host stepped onto a patch of packed snow with his expensive imported shoes. He almost smiled at the thought of Brant losing his footing before slamming the back of his skull against the steps of his house.

When the waking dream solidified in the mobster's mind, Maxley felt a twinge of guilt, a rare feeling for the man. After all, working for local mob boss Ben Pickern, and even with Al Capone's most enthusiastic endorsement, Brant didn't have to speak to him this morning. Brant had far greater responsibilities than giving the drug distributor an audience. Maxley promised himself to savor the fantasy of his boss's lifeblood pouring down the concrete steps and mixing with the snow later when he was alone. Maybe one day, it could happen for real.

"You're welcome. I'll pass on the word to my warehouse crew. It's nice to be appreciated." Maxley repressed his sarcasm as he smiled pleasantly.

Brant leaned back in his chair. "So, tell me about Sunday. Leave nothing out."

Maxley leaned back in his own chair. It felt good to confront this man inside this office, on Brant's home turf. "You read the files, and don't act surprised, Carlton. You stink at looking innocent."

"Well, I am surprised, Ray." Brant slurred his guest's name as an insult. "I never knew you had a backbone before. So, what was in the back of that car, and did you get a good look at the man who tore it apart?"

Maxley removed the tip of his own cigar cleanly with a silver-plated cutter, just as he'd seen his mentor, Ben Pickern, do. He pushed the device across the desk towards Brant, who ignored the proffered apparatus. Instead, Brant bit the tip free of his cigar before spitting the tiny speck of tobacco across the room, deliberately missing the wastebasket resting beside the desk out of spite to his cleaners.

"I talked to my delivery guy, once we were both conscious again." The gangster's eyes met Brant's. "You won't like what I'm about to tell you." Maxley paused to study Brant's stony expression. "It was the Terror." He took a slow puff on his cigar. "I know you two have history."

Brant didn't even flinch upon hearing the name. "Yeah, we do, don't we?" He nodded slowly as he struck a match along the side of the cigar box. Upon the flame's tip barely touching the wrapper, Brant turned his full attention to turning the cigar slowly, lighting it evenly as his inhalations pulled the flame into the center of the tobacco.

Maxley's patience evaporated rapidly as he studied Brant's casual attitude. "Don't try and fool me that you aren't scared, Brant. I have two guys from inside the warehouse still in the hospital, along with Cronin. One of them can't stay awake for more than two minutes at a time and the other jumps at anything louder than a mouse's squeak." Maxley contemplated his last words. "Then again, that toad Cronin usually is one good scare away from wetting himself. He used to be so tough." Maxley's expression and tone darkened. "I'm also out several thousand dollars for that shipment. You obviously don't know what I had to do to get that much horse out of Asia right now."

"Even more obvious is the fact that I don't care." Brant tilted his head back, pursed his lips, and released a perfect circle of gray-silver smoke. He watched it drift towards the overhead light fixture as he spoke. "I don't care about anything but the bottom line and results."

"Dammit, Carlton!" Maxley slammed his fist on the desk as he rose to his feet. "Pickern set me up with a legitimate, respectable business at no small expense. Do you only care about that company when you mess it up?" Maxley's heart beat more rapidly than his doctor would have liked.

Brant's eyes narrowed as they focused on Maxley. "I'm interested, okay? Especially when you try to blame it on the Terror. He's gone, you know."

Maxley reached into his suit jacket. He pulled out a dozen photographs and tossed them onto the blotter. "Your cop took these pictures." After Brant studied them for a few seconds, the career criminal continued, "Study that picture of the trunk lid very carefully. You might see some really deep indentations."

"Yeah," Brant confirmed, "they look just like fingers dug into it. I know you saw them when you woke up after the caped guy attacked you." Brant took another serious look at the photographs before stacking them neatly on edge like a deck of playing cards. A second later, he offered them to his guest.

"No, keep them." Maxley took another puff from his cigar. "It's possible there's more than one of his kind, you know. I mean he had that kid with him at one time. As it is, I'm always hearing about other mystery men across the country."

Brant nodded. "I read the papers too." Brant sighed as he contemplated the ash at the tip of his cigar. "So, what were you doing with all that horse?"

"The heroin was going to be processed for some legit purposes. We use a little bit in some of our compounds." Maxley took a deep breath. It wasn't standard protocol to question another made man's illegal intentions, probably due to not asking about the obvious. "It's all quite controlled and above board. It has to be."

"Oh, I'm sure of that." Brant grinned. "Even the stuff that winds up going out the back door?"

Maxley laughed before he continued, "Paperwork can be faked, records can be altered. At least that's what some of my more unsavory acquaintances tell me." Maxley narrowed his eyes as he spoke.

"Good." Brant took another draw on his cigar. "I want you to continue that, and you didn't hear it from me, got that?" He flicked the ash into a marble tray with a tap of his index finger. "That fits with my plan."

"Plan?" Maxley's voice took on a sinister tone. "Care to tell what you're doing? Or is this something I won't want to know about later?"

"No." Brant smiled. "Let's just say it'll contribute to the beautification of Raceway City when the time is right."

Silence filled the office and Brant's cheer faded swiftly. "Okay, but keep this on the QT. The west side is a blight on Raceway City, and it doesn't make me look very good." He cleared his throat. "Too much crime and too many people I don't like there. I want to give the police the wherewithal to step up operations." Brant leaned forward. "Want to know how I plan to do this, step by step?"

Maxley shook his head after he drew in another mouthful of aromatic smoke and let it out slowly. "Can't say I do, really. The less I know, the fewer lies I have to tell. Don't want to go to Hell for lying, you know."

"Just double up on your 'Hail Mary's' next time you're in confession." A fire burned in Brant's guts. He didn't enjoy sharing his plans with guys who could betray him and bring down the carefully constructed façade of his rule. But Brant knew clowns who asked questions were either idiots with a death wish or federal prosecutors. Maxley's absence of curiosity reassured him, and he made a mental note to call Ben Pickern later today and thank him.

Then again, every good businessman should have a patsy close by when the going gets tough and a judas goat was needed. Brant chuckled as he lifted his cigar to his lips. "And the best part is if it is the Terror, he might be helping us, whether he knows it or not." Brant leaned forward and whispered conspiratorially, "Don't tell anyone else, but I'm gonna let you in on what's going on…"

Elsewhere in the building, Jean Starr paused in her typing to look up at the man who entered her office. Without thinking, her bright-red lips curled into a perfect smile, and her blue eyes opened wide.

Dr. Bob Benton smiled at the secretary in what he hoped was a friendly, yet professional, manner. He pushed his glasses farther up the bridge of his nose as he admired her perfectly coiffed red hair, "Good morning, Miss Starr. Hope the world's treating you well."

"So far, so good, Doctor." She studied the pleasing curve of Benton's chiseled features and the gleam of obvious intelligence in his gaze. "What can I do for you today?"

"Just thought I'd come in and say hello," Benton said. He caught himself tugging at the knot of his necktie. "I was downstairs, paying my utilities. I thought I'd also pay my respects while I was in the neighborhood."

"Don't you have another neighborhood to be in?"

Benton grimaced as he recognized the voice. He glanced at Jean who aimed her strained smile at the intruder. "Hello, Mr. Clark," Benton said in a monotone.

Rodney Clark stood in the doorway, his brown overcoat resting over his right arm. The pencil-thin mustache on his upper lip curled in a parody of a smile and light from the fluorescent lights overhead seemed to dance along the waves in his brown hair. "The Comptroller's office thanks you for paying your bills. So, how's the drug-selling business these days, Benton?"

"F-fine, Mr. Clark." Benton inhaled deeply, barely controlling his anger at the stinging implication. He could pick Clark up like a rag doll and crush every bone in his body as easily as crumbling a saltine. However, Benton knew if he did, he'd not only be facing the wrath of law enforcement, but the government itself.

So would Tim and Velma.

Benton glanced back at Jean. She looked at him oddly as he attempted to discern the meaning in her eyes. "I think it's time I returned to my shop. Good day, Mr. Clark." Benton nodded at Jean. "Miss Starr." With that, Benton spun on his heel and walked towards the outer door.

Rodney Clark filled most of the doorway. His smirk silently

dared Benton to bump into him, to even graze against the expensive suit he wore. For a moment Benton imagined picking up this thorn in his side, holding him high over his head, then tossing him through the nearest window, just like in the comic books.

Just like in the comic books.

Bob Benton forced his gaze downwards towards the man's highly polished imported shoes. The pharmacist murmured, "Excuse me, Mr. Clark." After a long moment, he added, "Please."

With a chuckle, Clark stepped to one side, sweeping his hand towards the outer hallway with a leer. "Enjoy your day, *Mistuh* Benton."

Benton entered the hallway, aware of Jean Starr's eyes drilling holes into the back of his skull. The sensation followed him as he rounded the hallway to begin his shame-filled trek back to the west side of Raceway City.

Rodney Clark poked his head outside the office to make certain Benton left. He didn't turn around until the elevator doors closed. He chuckled as he caught Jean's gaze. "Aw, c'mon, Jean. I was just teasing."

"I don't like that kind of so-called humor, Rod, and you know it." Jean turned from Clark's smirking face. She wrestled with her conflicted feelings just as the inner office door opened. Jean's parents raised her with an open heart, to see different skins and beliefs to be nothing worth hating. Well, unless those beliefs came pre-packaged with hatred as their foundation.

Rex Maxley emerged from the innermost office, followed by the smell of cigar smoke. "Take care, Miss." He nodded at Clark as he passed. "Mr. Clark."

Clark smiled broadly as he made way for the mobster to leave. "Here, sir," he called out. "Let me call the elevator for you."

Jean Starr turned towards the inner office as Carlton Brant emerged. The cigar hung at the corner of his mouth as he spoke, "Please hold my calls for the next hour, okay, Jean?" He forced a smile onto his lips. "In fact, since your boyfriend's here, why not take a long lunch? I think I can hold down the fort for a couple of hours."

Nodding, Jean didn't correct Brant's observation concerning

her relationship. She pulled her purse from the bottom-most desk drawer before rising to reluctantly fetch her coat. Jean touched the ermine collar, a gift from Rodney Clark. She fingered the soft pelt as her eyebrows furrowed in deep thought.

The memory of Dr. Benton kowtowing to the Comptroller flashed in her mind. Jean immediately pushed it out of her consciousness as she slid her arms into the luxuriously warm sleeves. "I appreciate that, sir." Jean smiled at Brant. "I promise to come back as soon as I can, Mr. Mayor."

CHAPTER SIX

"I've Got a Job for You Tomorrow."

Tim Rowland's determined strides took him from Raceway City's business district into the residential area quickly enough. The streetlamps that illuminated what seemed to be every other building now grew even less frequent. Tim glanced up to see the broken bulbs, many of which were shattered by vandals months earlier. Even at his tender age, Tim already possessed a healthy skepticism about the urgency of their replacement.

Even at twelve, one grew up quickly, even in the lower middle-class neighborhood he lived in. Crime lurked in every shadow, whether it was around the corner from a broken overhead lamp or downtown at City Hall. Like many of his schoolmates, Tim possessed a well-developed sense of paranoia when the sun set.

Broken streetlamps didn't matter to Tim. His enhanced vision proved sufficient to pierce the darkness of the evening. He glanced towards the street where various automobiles deepened the ruts created by the packed snow and ice of the last few days. Many homes, mostly containing those too old or infirm to shovel their walks, still carried a thick layer of precipitation that crunched under Tim's footsteps. But the slickness below his shoes proved no impediment. Thanks to his heightened strength and balance, he moved through the short drifts and over the ice as if they didn't exist.

Light from a nearby front porch drew Tim's attention. An elderly gentleman stepped onto the concrete deck; his bathrobe pulled tightly over his lean body as protection against the cold. "Hey, young man," the man called out. "Does your momma know you're out at this hour?"

"She does, Mister Bates," Tim stated with a smile. "Had to run an errand, sir. But it's done and I'm on my way home."

Mr. Bates nodded once. "You best make tracks then. Don't

want you to catch your death out here."

"I won't," Tim assured the elderly man. "I appreciate your caring, sir. Have a good night."

Whatever Mr. Bates said next lost itself inside a gust of wind. With a quick wave and bone-deep shivering, he practically dove back inside his house, and locked the door. Tim smiled as he resumed his trek through the winter snow. Then his smile dropped as he heard a noise from farther ahead.

Half a block from his house, Tim dropped to one knee, seemingly to re-tie his shoelace. As he lowered himself, Tim took a glance to the left of him, then to the right. He focused his eyes on a man who stood two blocks away on the same sidewalk, almost in front of the Rowland home. The stranger stopped, pulled his cap down more firmly over his red hair, and took a step forward. Then ten more in the second that passed, followed by fifty more in the next heartbeat.

Before Tim could say anything, he launched himself at the stranger. He spread his arms wide, ready to seize the racing man in a running tackle. With his footwork a blur to any normal person, Tim covered dozens of feet with every second with no sign of slowing down.

Tim grinned in anticipation of the man's astonished expression. Instead, the stranger pushed himself off the ground and leaped above Tim with legs moving with the rapidity of an Olympic track champion. Tim dropped his feet onto the sidewalk, skidding in a straight line for another half block. He turned swiftly to see the older man move upwards in the night sky before executing a U-turn in mid-air to race downwards towards Tim.

As he suppressed the urge to analyze his pursuer's startling abilities, Tim braced himself for an attack and raised his fists to his chest, just like Bob taught him to do years ago. *Hope I'm not out of practice,* Tim told himself as he realized he'd not been Kid Terror for two years.

The man dropped to the sidewalk in front of Tim. His expression was neutral and for all his exertions, his breath emerged from his mouth as even drifts of fog rather than gray blasts that betrayed his fatigue. He opened his mouth to speak but before he could utter a syllable, a snowball splattered against the side of his head.

"You get the hell away from my boy!"

Both Tim and the stranger blinked in unison and turned their slack-jawed gaze towards the boy's front porch and the mama lion's roar that seized their attention.

Velma Rowland stomped down the steps of her front porch, broomstick in hand and fury in her rich brown eyes. Even with a little roundness in her face and the anger that only a loving mother could generate, she possessed a mature beauty that no makeup could enhance for none was needed. The wind whipped at the hem of her housedress, but her protective rage shielded her from the below-freezing temperatures.

She aimed the broomstick like a magic wand at the red-haired man. "You heard me! Tell me who you are or I'm gonna take this broom and turn you into a candy apple."

Tim breathed a sigh of relief. He turned towards the stranger and whispered, "Man, you're in for it now." The boy was faster, stronger, and tougher than any adult he knew, aside from Bob Benton. However, even he lived in fear of this magnificent woman's wrath and reveled in her love.

As Velma stormed onto the front walk which her son dutifully cleared earlier that day, both the man and Tim became aware of one porch light after another evicting the darkness from the street. Faces peered from behind curtains and dusty blinds. Several doors opened, pouring more light into the night.

The man frowned as he looked down at Tim. "I just wanted to talk. Didn't mean to scare you." He tipped his cap towards Velma. "Sorry to frighten you, ma'am. It won't happen again." Then he turned towards Tim, speaking softly, "Be more careful, Kid. Too many of the wrong people are watching you and Dr. Benton," before walking back towards downtown. This time, he did it with the speed of a normal human.

Velma wrapped her arms around her only son. Tim noticed she wasn't wearing her coat. "Let's get inside, Momma." His voice took on the maturity of someone several times his modest age. "We've got stuff to talk about."

Five minutes later, Tim sat at the chrome dinette in their small kitchen. Velma watched the early wisps of steam emerge from the silver kettle on the stovetop. "So, who was that?" she asked, unsuccessfully masking the concern in her voice.

"I don't know, Momma." Tim cradled the empty teacup in his hands. "Bob told me someone like this guy was in his pharmacy yesterday."

A faint whistle emanated from the depths of the kettle. "I thought we wouldn't be hearing from those government men again. You haven't been careless, have you, boy?" A frown crossed her lovely face. "And it's 'Doctor Benton.' You respect the man's accomplishments, got that?"

Tim nodded his head vigorously. "Yes, Momma. Sorry." Tim recalled his leap towards the red-haired man, the one that no ordinary boy could have made. "Well, maybe I got careless a few minutes ago when I saw the guy." He described, in brief, his encounter with the stranger. "But I think no one might have noticed me, what with a guy who ran on empty air."

"Let's hope." Velma continued to stare at the kettle as if her gaze could get the water to boil faster. As far as Tim knew, it probably could, given the number of times her loving eyes could render him as helpless as a newborn kitten. "We don't need that kind of attention again."

"Momma, you get the first cup, okay?" Tim smiled lovingly. "You didn't have a coat on out there. You're still shivering. How'd you know I was out there, anyway?"

Velma lifted the kettle from the flame, dampening the volume of its energetic whistling. She poured the boiling water over the strainer filled with loose black tea. She dipped the wire sieve into the water, savoring the aroma of the tea as the leaves surrendered their flavor. "Momma's intuition, okay?" Velma's smile dissolved. "I start worrying every time you leave the house, and don't you dare tell your momma that she's got no right to worry."

"Never. I wouldn't dare." Tim leaned forward and pushed his cup closer to the edge of the table. "I think I need to call Bob—Dr. Benton about this."

"Probably so." Velma dipped the leaves into the darkening water again and again. "I'll wait here until you're done so you can have some privacy."

"Thanks, Momma," Tim stated as he rose from his seat. "I won't be a minute."

Velma watched her son disappear into the front room. "Take as long as you need." She smiled softly as the sounds of the boy plopping himself onto the sofa and dialing the phone reached her ears. Velma rose to put the first mug of tea where she knew her boy would return. She then placed the kettle back over the flame and waited, trying not to worry about her boy as she puzzled over the stranger and why he fled.

She knew about the threat made by the trio of military men two years ago. Velma's son would have died before worrying her with the details of the government's intrusion, but Benton thought Velma deserved to know. Velma was glad to be included and active in any decisions involving her son, but none of this made her sleep better at night, particularly if an unfamiliar para-human was now involved.

The kettle's strident whistle soon drowned out the sound of Tim's dialing. Velma poured the boiling water onto a second set of tea leaves, grateful for the temporary distraction.

Meanwhile, outside the front of Dr. Bob Benton's pharmacy, the young druggist tested the doorknob. It didn't yield to the same strength any normal human being could apply. He heard the phone ringing through the door with his powerful senses, but decided whoever wanted him could wait until morning.

Now satisfied that the establishment was secure, Benton strolled towards home which just happened to be a few doors down from his place of business. He surveyed the length of the block, his senses at their keenest, before he let himself in through the apartment building's front door. Ever since the night he and Tim talked to the men of Operation Whitemask, Benton always made certain no one waited to follow him inside.

Once Bob locked the apartment door behind him, his face took on a stern expression, totally unlike the empathetic druggist who supplied medicine, vitamins, and other dry goods to his local patrons, along with friendly advice on their health and general well-being. "Maybe I should have saved all that money for college and bought a bar," he mused aloud.

Benton reached inside his icebox and withdrew an ice-cold bottle of cola. He placed his thumb under the lip of the ridged cap that encircled the bottle's mouth. With no more exertion than he'd use to open an envelope, Benton easily pried the cap free, sending it flying towards the ceiling. Before it could strike the tiles above, Benton swiftly pulled the cap from the air before casually dropping it into a trash can near the sink.

As the local neighborhood pharmacist, Bob Benton embraced the quiet lifestyle of service to his community. He once envisioned another existence of adventure and righting wrongs beyond the scope and ability of the law. A few missions as the Terror left Benton wondering how long he could sustain his activities before a criminal found a way to do him in.

Sure, he was tough, but despite his newfound abilities, he and Tim could still be injured, even rendered unconscious.

Now, Benton found himself drawn to the reality of his neighborhood and the need for his special talents once again. He felt a twinge of regret at the thought of possibly leaving a fairly normal, if rewarding, life behind.

Suddenly, another thought crossed Benton's mind. His eyes narrowed, and he swiftly flipped the light switch, plunging the room into darkness.

Moonlight poured in through a gap between his living room curtains as the clouds parted outside. Bottle in hand, Benton strolled towards the front window that overlooked the main street. He inserted a finger between the two sheets of cloth and gently nudged them apart to allow him a view outside.

Below, the red-haired stranger stood with his back pressed onto the streetlight on the nearest corner. He glanced upwards and his eyes met Benton's, sending a chill cascading up and down the pharmacist's spine.

At that moment, the phone rang, startling Benton. Through the parted curtains, he saw the man nod and casually walk down the street to disappear into the night. Benton took a long pull from the soda bottle as he crossed the room to lift the receiver from its cradle.

On the other end of the line, Tim Rowland's voice filled Benton's ear. "Bob, thank goodness you're home. The red-haired guy. He was here." The boy went on to describe his odd encounter with the stranger. Once his tale concluded, Tim asked, "So what's our next move?"

Benton sat in his favorite chair and spoke evenly, "Tim, I've got a job for you tomorrow after school."

"Oh?" Despite his best efforts to suppress his excitement, Tim's voice was thick with enthusiasm. "It's supposed to be cold out again tomorrow. Should I put on my...long underwear?"

Benton chuckled. The more sedate life of a pharmacist would never suit his youthful friend. "No, you don't need to do that."

He stopped himself before he could say, *"Not yet."*

CHAPTER SEVEN

"Nobody's Going to Hoist a Studebaker Over Their Heads But Us."

"Stupid," Dr. Bob Benton muttered to himself. "Stupid," he repeated with every step down the street. Only catching his lower lip between his teeth made Benton pause in his abusive self-analysis. His cheeks burned with humiliation, and he found himself growling as he anticipated opening up his pharmacy for the day. Hopefully, that might take his mind off current events.

Benton kicked himself for turning into an overly anxious schoolchild in front of Jean Starr the day before. There was a spark inside her, a vivaciousness that her businesslike demeanor couldn't conceal. He'd only seen her behind her desk for the last five months, the first two of which found him too tongue-tied to say much more than "Good morning" and "Have a good day."

Eventually, Starr took the lead in drawing Benton out of his shell. Their brief conversations often veered towards what occurred on the radio the night before or the events of the day. They shared many interests in music and programs, it seemed.

However, Benton reminded himself, they didn't share the same opinion of that mustachioed misanthrope, Rodney Clark. The only aspect of the city comptroller they shared was his attention, which could be focused on either one of them to the exclusion of all others in the room. But whereas he treated Starr like a fragile possession, Benton felt as if Clark would like to see the pharmacist swimming in a river with a cinder block tied to each ankle.

Benton could pay his utility bills via the mail, but he found himself heading to City Hall just to exchange a few words with Jean every couple of weeks. Doing this did wonders for his day. Benton managed to conceal his crush from Velma, but Tim and Benton's more perceptive customers could tell when Benton paid his water and power bills, just from his more cheerful demeanor.

I've never even seen Jean from the waist down, Benton told himself. *For all I know, she's got a wooden leg.*

He sighed and a smile played on the edge of his lips. *But I bet it's a* gorgeous *wooden leg.*

Unfortunately, Clark's open longing for the beautiful secretary was almost palpable, just as his hatred for Benton and the color of the pharmacist's flesh proved unmistakable and impossible to overlook.

Benton felt a cold breeze on his face. Because of the formic ether vapors in his blood system, Benton could feel, but only up to a point. He could register discomfort or pleasing sensations. But he'd never had to test the limits of his tolerance before. He hoped leading a quiet life, as directed by the government, would put off that assessment for a good, long time to come.

"Ulp!" Benton realized that even for the short distance between his apartment and his job, he'd been walking at a pace just slightly slower than most people could run. Fortunately, not many potential witnesses were on the sidewalk just as most businesses opened their doors. Benton forced himself to slow down to a normal man's speed as he approached the pharmacy.

An elderly lady awaited Dr. Benton's arrival. He took a deep breath before forcing his lips to configure a smile. "Good morning, Mrs. Clanton."

"Good morning, Doctor Benton." Ellie Clanton's slender face held so many wrinkles that the pharmacist imagined each line in her flesh represented every mile she ever walked in her ninety years of life. She clutched the top of her wooden cane with all ten of her gnarled fingers as if that was all that kept her from dropping onto her face, which it probably was. "I'm glad you open at ten." Ellie looked around before she whispered conspiratorially, "I think I need another treatment."

"Very well, Mrs. Clanton." Benton unlocked the door, opening it wide for his first customer of the day. He adored the older lady as she was one of the first in the neighborhood to welcome him on his first day as the former store owner's assistant.

Dr. Aaron Paris was the only Caucasian business owner in the west side business district back in the day. But everyone loved the man because he treated no one any better, nor any worse than their neighbors.

When Benton earned his PharmD diploma, which certified his expertise in the pharmaceutical arts, his request for employment with Dr. Paris was greeted in the affirmative. One dinner with the elder man later, both men knew each one would be a good fit for the other.

Benton learned quickly and he shared many an after-work meal and a laugh with his mentor. "You'll love these folks," Paris used to tell Benton. "Let them become your new family, once they take you in. You'll never regret it."

However, there came a day when Benton noticed the man behaving oddly. Paris spent hours in the back office, searching for listening devices, he admitted later. "Someone's watching us," Paris whispered over and over as he counted the day's receipts. He eventually stopped talking to Benton, except to ask a question or convey a request.

One day, a year and a half before Benton discovered the secret of the formic ethers, Paris awaited Benton in the back office of the pharmacy. A well-worn pair of suitcases lay on the floor beside the floor safe with a train ticket for New York City resting on top of them.

"I'm headed west," Paris sadly announced without a greeting. Before Benton could ask about the disparity in his boss' destination, the older man produced a set of papers. "Sign this, give me a dollar bill, and the business is yours, Bob."

A look of fearful desperation colored Paris' gaze. Benton found himself reading the lease agreement and the transfer of ownership for the business itself. Upon signing, Paris shook Benton's hand tightly. A feeling of peace washed over the elder pharmacist that even Benton could feel. "Thank you, and good luck, Bob."

Benton always wondered if Dr. Paris was approached by the men of Operation Whitemask before he and Tim. Were they somehow aware of Benton's experiments with the formic ethers? He would probably never know.

Mrs. Clanton remained outside in the cold long enough for the doctor to flick the light switches upwards and turn his sign from

CLOSED to OPEN. Once the store was ready for business, the old woman finally crossed the threshold.

Benton listened to the subtle hum of the florescent lights overhead as they warmed up and filled the room with illumination. "How's the family, ma'am?" he asked as he removed his overcoat. "Grandnephews and nieces, and all."

Mrs. Clanton smiled at the thought of her large and loving family. Although she and her late husband never had any children, and not for lack of trying, her younger sister made up for any shortfalls in the family tree. "I appreciate your asking, Doctor. Maisie's doing great. She's getting so many tips at the diner, you wouldn't know there's a war on. Donnie's gotten through basic training. I worry the boy's gonna be sent to Europe."

Benton grinned. "Those Nazis won't know what hit them. He'll be sending you postcards from the Eiffel Tower two weeks from now." The pharmacist folded his coat over his forearm and motioned with his other hand for his customer to follow. "Let me get into my safe, Mrs. Clanton. I'll meet you at the back counter."

Chuckling without conviction, Mrs. Clanton moved forward unsteadily. "Race you there, young man."

Benton hung his winter coat on a peg in the back room, pulled on his ivory lab coat, then stepped towards a combination safe resting in the rear corner of his office. He knelt to twirl the dial with practiced skill. A few seconds later, the tumblers dropped into their homes and the heavy steel door swung open easily. Dr. Benton removed a small metal box.

Cradling it in his right palm, the doctor closed the safe door and spun the dial several times before walking to his desk where he pulled two cotton balls from a tall glass jar. He then opened a bottle of rubbing alcohol and quickly poured a small measure onto the cotton, just enough to moisten each ball.

Mrs. Clanton lowered herself cautiously into a chair that rested at the edge of Benton's office door. Even with her best winter coat on, with all its padding, her hips didn't touch the armrests. Dr. Benton saw the effort it took for the woman to get here, and he found himself smiling at her work to remain independent. Benton placed the box on his desk and spoke softly, "So how's that warehouse job working out for that other grandnephew of yours?"

At the prospect of further talking about her family, Mrs. Clanton broke into a wide grin. "It's good money, Doctor. Davie's saving up for a car, although I want him to see about a college degree, maybe become a real doctor." Her eyes widened and she shook with embarrassment. "Ooh, sorry. I meant a real doctor like you."

"No offense taken, Ma'am. There's all kinds of doctors in this world, right?" Benton gripped the base of the box securely and lifted the lid with his other. Inside rested a bottle filled with a clear fluid and a small inhaler beside it. "We all serve the community in our own ways."

Benton carefully lifted the bottle and unscrewed its black metal cap as well as the one at the base of the steel inhaler. He poured a couple of drops of the clear liquid into the rear of the inhaler, onto the cotton wick packed inside. Setting the inhaler down on the table, Benton quickly secured the bottle cap and carefully placed the vial back into the box.

Dr. Benton smiled at his client while running one of the cotton balls around the exterior of the inhaler. "So, is Davie picking up any overtime? I worked a lot of it when I put myself through school. It's good discipline."

Mrs. Clanton frowned. "Yes, the boy's gonna get some extra hours tomorrow night. It seems something happened on Sunday, something about a car that got into an accident that tore its trunk lid right off. I think they want some extra help to carry in the boxes from the trainyard or something. It's some kind of special shipment. He doesn't talk about it much." Mrs. Clanton leaned forward and whispered, "I don't think they tell him a whole lot about what goes on there."

"Sorry to hear about that car. Shame it had to happen." Benton walked over to the sink and filled a small glass with water. Then he stepped toward a rack of large bottles. He found one on the top shelf and carried it to a metal tray. The pharmacist poured a measure of small, white sugar pills and counted out a month's worth of "dosages," using a flat metal ruler. Benton then herded the pills into a waiting glass jar.

Next, Benton moved to a sink in the back of the pharmacy where he mixed various medicinal compounds for his customers. He poured some cool water into a paper cup. With the vessel in one hand, Benton picked up a spare sugar tablet in the other and carried his cargo to the waiting woman.

"I'm gonna tell that boy to be careful, not that he listens to me." Mrs. Clanton took the water glass from the doctor. She then accepted the pill and swallowed it quickly, washing it down with the rest of the chilled liquid. "Nobody's got business hanging out at the railyards at one in the morning. Nobody that isn't up to something, you know."

"I'm sure someone will be looking out for Davie's safety. Now let's make sure those sinuses are clear," Dr. Benton stated. He waved the inhaler under her nose. "Now take a few deep, deep breaths."

Mrs. Clanton closed her eyes and filled her lungs with the vapors from the inhaler. A smile crossed her lips just as Benton stated, "That should do it, Mrs. Clanton. How do you feel?"

"I feel pretty good, Dr. Benton. I think I'll make it for another month."

"Good." Benton handed Mrs. Clanton the pill-filled jar. "Here are your vitamins. Remember, take one just before breakfast and you'll be fine." He placed a supportive hand under her elbow and the other on the small of her fragile back as she strained to rise to her feet. "It'll take a few seconds before the formula take effect."

Mrs. Clanton dropped the bottle into her purse and withdrew a couple of bills. "Keep the change, Doctor."

The amount sitting in Dr. Benton's hand wasn't enough to cover the tab so he slipped the money into her coat pocket before she could notice. It was probably all she could afford, but Mrs. Clanton didn't want anyone to think she would welch on her bills. *She'll just think she found the money*, Benton thought, *just like every month for the last three years.*

"Thank you kindly, Mrs. Clanton. Let me see you out."

As the pair approached the front door, it swung open as Tim Rowland stamped the last of the snow from his shoes. He looked up and smiled politely. "Morning, Bob. Good morning, Mrs.

Clanton. You're looking well."

"Feeling great," the woman confirmed. "Thank you for every-thing, Dr. Benton. See you next month."

Tim held the door for the old woman who left the store. Bob stepped out onto the sidewalk to watch Mrs. Clanton quickly walk down the street towards her home. She tucked her cane under her arm as her pace increased.

"When--?" Tim began, but his mentor cut him off.

"I have a few customers who get a *very* diluted version of the ethers so don't panic, Tim." Benton clapped the boy on the shoulder. "Nobody's going to hoist a Studebaker over their heads but us. Let's get inside."

Tim followed his mentor towards the rear of the store. "What do you mean you're sharing the formic ethers? That's crazy, Bob."

Before he could answer, the bell over the front door sounded. Benton and Tim spun on their heels towards the ringing. They each narrowed their eyes, focusing on the man standing in the doorway.

"Dr. Benton." The red-haired man entered the pharmacy. As the metal and glass door slid firmly into place behind him, cutting off the chilled winds that still howled down the street, he tipped his cap at the men. "Tim. Sorry for the scare the other night. Sometimes, I forget what I can do." He paused and locked his gaze with Benton's. "What we can do."

Benton stepped in front of Tim, acting as a barrier between the stranger and his young friend. "I'm getting good and tired of the mystery man act. Make your statement and go."

"Mystery Man." The man chuckled as the words passed his lips. However, his amusement vanished like the snow under the morning sun. "Listen, I know about the delivery tonight at one. You just stay put." Benton opened his mouth to protest, but the man held up his hand for quiet. "You got lucky the other day. But if someone gets a good look at you and gives a description to the police, you're going to mess things up for a lot of people." He unintentionally glanced at Tim.

"You tell your boss that—" The words caught in Benton's throat. "I think you need to leave." His eyes narrowed. "Consider never coming back."

The red-haired man nodded. "Don't give me a reason to return, and I won't." He looked past the doctor at Tim. "I'm really sorry about last night, kid. Hope your mom wasn't too upset." The sincerity in his voice stayed Benton's hand long enough to allow the stranger to exit the building.

"So, what are we going to do, Bob?" Tim studied Benton's face. "Do we put on the suits tonight?"

"I don't think so." Benton led Tim towards the back of the building. "Aren't you supposed to be in school?"

"Naw," Tim said with a grin, "snow day. So, if you need someone to run the soda counter or cover your lunch, Mom said I could."

Benton chuckled. "Who am I to contradict that fine lady?" His smile faded. "Tell you what, I'll let you close the store today, all right?"

Tim frowned. "You mean you're handling this one o'clock adventure alone?"

"Did I say I was going to be at the railyard tonight? Especially since one of the thugs in the warehouse spilled his guts to the Terror on Sunday about the meet?" Upon entering his office, Benton moved towards the safe again. A few spins of the dial later, the door swung open, and Benton removed two zippered leather bags.

Benton handed Tim the bags, each containing the day's starter change. "Fill the cash drawers for me, please."

"Sure." Tim opened the pharmacy counter cash register and placed each denomination in its proper slots.

Benton found himself smiling as he watched the boy work so effortlessly in the hopes of hiding his own concerns. Tim knew a lot for a boy his age and the kid didn't get fooled very often. For one thing, Benton knew Tim was certain where his mentor would be late tonight, and it wasn't in his own bed. Benton also knew it chafed the action-craving young man to be forbidden to accompany his costumed persona on this mission.

As Tim moved to the cash register resting on the modest soda fountain counter, Bob Benton re-entered his office and knelt beside the combination safe again. He reached under the steel box and easily raised it with one hand while he lifted a section of wooden flooring upon which the safe rested.

Benton moved a square of glued wood that passed for some floorboards and pulled out a brown paper grocery bag. Seconds later, the flooring and the safe resumed their proper places and no one, except Benton, would know they'd been moved in the first place.

"What if I don't want to go home tonight, Bob?" Tim closed the cash register drawer and walked toward the office. "Maybe I'll let you cook dinner. Whatcha serving up tonight?"

The pharmacist reached inside the bag and pulled the contents free. Benton held aloft a fistful of silken ebony fabric with one hand, allowing it to unfurl completely.

Benton found himself smiling as grim thoughts crossed his mind. No, he wouldn't be making the rendezvous tonight as a quiet pharmacist. He stared at the ivory skull on the front of his midnight uniform and whispered one word...

"Terror."

CHAPTER EIGHT

"Charlie Will Probably Have a Heart Attack."

The not-much-above freezing temperatures of the afternoon vanished as the sun dipped below the horizon. Shortly after midnight, what melted during the day became ice once more. At this time of night, during the tail end of a Raceway City winter, the world shone with silver when bathed in moonlight.

However, on the south side of town, while still coated in an icy shimmer, the night wasn't exactly quiet.

A pair of boxcars slammed together at the far end of the railyard, drowning out Charlie Cronin's footsteps. He trod carefully, feeling the soles of his shoes maintain their precarious grip on the ice-covered ground. He swept his gaze over the yard until his neck muscles began to burn from the exertion. With another glance at his watch, Cronin tromped towards the far side of the yard with his arms extended from his sides, like a tightrope walker.

Cronin grew up taller and meaner than most of his schoolmates, albeit less muscular. When he was just a kid, the guy his mom claimed was his dad headed to France to shoot at strangers from the safety of a trench, or so he said. Cronin never saw him again, although the man sent money every now and then from an Arkansas address.

Without an older, somewhat responsible male to ask questions of, Cronin relied on the rumors and bad advice of his peers. Sometimes, the boys he interrogated didn't appreciate Cronin's inquisitive nature. When they made an issue of his questioning, Cronin used his fists to end many of those unpleasant encounters.

When his schoolmates proved to be no physical or mental challenge, Cronin turned his attentions to his teachers. He was expelled at 15 for trying to intimidate the school's staff The rumors flew that Cronin had put more men in the hospital than the

Spanish Flu. At least those were the rumors Cronin himself started.

Cronin enjoyed the notoriety and parlayed that into freelanc-
ing as a warm body for hire. You wanted someone to keep the
getaway car's motor running? You needed a delivery with no
questions asked about the contents? You wanted some smokes
for later? Cronin became your man and all of Raceway City's
underground knew it.

Although Cronin stayed good with his fists, getting tossed
around so easily by that guy in black rattled him. Sure, there were
mugs who could outfight him, but no one could fault Charlie
Cronin for not standing his ground. But that was a couple of
nights in the past.

Tonight, however, Cronin's pulse raced with every fresh noise
that filled the frigid night's air. The movement of goods in and
out of Raceway City on the steel rails that vivisected the city
didn't end at sunset. A lot of commerce entered and exited
around here under the moon's silver gaze every night of the
week, even on holidays.

A cry of greetings from one engineer to another sent fresh
chills up and down Cronin's spine. Despite the cold of the night,
Cronin broke into a sweat. He knew the truth, that he was as safe
as a battle-shocked thug could be in an active railyard, every
sound triggered a feeling like that monster in black, red, and silver could launch a new attack at any second.

Cronin's head still rung from the blow he received from that
costumed lunatic, but no learned doctor or pretty nurse could
have made him spend one more day in a hospital. Well, maybe
the nurses could, but none did so he checked himself out.

The career criminal unconsciously patted the handgun in his
jacket pocket as he approached the boxcar, reaching for his cigarettes with the other. He knew his nerves could use the nicotine
and hoped the pistol would stay in his pocket until he got home.

Cronin stopped in his tracks as he noticed someone at the edge
of his vision. He laughed briefly and inwardly cursed his newfound cowardice.

Someone sat on the metal steps attached to the back of a passenger car. Cronin couldn't tell if the man stared at him from under the slouch brimmed hat he wore. "What're you lookin' at?" Cronin called out, plunging his hand into his pocket to grip the revolver, just in case.

The black man raised his shoulders and hands to indicate he would prove no challenge to the criminal. He casually rose to a standing position and walked up the iron steps and into the car, slamming the door behind him.

"Yeah," Cronin stated in a whisper, "move along, pal." He checked his wristwatch. "I'll deal with you if you're still around later."

Cronin checked his watch yet again. The hands rested on five minutes until one and Cronin didn't want to be late for his clandestine appointment. He deftly stepped over the numerous rails that ran the length of the yard, making his way towards a lone boxcar at the far end.

But unseen by Cronin, inside the unlit passenger car, Bob Benton pulled off his hat and shrugged away his long coat, exposing the skin-tight costume with the ivory skull adorning his chest. A few seconds later, he stepped out of his trousers before folding his clothing quickly and neatly one item at a time. After dropping his hat on the pile, Benton shook his blue and red cloak, making certain it flowed freely.

After pulling the ebony mask over his eyes, Bob Benton took on another identity, one that existed now only as erroneous comic book fictions...*The Terror!*

It felt good to be in costume again, the Terror admitted to himself. Then his expression turned as grim as the task that lay before him.

Checking through a window, the Terror watched Cronin climb over a coupling between two boxcars to disappear from sight. The Terror stepped out into the night quietly, drawing the blue exterior of his cloak close to his body. Then he bent his knees slightly and launched himself upwards from the rear of the passenger car to land a good fifty feet from where he started. From there, the Terror sprinted across the trainyard, his footfalls silently pressing into the ice and what remained of the snow without a sound.

Upon reaching the boxcar where he last saw the criminal, the Terror unhesitatingly lifted a leg as if attempting to leap over a mud puddle. Instead, the costumed man vaulted into the air as if propelled by a cannon. The Terror easily reached the top of the wooden box, alighting upon it gently. With the moon at his front, even if the clouds would part long enough to allow some light, his shadow would never strike the ground to risk warning his prey. He knelt atop the railcar and watched Cronin make his way to the far edge of the railyard where a single boxcar awaited him.

Charlie Cronin approached the lone car. From here, the multiple rails unified into three leading out of Raceway City. He checked his watch and smiled. Three minutes to spare. Cronin took in a chilled lungful of air and enjoyed the distant noises of trains moving at the other end of the lot.

As if to reward Cronin for his punctuality, a half dozen men emerged from behind the car. Their wool caps covered their faces from the eyebrows on up and scarves concealed all but their eyes. Each man lumbered into the sparse light with fists clenched, their eyes focused on their visitor and no one else.

Six men, thought the Terror, *and Charlie Cronin too.* He smiled, knowing the fight he hoped to avoid would cost him no more than thirty seconds' worth of violent effort, not counting the five seconds, or less, it would take to close the distance. *After Sunday, Charlie will probably have a heart attack when he sees me.*

The Terror caught a glimpse of a seventh man lurking back in the icy shadows of the boxcar. His slender shadow made the Terror think of a long coat and with the obvious brim of a fedora, this man wore his money for all to see. *Probably the boss who'll be the first to bolt while I take out the muscle.* The Terror squatted down and listened to the men as they approached the now-halted Charlie Cronin.

Cronin raised his hands and allowed three of the men to pat him down. Each thug thrust their hands into his pockets with much-practiced efficiency in their search for weapons. One pulled out a snub-nosed .38 as another withdrew a thickly packed envelope. A quick rifling through the packet's contents and a nod later, the searcher placed the envelope inside his own jacket with a reassuring pat to seal the deal. The pistol, however, remained in the new possessor's grip.

"You got the goods?" Cronin asked the man in the darkness. He winced and hoped no one noticed his voice cracking out of nervousness. Something was wrong, but Cronin couldn't articulate what it could be. This feeling filled him with dread, but he didn't know why. Did it have to do with the stranger he saw? Or the man who stayed in the shadows?

After a long pause, the mysterious gentleman spoke through his face scarf as he stepped into a thin beam of moonlight. "We have it inside." He indicated the boxcar with a wave of his hand. "The money?"

The man who handled the envelope nodded once. Satisfied, the shadowed person snapped his fingers.

The other henchmen pulled at the boxcar's heavy wooden door. The wheels squealed in protest as they moved in their tracks, revealing two small brown paper bags sitting on the dirty floor.

Cronin bit his lip as he stared at the small satchels. The size of each made him think of two railroad workers going hungry to-night without paper bags to carry their lunches. "I see the usual delivery, but what about the other stuff?" Cronin asked. "You know, about replacing the delivery stolen the other night? My boss will want to know."

"You take on the replacement costs, not us." The shadowed gentleman's voice turned colder than the ice under his feet. "You got it to the warehouse and then it's not our problem that part of it got nabbed." An undertone of annoyance colored the stranger's speech. "You have the chemicals for your legitimate businesses." Then his tone softened. "The other here will tide your employer over until you fork over more cash."

Cronin shook his head in confusion as the Terror flexed his legs and calculated the amount of power he'd need to reach the closest bad man. A broad grin crossed the Terror's face as he re-assessed the strength of his legs. He savored the crisp night air, the pounding of his heart, the challenge of the situation and didn't realize until now how much he missed this.

The six hired hands reached into their jackets for their weapons with the kind of speed and unwasted effort that only years of practice could bring. But the exposure of their weaponry found itself delayed as they noticed the ebony-clad man leaping upwards and toward them.

Unlike most men, the Terror didn't fall to earth but kept rising in the air. He spread his hands as he ascended, and the scarlet underside of his cloak caught the night breeze to unfurrow like a flag. Mesmerized by the sight, the thugs hesitated for almost a full second, even as the Terror landed beside the boxcar.

The first henchman caught a right that spun him in place like a drill bit. As he fell to the ground, the Terror stepped quickly to the guy next in line. The thug's pistol already cleared his jacket but before he could aim the piece and pull the trigger, the dark-clad adventurer seized the gun. The Terror turned the handgun like a doorknob and instantly broke the crook's trigger finger. A lightning-fast left rendered the man unconscious, unable to feel his broken jaw.

Charlie Cronin fled towards the center of the trainyard to the Terror's complete lack of surprise. The cloaked man continued to squeeze the pistol and with no more effort than it would take to juice an orange, the Terror transformed the handgun into a mis-shapen parody of a ball. He took a second to backhand the last man guarding the boxcar, lifting the criminal a couple of inches off the ground when doing so.

As the unconscious gunsel landed hard on his back, the Terror reared back his arm and let the metal lump fly. The former handgun struck Cronin at the base of his spine and the fleeing man dropped like a sack of potatoes, face-first into the dirt and ice.

By the time the remaining trio realized their peril, two of them felt steely fingers dig into their shoulders. A second later, the third man witnessed his cohorts being slammed into each other like a pair of cymbals. The last crook left standing backed up, his eyes wide with fright. He stammered unintelligibly, raising his hands in a shaky effort to ward off the Terror's potential attack.

The Terror's grin faded. This escapade took too long. His enhanced hearing registered the shadowed man's footsteps hurriedly fading from the range of his perceptions. He pulled back his fist, ready to send the last hired gun to Dreamland.

But the Terror's hand didn't move. He attempted to complete his attack. However, something that felt like a manacle surrounded his wrist. The Terror turned to see what could hold him so thoroughly.

To his astonishment, it wasn't a thing of metal that kept his fist in place. It was another human hand gripping his wrist in its adamantine grasp. It appeared to be a man of comparable height who wore a navy-blue hooded jacket with matching pants, as well as scarlet gloves and jet-black boots, with crimson goggles that concealed most of his features.

With the moon now traveling towards the western sky, shadows extended from below the brim of the attacker's hood to conceal his face. But the silvery illumination from overhead now highlighted the outer edges of the cloth from which the man's bright red hair emerged.

CHAPTER NINE

"There's More Going On Than You Know."

"How—?" was all the Terror managed to utter before the red gauntlet struck him in the face. The process that gave the masked hero and his youthful sidekick their incredible abilities made Dr. Bob Benton tougher than any man alive that he knew of.

However, the Terror couldn't recall ever being hit this hard, since he'd created the formic ethers compound. Pain overwhelmed him for a fleeting moment until the red-haired man's fingers dug painfully into the Terror's wrist once again. If the pharmacist-by-day had been a normal man, the pressure would have turned his bones into powder. As it was, pain shot up the Terror's arm and made him wonder if he'd get to keep the appendage.

"Let go of me," the Terror commanded through gritted teeth. "He's getting away."

"Let him," the stranger growled back. "You don't know all that's going on."

"How about you telling me, then?" The Terror winced as he heard an automobile starting up on the far side of the boxcar. The sound of wheels spinning on a patch of ice before finding purchase and vanishing into the night filled the Terror with acute disappointment and fury. He growled as he yanked back his hand, freeing it from the red-haired man's grasp.

Rubbing his wrist to restore the circulation, the Terror looked at his attacker. His back curved, his fists rose, and his knees bent slightly in a boxer's stance. "The boss is getting away, you idiot. So, either step out of the way or get knocked over."

With a quick shake of his head, the stranger stated in a low voice, "Wrong. But your choices are to get the hell out of here." A quick smile disappeared as quickly as it arrived. "Oops, never was good at math." Sensing a fight in the offing, the man swiftly smacked his scarlet-covered fist into his open palm.

The Terror noticed that his opponent wore slacks and a hooded jacket, both in cobalt-colored fabric that glinted in the scant moonlight like chainmail. The stranger adjusted the scarlet goggles over his eyes, then he pulled his hood over the top of his head and quickly tied it into place so swiftly that even the Terror barely saw his fingers.

What looked like a navy-blue beetle served as the belt's buckle while a pair of highly polished jet-black leather boots completed the man's costume.

"So, what do I call you and which circus do you belong to?" the Terror asked.

"I'd throw fewer stones if I was you." The stranger gave the Terror's uniform a visual once-over and smirked. "Try calling me the Cobalt Scarab...assuming I leave you any teeth."

He's right. I'm no one to criticize anyone else's fashion choices. The Terror gritted his teeth and launched himself at the Cobalt Scarab. He pulled back his fist, certain he wouldn't—couldn't—hold back for once.

But when the Terror threw his punch, the Scarab stepped out of the way, barely avoiding the blow. The man's lips pressed together in a thin line of flesh, masking his surprise.

The Terror followed through and tried to leave his attacker behind so he could apprehend the well-dressed man in the shadows. But the Terror's momentum ended as he felt his cape and the fabric around his collar go taut. He spun to see the Scarab gripping the blue and red cloak with both hands, the strain of holding onto the Terror visible on his face.

"I said—" The Terror launched another blow. With his hands engaged, the Cobalt Scarab took the punch right in the jaw. He released his hold on the cloak and stumbled back, his hand pressed up to his aching chin.

"—Let go." The Terror raised his fists again. His enhanced strength could pierce an oak door easily, but he never used it against normal human men, which this interloper clearly wasn't. Regardless of his medical standing to do no harm, the Terror refused to take a human life if he could help it. And almost every time he entered combat, the Terror could help it.

As it was, the Scarab rubbed his jaw and shook his head to clear it. From the expression on the lower half of his face that he could see, the Terror guessed the red-haired man was more surprised to feel this much pain than he was to receive an attack of that magnitude.

"I don't accept interference when Raceway City's in danger," the Terror snarled. "And I won't warn you again. Back away."

Growling in frustration, the Cobalt Scarab turned on his heel and kicked up a spray of frozen soil and dirty snow as he sprinted away from the Terror. He raced toward the boxcar at the speed of an express train. But once past where the satchels remained unmolested in the dirt and ice, the man's feet left the ground and he appeared to run on an invisible footpath that took him twenty feet into the air.

The stranger leaned to his left, pumping his feet furiously. He moved in a tight oval overhead until he could see the Terror again. At that point, the man leaned forward to execute an accelerated power dive towards the Terror.

Instinctively, the Terror lifted his forearms to cover his face and he braced for a full-body impact. A heartbeat later, the Scarab's fist got past the Terror's defense and connected with his chin. He felt his head snap backwards dangerously as he struck the frigid ground. Rolling over again and again, the Terror tumbled, striking several steel rails before he came to a halt, landing with his backside higher than his head.

He's as powerful as I am. And this is embarrassing. The Terror's grogginess vanished as he executed a tip-up to land on his feet. He swiftly unwrapped his cloak from around his body and tried to brush off the dirt and snow from his uniform. *And I sure as heck can't fly.*

"You're stronger than I thought." The Scarab's voice was tinged with a combination of astonishment and no small amount of respect. "But you've got to get out of here. There's more going on than you know."

Under other circumstances, the Terror might have paused to listen to an explanation. Instead, his anger drove him to close the distance between them. He aimed for his foe's midsection, hoping to drive the air from the Scarab's lungs and get the challenger into a position to receive a devastating uppercut.

However, once the Terror came within striking distance, the Cobalt Scarab quickly reached down, seized a fistful of dirt, and tossed it into the dark-clad man's eyes. Blinded, the Terror braked, which gave the Scarab another opportunity to attack.

The Terror felt a pair of powerful hands clap his ears. Deafened, doubled over, and blinded by the ultimate Fourth of July fireworks display behind his eyes, the Terror couldn't stop the Scarab from grabbing him by the shoulders to bring him to a full standing position. Then the costumed man felt the worst pain a man could feel in the most sensitive area of all. The Terror gasped, barely aware of his knees coming into hard contact with the ground.

Momentarily unable to defend himself, the Terror barely felt his feet lose contact with the frigid ground. A couple of hard slaps across his face brought the hero back to reality. He realized several male voices cried out in confusion behind him as the volume of their unintelligible shouts grew louder and quickly.

With a pained grin spreading over his face, the Terror looked up at his attacker. "The railroad workers. Looks like we've been caught."

"That's why I'm doing this, to make it look good." The Cobalt Scarab shook the Terror like a rag doll before dropping him. "Listen," the Scarab growled, "get the hell out of here. You don't want someone to identify you."

But the Terror's knees couldn't yet support his weight. "Why...?" he mumbled, still trying to catch his breath. "How are you...?"

With a growl, the stranger grabbed The Terror's belt. With no effort whatsoever, he hurled the black-clad hero through the open side door of the boxcar. The Terror struck the far interior wall with enough force to almost knock him out. Stars danced behind his eyes and his muscles felt like wool.

A pair of objects whizzed past the Terror's head. He glanced behind him to see the satchels left behind when the clandestine meeting broke up. *If I could just get to my feet, I could...*

The Terror struggled to lift himself to a kneeling position as the side door slid shut. Able to see from just a few slivers of moonlight reflected from the icy ground outside, the Terror crawled over to the door. He moved only a few feet when he realized the boxcar was now in motion. The Terror dug his fingers into the wall as he realized the reason for the boxcar's movement.

"Dammit, Scarab."

Unsteadily, the Terror glanced down at the twin bags and looked in every direction for a quick way out. The door would be the easiest, but the racket from it being torn from its hinges would give his opponent too much warning. And until he could learn to run on air, which wasn't going to happen in the next ten seconds, the Terror decided on another means of egress.

Outside, the Cobalt Scarab pushed against the back of the boxcar. Overcoming the box's inertia wasn't the easiest thing he'd done all week, but with his maximum effort, it now moved quickly over the steel rails under its wheels. The Scarab looked down to place his feet against the forward side of the ties with each step, pushing against the hard wood to increase his speed.

"This should keep you occupied, pharmacist," the Scarab muttered.

After just a few seconds, the boxcar gained velocity on a slight downhill incline. Pushing with his unnatural strength urged the railcar's speed beyond that of an Olympic sprinter's. The stranger pushed even harder until the voices of the railyard workers grew fainter. Soon, all the Scarab could hear was the hypnotic drone of steel moving over steel.

The pathway curved slightly, and the Scarab craned his neck to see around his burden. In just a few seconds, the boxcar would strike a steel buffer stop, a device designed to absorb the kinetic energy of a moving train and prevent the cars from falling off the end of the track. That was, if the engine wasn't going as fast as the boxcar now traveled.

For a moment, the Scarab considered bringing the railcar to a halt, to see if his prodigious strength could brake this multi-ton car's moving weight. Before he could come to a decision, a flash of movement at the edge of the Scarab's vision distracted him. Startled, he stumbled on the railway ties before he lost his grip on the rear coupling of the vehicle.

As the Scarab pushed himself to his feet again, the boxcar raced relentlessly toward the buffer stop. Unable to tear his gaze away from the impending disaster, the Cobalt Scarab grimaced, thinking of the Terror inside. As the boxcar struck the steel buffer, the night air filled with the din of what Armageddon must sound like as the wood and steel of the vessel flew in a dozen different directions.

Ignoring the shouts of the approaching railyard workers, the Cobalt Scarab raced towards the destruction. The roof of the boxcar landed on its side, imbedding itself a foot into the frozen soil. Shards of metal and wood rained down like seeds sewn by a blind man. The Scarab reached the boxcar and pulled the wooden side door away, tossing it like balsa. "Terror!" he cried out; his voice thick with concern. "Benton?"

As the Scarab searched what remained of the boxcar's interior, he gritted his teeth. Whatever was inside there, including the two satchels, were nowhere to be seen. No blood, no costumed body, no sign of anyone being inside at the critical moment of impact.

The Cobalt Scarab turned his attention to what remained of the boxcar's roof. He noticed a hole torn in the center of the wood and what appeared to be fingerholds dug into what used to be a steel crossbeam. *The Terror must have jumped towards the roof, buried his fingers in the beam, then punched a hole through the ceiling,* the Scarab deduced. *He must have leaped to safety while I was trying to move the car.* Another thought crossed his mind. *Damn him twice,* he thought, *Benton made off with those bags.*

"Hey! Stay right there. The police are gonna wanna talk to you."

The Scarab looked toward the voices. A mob of men crossed the railyard, some with iron levers, others with clubs, and a few with small caliber handguns.

However, they weren't coming for the Scarab who turned his gaze to where the boxcar had rested.

The Terror grabbed one of the mobsters and tore the man's pocket open. A moment later, he pulled an envelope free of the fallen crook's care, tucked it into his belt, then looked up at the approaching mob.

With a wave to the Scarab, the Terror flexed his legs and pushed himself into the air and away from the railyard. Once the advancing rail workers saw this, and their amazement wore off, one of them pointed at the blue-clad intruder and said something to his fellows. At that moment, the mob changed direction and marched toward him.

The Cobalt Scarab decided he didn't want to answer their questions. He especially didn't wish to meet anyone from the Raceway City Police Department, not quite yet. The man turned quickly and easily leaped over the chain link fence that enclosed the property. A few leaps later, the man took to the air, running thirty feet over the ground and into the night.

Several minutes later, the Terror entered his pharmacy by the rear door. He didn't dare turn on the lights for fear of someone seeing him in his uniform. The faint light from the electric clock over the entrance gave his enhanced vision more than enough illumination to work with. Soon, the Terror lifted his office safe, placed the two bags inside the hidden space below the floorboards, then set everything back where it belonged.

The Terror removed his uniform with an unnatural speed. A swift look at the ebony fabric revealed no patching was needed but a good wash would do wonders to spruce up the costume.

Planning the next move would also be a good idea, but that could wait until the morning.

CHAPTER TEN

"You've Got a Job To Do."

"He grabbed *what*??? I want to hear your version of this nonsense."

Ben Pickern pinched the bridge of his nose and turned away from the light on his bedstand. "You heard me, Brant. My guys almost got pinched and the shipment was stolen, along with the money."

Mayor Carlton Brant cradled the telephone receiver between the side of his chin and his shoulder as he awkwardly put on his bathrobe. "My representative told me the same thing. Fortunately, for both of us, he managed to make his escape."

"Good." Pickern took a deep breath. "Listen, I just wanted to give you the details. We've got a larger problem than just the dope and the money."

A few seconds passed before Mayor Brant spoke again. This time, he'd regained his composure. "I'm sorry, but this whole affair is getting to me." He paused for a few seconds. "This wouldn't involve the parahumans, would it?"

"Pair-of-humans? If it's those costumed freaks, you got it in one," Pickern admitted. "I thought everyone was toeing the mark, keeping quiet and inactive. But the trunk lid didn't tear itself off. And you don't want to know what happened in the train yard."

"Don't worry, Cronin gave me most of the railyard story twenty minutes ago. Did you get a description of the guy?"

"Guys," Pickern corrected. "Hey, let me pick up the other line, okay? I need a drink." Without waiting for an answer, the mobster set the receiver down on the pillow gently. Pickern stepped into his house slippers and made his way to his study at the other end of the hallway.

Once inside the spacious study, Pickern poured himself two fingers of Kentucky whiskey, omitting the ice. He plopped into his favorite chair before picking up the extension phone. "Okay,

I'm ready."

Mayor Brant altered the tone of his voice to conceal his mounting concern, as well as how much Pickern intimidated him. In moments like this, Brant's political training served him well. He could conceal his fury and bewilderment in a manner more suitable for ordering dinner at a fancy restaurant.

The mayor recalled when the bedside phone rang less than half an hour ago. Charlie Cronin's voice shook like the man just hit puberty. After a minute of useless stammering, the mayor hung up and then called one of the rail workers, the one who arranged for the car to be placed at the far corner of the yard to ensure a degree of privacy for the exchange. That conversation proved far more fruitful, although the results were equally disappointing.

Brant now relayed similar information, just as he received it. He braced himself for the emotional explosion on the other end of the telephone line.

Much to the mayor's surprise, Pickern's voice came across as calm, almost difficult to hear, as he punctuated his half of the conversation with the occasional "Uh-huh" or "Mm-mm." Brant continued his narrative until he described the stranger in blue with the strength to push a railway car at a speed that rivaled an automobile.

The career criminal waited for Brant to conclude his narrative before speaking. "So, the money and the dope is in someone else's hands."

"So it would seem." Mayor Brant still waited to hear an ear-shattering string of obscenities. After a brief wait, he added, "I think the one in black with the skull on his shirt, he's the one who took the goods and the loot. The other one leaped away until he was out of sight." Brant decided it wouldn't be a good idea to relay the worker's assertion that one of the parahumans could fly.

"Describe these men to me," Pickern commanded.

"Both guys were around six feet tall, athletic from what I was told."

Mayor Brant took a deep breath on the other end of the phone.

"One guy was white wore a weird jacket with matching blue

pants. They both looked like something out of the funny pages."

Pickern inhaled deeply one more time.

"The other was dressed in tight black satin, I think, with a big skull on his chest. He had a blue cape lined with red." Brant paused for a couple of seconds. "And I'm told he was black."

No sound came over the earpiece as Pickern digested this information. After what seemed like a half hour, but was only a few seconds, Pickern broke his silence. "If you're waiting for me to tear your ear off, don't worry." The mobster's voice was as even in tone as the mayor's, much to the latter's surprise. "If they're who I think they are, your guys couldn't have stopped them anyway."

Brant found himself nodding, even though he knew Pickern couldn't see him. "If nothing else, I want to get that money back." He chuckled. "I'll meet you for lunch at the Club. I'll reserve the back room." He paused. "There's stuff you need to know about what and who we're facing."

Pickern almost asked how the politician knew anything about these bizarre men but thought it wiser to keep his surprise to himself. "Well, I'm glad we're comparing notes. So, what's our next move?"

"We will discuss that at noon, sharp." Brant cleared his throat as he felt the need to take control of this conversation, as well as the situation. "I think I know who one of them is, for sure. I've had dealings with him in the past. The guy who busted up the boxcar, however, I'll need to know who that is."

"Get Cronin to ask around, "Pickern offered. "Anything else?"

"Not yet. See you at lunch."

Then the line went dead in Ben Pickern's hand. He replaced the receiver in its cradle, knowing he wouldn't get back to sleep now.

Back in his mansion on the east side of the city, Carlton Brant ran his tongue along the edge of the crystal glass, savoring the taste of his finest scotch. Although he rarely took a drink of spirits before five in the evening, a fouled-up deal like this made him question his commitment to sobriety at this hour.

It was supposed to be a simple exchange at the railyard. Five figures worth of cash in exchange for what could become at least six figures of horse. It should have happened smoothly on Sunday, except that jerk in the black Halloween costume foiled everything.

Mayor Brant grimaced. *I thought the Terror had been dealt with two years ago. It's time to remind that clown of his place and the wisdom of staying there.*

Some help that damn Mayor's been lately. Far from the mayor's mansion, Pickern contemplated the irony of having helped Brant get into office just two terms earlier, thanks to rigging the vote in certain precincts, but now the mob boss had to tread lightly around the man. *Wish I'd never set him up. He's too friggin' clever for his own good, or mine. He also keeps forgetting who's on which rung of the ladder in this town.* He stood up and placed the glass, rim down on the bar, closed his dressing gown, and walked towards the door.

If nothing else, he thought, *I could catch a couple of hours more sleep.*

After turning out the lights in the study, Pickern ascended the stairs. His mind raced through all the options available to deal with the Terror and that guy in blue as well. He promised he'd call Charlie Cronin himself when he woke up again. He envisioned the man lying on the floor of the apartment, nerves shot to hell, curled up in the fetal position, clammy hands clutching a bottle of back-room hooch that probably came from that dive Cronin haunted.

Once inside his bedroom, Ben Pickern removed his robe, ready to hang it carefully on the back of his door. Then he turned towards his bed and saw something that made his jaw drop and the robe slide from his hand and onto the floor.

The telephone receiver rested on the bedside table.

Pickern's manservant prepped breakfast in the kitchen. The butler didn't know all of his boss' cronies and hardly anything that could be used against him in a court of law. The butler enjoyed his paycheck too much to think about nosing into Pickern's businesses, however.

The mob boss knew the man's loyalty was well and truly paid for, so it couldn't be him that moved the receiver.

Pickern's hands shook as he reached between the mattress and springs to pull out a snub nosed .38. He checked his window, relieved to find it still locked up tight, just as he left it. He examined both the closet and the attached bathroom, his revolver at the ready. However, no one was in either space and Pickern wanted to know not just who invaded his home, but how.

How much did he hear? Pickern picked up the receiver and dialed as quickly as his trembling fingers would allow. He listened as the phone rang on the other end of the wire once, twice, then a third time before being picked up.

Without waiting for a reply, Pickern growled into the mouthpiece, "Cronin, get your backside off the floor and sober up fast. You've got a job to do."

As Ben Pickern growled his commands to Charlie Cronin, a lone lightbulb shone in the back office of Benton's Drugs.

Inside, Bob Benton rose from his chair after some time, contemplating tonight's events in the near darkness of his office. Determined to finish his business and soak for a while in the bathtub, the pharmacist knelt behind the cast iron safe in the corner of the room. To get it through the front door and into his office at the rear of the building, two strong men almost gave themselves hernias as Benton watched with concern for their wellbeing.

Today, Benton easily raised the safe a couple of feet above the floor with one hand. A moment later, he lifted a small square of flooring and dropped both brown bags from the railroad car, along with the envelope filled with illicit money, into the gap before lowering the wood once again. After lowering the safe's legs onto the indentations it created long ago, Benton began to breathe again.

Benton picked up the black, white, and gold uniform from the floor where he tossed it. Clods of dirt dislodged themselves from the silken fabric and struck the wooden surface, each with an all-too-loud PLOP! A further examination showed the cloak suffered some damage from either his tumble over the icy ground or being slammed into the back wall of that boxcar. Either way, it wouldn't do to be seen in a cape with so many tears in it.

Actually, Benton hoped the railyard workers didn't get a good look at him or if they did, they thought he might be some kook dressed up like a comic book character.

The thought of comic books sent a wave of anger through Benton and he closed his eyes, took a deep breath, and brought his pulse back under control. *I can't change the last couple of years,* he thought. *However, I can alter the course of my life from this point on.* He paused, then added, *I hope.*

Benton held up the cloak once again, noting the light pouring through the shredded material, and sighed.

But one thing I can't do is sew.

* * * * * *

A late-night bath, a few hours' sleep, a hearty breakfast, and most of a pot of coffee later, Bob Benton dressed and readied himself for another day in the pharmacy. He slipped on his glasses and then his overcoat before he exited his apartment. Actually, when he took in the formic ethers and his entire musculature became super-charged, that included his ocular muscles. He kept the glasses on as a distraction from anyone guessing he was the Terror.

Not that too many people on the free side of prison bars knew his alter ego existed because of Benton's caution during his two years of adventuring. *Or freelance social engineering, if you will,* he thought with a grin as he stepped onto the sidewalk.

The sun painted an early morning orange patina over the gray snowbanks that lay on the ends of each block. The radio earlier claimed the start of another above-freezing day would turn what little slush remained from last night into a solid block of ice by tomorrow morning as temperatures dropped again after sunset.

However, the news reader made no mention of any altercation in the trainyard overnight. Benton's brow furrowed in confusion as he contemplated that. Surely a super-powered man pushing a boxcar to its destruction would warrant a mention.

Better concentrate on making it to the end of the block. I don't want to start sprinting and finding myself downstate before I know it.

Once inside his business establishment, Bob Benton turned on the overhead lights without even glancing at the wall switches. He quickly pulled out the day's starter change and made a note to drop off the last couple of days' receipts in the night deposit after work. Tonight, Benton promised himself a night off from costumed heroics. Maybe he'd cook a steak and listen to some music before hitting the hay early.

Soon, the regular customers entered to fill their prescriptions or to buy supplies. Dr. Benton enjoyed this part of the day, talking to people he came to know as more than just customers, but as friends and neighbors. Occasionally, he'd make a fresh pot of coffee. The lunch counter didn't really open until Tim came home from school. Fortunately, he was a good student who got his homework done early and Benton was pleased to have his company.

Just before lunchtime, Dr. Benton heard the bell over the front door ring. In walked a gentleman in a fur-lined coat, wearing black leather gloves and a jet-black homburg. He kicked the snow from his shoes before entering. Benton focused his eyes on the man, keeping his expression impassive as the visitor studied a shelf filled with various brands of aspirin.

After he finally made a selection from the pain killers, the gentleman approached the rear of the store. He tilted his head back and flashed a lustrous grin at the pharmacist who returned it.

"Davie? Davie Clanton?" Benton emerged from the back to shake the younger man's hand. "You were just a kid, last time I saw you." Benton stepped back to admire his visitor's ensemble. "You look good, I must say."

"Thanks, Doc. It's 'Doc' now, right?" Davie grinned a perfect smile. "I think I was a brat when you bought the pharmacy."

"Yes, on both parts" Benton agreed with a chuckle. "I'm told you got a good job at Raceway Distribution."

Davie chuckled. "It sure is. Mr. Maxley's been really good to me. You know him?"

"Only by reputation," Benton stated as his smile wavered for a moment. The pharmacist gestured towards his visitor's ensemble. "I see he pays well."

"I won't get rich working there," Davie said, a fresh seriousness in his voice. "But I grew up watching my friends become al-kies or hop heads. I told myself I'm not going down that path." The grin returned as he opened up his coat to expose the bright red silk lining. "But I figured if I'm going to have some kind of vice, how about good clothing? I mean if someone asks me how I got these fine threads, I'd tell them to work hard for the right people so you can lift yourself into a better life."

"Words to live by, Davie." Benton paused. "When one has earned so much, the best way to pay back your benefactors is to share with your people, I believe."

Davie nodded with a soft smile. "That's why I came back to Raceway City, Doc." He hefted the bottle of white tablets. "I promised Grandma Ellie I'd be back right away, so I better pay for this."

Benton took the bottle, rang it up in the cash register, and bagged Davie's purchase as the gentleman paid in exact change. "I'll probably be running more errands for Grandma, Doc. See you around?"

"Definitely." Benton handed the bag to Davie. "Tell your grandmother I said hello."

As Davie walked out of the pharmacy, the doctor studied the other man's silhouette. *Not the same cut of clothing as the guy from the other night, that's for sure.* Benton sighed with relief as he resumed his contemplation of a night's worth of relaxation and a good steak.

CHAPTER ELEVEN

"How Odd Could It Be?"

The end of the workday couldn't come soon enough for Bob Benton. After locking the drug store's front door, the pharmacist prepared a deposit for the day's receipts. As the week concluded, this money would just cover the rent and the cost of new merchandise for the last week and that was okay for the pharmacist. While the government talked about rationing many staples of American life, people still needed their prescriptions filled.

However, if he made just a little more money, Benton contemplated hiring someone to man the lunch counter…well, at lunch, perhaps. Then again, he reasoned, it would be one more person to be secretive around. It was tough enough with just two other people, the Rowlands, knowing of Benton's dual identity.

Not counting, of course, anyone connected with Operation Whitemask. But the more Benton thought about this shadow organization in his own government, the less sleep he got at night. Thus, Benton pushed this train of thought off its rails and into the back of his mind.

While no one in this neighborhood could claim to be wealthy, Tim's mother, Velma Rowland, worked a decent job at the neighborhood bank. It didn't allow for many luxuries for herself and her son, but Tim never lacked for clean clothing or a hot meal.

After checking his figures three times and filling out a deposit slip, Benton inserted the money into a zippered bag. Once everything rested in place, he pulled the fastener shut before he secured the contents with a small padlock that fit through the zipper's pull tab and a brown leather loop at the end.

Before closing the safe, Benton withdrew the Terror's torn cloak and placed the fabric inside a large grocery bag without bothering to straighten it. He quickly folded the brown paper sack and placed it under his arm. Then he dropped the deposit bag into his coat pocket before he turned off the overhead lights, locked the front door, and left for the night.

Benton's Drugs and The Second National Bank of Raceway City where Velma worked kept the same hours so he often availed himself of the night deposit box unless he could talk Tim Rowland into watching the store for a half hour. *The boy never complained, God bless him. He probably likes being in charge.* Once the money entered Benton's account in the morning, the bank was kind enough to mail his receipt back or Velma might drop it off on the way home, if time permitted.

As Benton strolled amidst the rush hour pedestrians, he enjoyed the cool wind on his face. To many, the stiff breezes proved unpleasantly cold, even though the temperature reached the low forties by mid-afternoon, the warmest they'd been in two weeks.

The sound of water dripping from icicles attached to the overhanging business signs created a gentle percussion that Benton found almost musical, thanks to his enhanced hearing.

For Benton, the several blocks of walking barely proved any exertion at all. Upon reaching the bank, Benton opened the night deposit gate as his hand dived into his coat pocket for the bag.

"Fancy meeting you here."

Startled, Benton released the handle on the night deposit. The door slammed shut with an impossibly loud *CLANG!* He whirled about, scarcely able to believe the voice's owner.

"Jean Starr." Benton stopped his voice from quavering as he laid eyes on the woman. He could punch a hole through the slats and metal supports of a boxcar's roof with relative ease compared to feeling weak in the knees when this beautiful woman smiled at him. "What brings you here?"

"The city comptroller asked me to drop off some paperwork at this bank." She held up a large envelope with the city seal printed on its back. "I was told I could just drop them in the night deposit and the president of the bank would look at them tomorrow."

Benton smiled as he gestured gallantly for Jean to approach the night deposit. She stepped forward and released the paperwork into the darkness of the box. Benton imitated her action by surrendering his money to the bank's care and then releasing the door, this time with far less racket than a minute ago. "So, you're working for the comptroller's office, running errands after hours? Is that part of your job description?"

Jean looked away demurely. "Rod doesn't—well, he is a busy man. I'm sure you understand."

"Oh, I understand, all right." Benton mentally kicked himself, hearing a rare edge in his voice. He wanted to add an apology, but the look in Jean's eyes told him it was already too late.

"He's not what you think he is," Jean stated, adding her own edge, one that sliced Benton to his core. "He's direct and some people can't handle that. In addition, he doesn't have a lot of patience with certain types of people." Her eyes blazed as she stared into Benton's, not needing to add, *I'm sorry you're one of them.*

"Jean—Miss Starr, you've seen the way he disrespects me. I've also seen him treat Otis like he's more of an annoyance rather than a working stiff like the rest of us." Benton paused. "Do you know who Otis is?"

Her cheeks flushed, Jean crossed her arms across her chest. "He's married, has four children—three boys, one girl—and he's worked in that building for seventeen years. So, yes, I do know Otis. Are you going to tar me with the same brush as you do Rod?"

Benton turned away. All thoughts of a quiet evening now vanished; he took a deep breath as he cautiously formed his next statement with the realization of how little he had left to lose. "I do sincerely apologize, Miss Starr. I overstepped my bounds. I have no right to criticize the people you are romantically attached to, and I wish I could take back every word about your hard-headed, bigoted, addle-pated, bonehead of a boyfriend."

Jean's jaw dropped in astonishment as Benton's words penetrated more than just her ears. She covered her mouth as she said, "I accept your apology, Dr. Benton. I will, however, take issue with your assertation of my so-called 'boyfriend' being a bigot when he's arrogant and annoying to everyone, regardless of race or creed."

The Terror might be able to punch his way out of a boxcar, but Bob Benton lacked the strength to hold back his amusement. He tilted his head back and roared with laughter, loud enough to attract the attention of every passerby within a hundred yards. He wiped tears from his eyes and attempted to compose himself. "It's…heh…it's good to see you aren't blind to his faults."

Jean chuckled for a moment and turned to watch the cars slowly make their way forward during the rush hour traffic. "I don't consider him a boyfriend, really." Her smile faded. "He seems to have attached himself to me and I guess I let him." Jean sighed. "He's good to me," she offered as her only, half-hearted defense. "And I'm sorry for the last few minutes too, Dr. Benton. Any chance to regain our lost ground?"

"I think so." Benton shifted his weight from one foot to the other and transferred the brown paper package from the crook of one elbow to the other. "How about you start calling me 'Bob'?"

"Call me 'Jean' from this point on and we're golden." A gentle smile lit up her face as her eyes darted to the package under his arm. "Is that your dinner by any chance?"

Adrenalin coursed through Benton as he realized he was about to tell this gorgeous woman a bald-faced lie. "No, that's still in the icebox in my apartment. This is just some sewing I need done."

Jean reached for the package, but Benton instinctively pressed it tighter against his ribs. "I'm pretty good with a needle and thread, Bob. I made the dress you saw me in a couple of days ago."

Benton gulped audibly when he recalled the fit of Jean's dress. The fabric hugged her curves like a finely tuned racecar with a fresh set of wheels. "Um, good work, Jean. No, I was going to take this to a lady who works on odd sewing projects for me."

"How odd could it be?" Jean's fingers touched the end of the package. "Please let me apologize by fixing it for you."

"I can't impose upon you, Jean." Benton's courage fled as he contemplated Jean seeing the blue and red cloak inside. "My friend Velma loves being busy. She's a widower, you know. Keeps her mind off her grief."

"More like 'good grief.'" Jean seized a handful of the bag and pulled. Not wanting to tear the bag and expose its contents, Benton relieved the pressure from his elbow, allowing the package to slide free. He reached forward to retrieve it, but Jean moved the bag behind her back. "If it's your underwear, I promise not to tell anyone about the pink flowers on your boxers."

"Jean, I really—" But Benton's statement was interrupted by a series of short bursts from an automobile horn, punctuated by a longer blast that demanded both his and Jean's immediate attention.

Rodney Clark leaned across the passenger's side of the front seat of his obviously expensive automobile. He threw open the door and aimed his hottest glare at Jean. "Jean, I told you to return to the office immediately. The restaurant won't wait forever, you know. How often do I—?" He noticed Benton as if for the first time and although his expression didn't change one iota, his tone softened in volume if not in intent. "Benton," Clark said in a tone that let the pharmacist know in no certain terms that he didn't appreciate seeing the man.

Jean turned to Benton, her eyes filled with regret and no small amount of unease. "I'll be in touch, Mr. Benton." Before he could reply, she'd covered the distance between the bank and the waiting automobile. Knowing his next words could do more harm than good, Benton remained quiet as the car peeled out, moving into the thick traffic.

Benton imagined the conversation inside the vehicle and how unpleasant it had to be for Jean. Then he slapped his palm against his forehead, almost knocking off his hat.

He moaned, "My cape…" and felt his heart race faster than a cargo plane.

Two hours later, the smell of steak filled the Rowland household as Tim leaned forward on his mother's sofa. "Bob, you really messed up big this time."

Benton grimaced. "I'd turn you over my knee if you weren't so right." He paced back and forth in front of the fireplace, stroking his chin as he contemplated his options.

Velma entered the living room, untying her apron. "Dinner's ready." She smiled sympathetically. "And Tim's right. So, what are you going to do to fix this that doesn't involve my only child endangering himself?"

Benton lifted his hands as if surrendering to his fate. Her gaze was much more painful than any blow she could muster. "I can't see any other option than to break into her house tonight and take my cape back."

"That's a stupid plan," Velma announced before she spun on her heel and returned to the kitchen.

"It is a stupid plan," Tim concurred.

"It *is* a stupid plan," Benton agreed. "But I don't see any other way. And that assumes she hasn't opened the bag yet." *Or worse,* Benton thought, *Rodney Clark tore it open and somehow recognized who it should belong to. Can I hope he only thinks I'm more of a lunatic than he realized?*

Velma Rowland returned to the table with an ivory China plate topped with still-sizzling steak in one hand and a two-pronged serving fork in the other. She speared the topmost piece of meat and dropped it onto Tim's plate. As she selected the larger of the other cuts for her guest, she looked up at Benton. "I'm glad you came here with your wonderful steak instead of worrying all by your—" Velma glanced past Benton. "Did Tim go to wash his hands?"

"Tim?" Benton spun around but Tim was nowhere to be seen. He looked down the hallway, but the washroom door was wide open, and no light burned from inside the lavatory. Gazing farther down the hall, Tim's room was also dark. But what emerged was the sound of the boy's bedroom window slamming shut.

Benton whirled around to face Velma. She dropped the last piece of steak onto her plate as she asked, "Do you think Tim's doing what I think he's doing?"

Benton closed his eyes and sighed. "I think Tim just came up with the only plan worse than my own."

CHAPTER TWELVE

"Or I'll Have the Hand Holding It."

Tim Rowland hadn't felt the cold for around four years now, thanks to the formic ethers. As he sprinted from his bedroom window and through an alley heading east, he barely noticed the drop in temperature, especially since he wasn't wearing a jacket. In fact, his running speed exceeded the posted limit for cars, but the impossible exertion didn't even leave him winded.

He knew this was an idiotic idea, but he couldn't allow his mentor to undertake it and ruin his reputation or his business if he got caught. Being a juvenile, Tim hoped he could be granted some kind of leniency if he was arrested, assuming he *could* be caught.

Then again, Tim's knowledge of the law consisted of whatever he heard on the radio. Tim could hear his mentor griping in his mind's ear that you couldn't believe what you heard on "the idiot box" unless it came from Edward R. Murrow.

Despite the snow and dampness on the parallel dirt trails that comprised the alleys of Raceway City's oldest section of town, and now their poorest, Tim maintained his footing as if the trail was completely dry. He barely slowed down to turn left at the mouth of the alley to run down the center of the street. His eyes darted from side to side, making certain no one looked out their windows and that the closest headlights were still blocks away. Still, he pulled his cap tight onto his head.

By this time of the evening, most people were home from work. Even if someone looked outside, the city tended to neglect replacing any burned out or busted streetlights. For such a prosperous municipality as Raceway City, no one wondered how the powers that be couldn't find the money to keep the west side lit the same way as every other neighborhood.

Tim knew why also. Thanks to his mother's guidance, Tim held a positive outlook in most matters, but was far from naïve because of the heartfelt discussions with Bob Benton and his own mother.

Knowing the discovery of his own dual identity could lead the authorities to Bob Benton's, Tim congratulated himself on being reasonably cautious, for him at least, as he leaped to the sidewalk and remained in the shadows of the trees that lined the street, never once missing a footstep. Tim's arms now pumped so swiftly, only he could see them, and he passed the houses as a blur.

Tim luxuriated in the use of his abilities. He loved the feeling of strength and speed the formic ethers gave him. He missed the adventures he and Bob fearlessly shared until two years ago.

However, the only part of this escapade the boy feared was confronting his mother later. But he promised to burn that bridge when he neared it. Until then, his footsteps brought him closer and closer to the north side of town.

* * * * *

"Okay, Velma, I'm sorry. I said I'm sorry and I'll say it again." Bob Benton reached for his coat and hat. "I'm sorry."

"Fine. I accept your apology, Bob" Velma Rowland said from her dining room as she placed a plate over the platter upon which sat the now-cooling steaks. "Now, how are you gonna get my boy home without a bail bondsman?"

"I'm working on that, okay?" Benton placed the hat on his head before pulling it off again and tossing it onto the sofa. "Honest, Velma, you're the only person I can talk to about this, and I appreciate that."

Velma walked towards Benton; her lips pulled back in a gentle smile that didn't diminish the fear in her eyes. "I know. But I'm scared, Bob. You know why." She seized Benton's arm. "They can't hurt my boy."

As if they could...I hope, Benton thought. He doffed his coat and let it lay over his abandoned chapeau. "I'm going after Tim." He loosened his tie and undid the top button of his dress shirt.

"In your underwear?"

Benton glanced down at his exposed t-shirt. A wave of embarrassment washed over him, and he realized he left his Terror uniform back at the pharmacy. "Dammit! I'll have to go as I am." He began buttoning up his shirt.

"No!" Velma gripped Benton's arm even more tightly, although he couldn't feel her fingernails digging into him. "There's got to be a way. You know what could happen if you're caught operating as the Terror again."

"I've been the Terror again, Velma." Benton moved the woman's hand from his arm and fought the urge to lift her chin and close her mouth. "I have been for about three weeks now." Before the woman could protest, Benton interrupted her. "I got wind of some bad activity, and I can't just let it happen to Raceway City, not to our people."

"What???" Velma's eyes widened in fright. "Wasn't the last time enough for you? You could have wound up in Federal prison, you idiot." She resisted the urge to punch his arm, to get him to listen to her. "Let the police handle this. They're trained to handle the drug problem."

Benton moved quickly through the dining room and into the kitchen with Velma a step behind him. "They won't help us. The city doesn't care about the westsiders. They would just as soon we…stay in our place." The words stung like venom on Benton's tongue. "I've been given a gift. I have to do what I can for Raceway City." Benton's voice dropped into a whisper. "Nothing will happen to Tim. I'd die before I let that happen."

Velma looked into Benton's eyes, nearly blinded by her tears. "You do what you have to do, Doctor Robert Benton. You bring my son home to me. And you better be with him."

"I promise." Benton gave Velma's shoulders a quick, supportive squeeze before he opened the back door and disappeared into the night. Velma stood in the doorway, her trembling having nothing to do with the temperature outside.

* * * * *

"You're right, we are not going to have this conversation again."

Rodney Clark forced his fists to open and his anger to abate.

His rage could barely be contained, and he knew it. He hoped, however, to be able to conceal it more skillfully as he prowled the area by the apartment door.

On the other hand, Jean Starr gave full vent to her fury. "I agree, Mister Clark." She walked to her dining room table to divest herself of the package and her overcoat. "I was trying to do you a favor and you rudely wind up kidnapping me."

"I intended to take you to dinner, Miss Starr," Clark countered. "Hardly kidnapping, and certainly not rising to the level of your refusal."

"Then you should have asked me instead of assuming I'd not made other plans."

Clark growled, "We always go out on Thursday nights." His eyes fell on the package and his gaze lingered on it. "Instead, I find you sharing a laugh with that n—"

Jean's voice turned colder than a glacier as her eyes narrowed. "You finish that word and I'll toss you out the window or have fun trying."

"You couldn't—" Clark's voice halted as he contemplated the vision of this woman trying to lift his brawn from the floor and flinging him out of her fifth-floor window. The very notion of it dissipated his ire as he threw his head back and laughed uproariously.

The sound of Clark's laughter disarmed Jean. Although she couldn't know what he was thinking, his honest amusement stole her emotional momentum. However, she refused to allow her face or voice to reflect this. "Maybe I couldn't, but I'd let you know you were in a fight." She paused to collect her thoughts. "Besides, we don't go out every Thursday unless *you* want to go."

Clark walked towards the table, his eyes still on the brown paper bag. "So, what could be more fun than hitting The Brown Derby for dinner and drinks tonight?"

With a quick sweep of her hand, Jean picked up the package and tucked it under her arm. "I promised to do some stitching for Dr. Benton. So, stop staring at it, okay?"

"Forget him." Clark insisted as he wrapped his arms around

Jean. "Let's go have some fun, okay?"

The warmth of Clark's embrace almost made Jean forget about her task for the evening. Still, something about him felt comfortable, but not quite right, like an old injury that rarely flared up unless the weather turned bad. "Come on, Rod. I gave my word."

Clark ran his hands up and down Jean's back. "Your word means nothing to his kind. Let him take it to his mammy, okay?"

"That's it!" Jean pushed herself out of the hug, her full anger now restored. "I am sick and tired of your bigotry, Rod. I think you should—"

A sound like footsteps came from Jean's bedroom and interrupted the argument. They both turned towards the rear of the apartment before looking into each other's eyes with shared confusion. Jean broke the gaze to move cautiously toward the closed bedroom door. As she passed the dining room, she placed the paper bag on the table before heading down the hallway.

Rodney Clark reached into his pocket, finding the comforting coolness of the pearl grip on the snub-nosed .38 he carried. He pulled the handgun free and thumbed the safety off as he quietly closed the gap between himself and Jean.

Jean reached for the doorknob to her bedroom slowly. Without waiting to see where Clark stood, she wrapped her slender fingers around the cold metal.

But before she could get a firm grip on the handle, the door moved away from her like a bolt of lightning. She gave a soft gasp as she saw the person holding the door from the other side.

The light from the hallway behind Jean framed the figure as he stood in the doorway. He wore a blue jacket with an attached hood that covered all but his face. His trousers matched the azure fabric of his jacket while red leather gloves covered his hands. With the scarlet goggles over his eyes, only the grim expression on the intruder's lower face could be seen clearly.

Jean's mind raced as she attempted to take in this odd figure with his wide stance and an outfit unlike anything she'd ever seen this side of a Saturday morning serial.

The Cobalt Scarab stepped around Jean to walk toward the table where Benton's package lay. But when the Scarab reached for it, Clark snatched it away and stepped back so Jean stood between him and the oddly dressed man.

With a lopsided grin, the Scarab said calmly, "I'll take that package, Mr. Clark, or I'll have the hand holding it."

And from his tone of voice, both Rodney Clark and Jean Starr held little doubt this man could make good on his promise.

CHAPTER THIRTEEN

"I Don't Want to Add Lying to My List of Sins."

Bob Benton kept to the alleyways whenever possible, especially when an automobile approached. The need to walk at the same speed as a normal man hurt like hell, knowing how far ahead Tim Rowland raced ahead. But the most direct route to Jean Starr's apartment forced Benton to stroll, instead of sprint, through the north side neighborhood. Times like this made him regret he didn't own an automobile.

It's not like I have a lot of places to visit, Benton reminded himself. *Hell, it's not like I can take time off from the pharmacy. I can't afford to hire an assistant and I'm sure not letting Tim pretend he's one. He's already in dutch with me and his mother.*

As he thought of his young friend, a thousand different scenarios ran through Benton's mind. The success of Tim's scheme was not one of them, however. The boy could be hot-headed, as evidenced by his actions tonight, just like it had been during the days when the Terror and Kid Terror righted wrongs from the shadows of Raceway City.

Benton's mind sifted through the options of Tim's arrest, the boy's identity being revealed, his mother's heart breaking, reprisals from the criminal elements the Terror and Tim previously put out of business, the end of Benton's pharmaceutical career, and probably more calamities than he could envision. He forced himself to calm down and focus on the matter at hand, namely getting through this neighborhood without raising a ruckus.

And people lived in the upper echelons of Raceway City who could make more trouble for Benton and the Rowland family. Operating beyond their notice was all that kept Benton alive, no doubt.

But now, Benton entered the north side and noticed the houses had more space between them and he could see more expansive back yards for their better-off children to play. In his own neighborhood, Benton would draw little to no notice as he walked determinately along the sidewalk. But here, he noticed the cracks in the pavement becoming fewer as he approached the local business district.

The sight of a black man walking through a white neighborhood would often draw enough unwanted attention. It didn't help that in his haste, Benton didn't put on his overcoat, mostly because it was still inside a railway car from last night, along with a rather nice hat of his. In fact, he didn't even want to spend the time to race back to the drug store to retrieve his Terror uniform. Tonight, every second counted and even knowing that, Benton felt as if he was already too late to save Tim.

No, don't think about that. The kid is smart and almost as strong and fast as me.

Whereas the west side pretty much shut down after six p.m. five nights a week—Friday and Saturday being the exceptions to the unwritten rule—the north side kept extended hours for their people to dine and dance and forget about the War for a couple of hours. Shoving his hands into his pockets, Benton walked as quickly as he dared and stared forward, never making eye contact with the narrowed eyes of various passersby.

At this pace, Benton estimated he wouldn't reach Jean Starr's apartment for another twenty minutes. If he could run full tilt, he could close the distance in a fraction of that time. And if he could run on air like the red-haired man, he'd have been there ten minutes ago.

"Hey! Mister!"

Benton stopped in his tracks. He pulled his hands from his pockets and let his arms go limp at his sides. He slowly turned, preparing himself for a confrontation.

An elderly man with a long gray beard limped towards Benton. His brown eyes met the pharmacist's with no hint of fear or curiosity. Wrapped in a well-worn raincoat with more than one sweater underneath, each layer of fabric valiantly keeping the elements at bay, the gentleman's eyes shone with compassion. "Are you okay, young man?"

With a relieved smile, Benton replied, "I guess I'm in a hurry. I need to see someone and I'm already late for our appointment."

"So much in a hurry, you forgot your coat?"

Benton chuckled as nonchalantly as he was able. "I don't feel the cold like others do, sir."

The man's smile slowly melted. "So why are you in *our* neighborhood."

"Because it's on the way to my destination and I have the same right to be here as you do." Benton added a half second later, "*Sir*." He braced himself for a rebuttal or a call to the authorities. He felt the eyes of strangers rake over him as they walked past. Their eyes narrowed, studying him like a particularly virulent strain of bacteria. Although tougher than most humans due to his parahuman abilities, their gazes sliced at him like scalpels.

The old man looked deep into Benton's eyes before he nodded. "You're right. Sorry to bother you." The smile returned to his face as he took a step back. "Just be careful, okay? Have a good night."

"You, too." Benton turned and resumed his trek towards Jean's apartment. He bit his lip, wondering if he was already too late.

At that moment, many blocks away, the red-haired stranger stepped into the fifth-floor hallway. He quietly lowered the outside window before moving toward a specific apartment. From following Bob Benton, the Cobalt Scarab noted the man's puppy dog yearning for the Comptroller's secretary. It was adorable and painful to behold, depending on the Scarab's mood.

Lunch with Otis taught the Scarab Jean Starr's name and a search through a local phone book took him to her home address. When Benton lost the paper bag under his arm to the woman, a look of horror crossed his face for a second, just long enough for the Scarab to guess how important the package must be, leaving him glad he thought to tail the pharmacist.

And with one task completed outside and five stories below, the Scarab moved down the hallway. He crossed his fingers, hoping no one chose to open their door as he passed, searching for a specific apartment number.

The Cobalt Scarab stopped in front of Jean's apartment and listened, hearing nothing. He pulled a set of lockpicks from a pocket inside his azure belt. Seconds later, with the lock defeated, the Scarab stepped inside and secured the door once more.

However, the sound of an elevator gate opening from down the hallway drew the Scarab's attention. He heard two sets of footsteps approach the apartment before a key slid into the apartment's lock, which informed him that he'd have company soon. "Crap," he whispered just before he moved swiftly into Jean's bedroom.

Once Jean and her companion entered the apartment, The Cobalt Scarab stepped toward the bedroom window, but not as quietly as he wished. He hoped he wouldn't have to crash through to escape, but he decided to see how easily the young lady surrendered the package before making a decision.

Then again, if that bundle was as important as he feared it was, the Scarab couldn't imagine leaving without it.

With his presence now known, Jean gave out a short gasp as the business end of Clark's handgun found itself aimed at the oddly garbed stranger.

"How cliché," the Scarab stated. A smile crossed his face as he approached the couple.

However, Jean Starr stood her ground as Rodney Clark kept his handgun at the ready. If the intruder was impressed in the least, he didn't show it.

Clark affected his toughest tone of voice as he said, "I don't know who you are or how you got up here, but you better put your hands up."

The Scarab chuckled. "Step out from behind the skirt and I do mean now. Otherwise, I refuse to take you seriously."

"What do you want?" Jean asked. "I don't keep a lot of money in my apartment."

"I want the package you picked up earlier today," the Cobalt Scarab stated as he held out his hand. "I take it, then I go away forever." *Maybe*, he mentally added.

Clark held the package in the air. "You mean this? What's so important about some sewing?"

"Lower that gun, pal," The Scarab demanded as he neared the comptroller. "Then hand over the package and you can go back to pitching woo with the pretty lady with both arms working."

Instead of putting his gun away, Rodney Clark leveled it at the Scarab's chest. Before he could pull the trigger, the colorfully costumed stranger closed the distance between them in less time than it would take to blink. Clark felt a searing pain in his right hand as the Scarab inserted his index finger behind the trigger, effectively preventing it from moving. The comptroller pulled gently at the sliver of metal, then he squeezed with as much force as he could muster. But Clark could move the trigger no farther than he could the Rock of Gibraltar.

"You had to make this difficult, didn't you?" The man in blue pulled the trigger toward him, bending the metal. Clark cried out in pain as his finger was pinned hard against the trigger guard. One twist of the wrist later, the comptroller's pain eased slightly as The Scarab now held the gun.

Without taking his eyes from Clark, the Cobalt Scarab flipped the pistol upwards and caught it in mid-air, barrel down. With a flick of his thumb, he pushed the cylinder to one side and shook out the six bullets within. Once the last cartridge struck the floor, the Scarab tilted the handgun so the cylinder fell back into its housing. Then he wrapped his fingers around the metal and squeezed gently.

Jean pressed herself against the wall as she watched the Scarab's fingers dig ridges into the steel, rendering it useless. Upon opening his hand, the twisted pistol dropped to the floor, bouncing once.

The Cobalt Scarab held out his other hand to Clark. "That package. Now." He tilted his palm slightly. "Or would you rather shake my hand?"

Clark hesitated and he kept Jean in the corner of his eye. He felt a cold breeze strike the thin layer of sweat that formed on his brow.

"Give it to him, Rod." Jean's voice was firm, fearless. "It's not worth our lives, I'm sure."

"Don't be so certain," the Scarab stated evenly. "How about it, Roddy? Either shake my hand or drop the package into it." He took a deep breath. "I don't have all night and you have five seconds to decide."

With a grimace, Rodney Clark placed the brown paper bag onto the stranger's palm. The Scarab gave the package a squeeze. He looked at Jean. "Did you look inside?"

"No," Jean admitted. "What's so important that you're threatening a city official?"

The Cobalt Scarab chuckled. "For me to know, beautiful." He took a step backwards, "Go ahead and call the cops when I leave. They won't be able to catch me anyway."

Before Jean or Clark could react, the man in blue sprinted down the hallway and raised a window at the far end before diving through it. Jean gave pursuit with Clark close on her heels.

Despite her sensible heels, Jean Starr reached the open window first. Clark moved her out of the way to gaze downward in the expectation of seeing a shattered corpse in the alleyway five stories below. But no sign of a body could be seen.

Clark shivered and not just from the wind as he pulled the window downward to close it. "I'll call the police," he offered.

"I don't know why you'd bother," Jean said as she willed her pulse to slow down. She might have looked like a cool customer, but she fought the urge to find a strong drink to calm her nerves. "He wore gloves so there's no fingerprints and I certainly didn't see any identifying features, aside from his odd fashion choices."

"Let's get back inside." Clark strode towards Jean's apartment door, bending over to scoop up his now-useless revolver upon his arrival. "I've got a phone call to make, if you please."

Two minutes later, as Jean checked her makeup in the bathroom, Rodney Clark dialed a second phone number from the living room telephone. Jean listened as Clark spoke. "It's Clark. We've got a problem." Then his voice dropped in volume.

Jean made out the words, "mystery man." She turned off the bathroom light and approached Clark, but just a quick glance stopped Jean in her tracks. He cupped his hand over his mouth, speaking softly while keeping an eye on Jean.

Giving up on hearing anything useful, Jean silently wondered why the city comptroller carried a pistol. She also pondered why he was unsurprised to see an oddly dressed man with this amazing strength.

Jean realized there was a lot she didn't know about Rodney Clark, and she wasn't certain she wanted to find out.

* * * * *

Bob Benton finally reached the apartment building. Five stories tall, he decided to circle the building in the hopes of discovering Tim's point of entry, assuming he found one, or if he created his own.

Once out of the streetlights' glow, Benton hurled himself down the alleyway that ran between the apartment building and a smaller one next door. His eyes adjusted instantly to the darkness as he ran past a row of trashcans resting at the rear of the building.

Benton looked down to see a set of small footprints that ran from the far end of the lane to a spot behind another half dozen garbage bins behind Jean's apartment building.

Lying there, nestled between two overflowing cans, was Tim Rowland. His shirt was open, exposing an ebony uniform with a large ivory skull emblem on the chest, the mirror of Benton's own. Tim's black domino mask was pulled over his eyes, one of which he opened slowly. Taking a moment to focus, Tim broke into a smile. "Bob," he said, gripping Benton's outstretched hand.

"I'd tell you I can explain everything," Tim said, rubbing the back of his neck, "but I don't want to add lying to my list of sins."

"Don't worry about the Almighty," Benton whispered, visibly relieved to find his young friend. "At least the Almighty will forgive you. I'm not so sure about your mother."

Tim would have gulped in fear, but his reaction to his mentor's words died in his throat as something struck him on the head from above.

Benton picked up the familiar brown paper bag, feeling the cloak bend inside. In the moonlight, Benton could make out three words written in large, penciled letters: TOMORROW, AT WORK.

The younger man followed Benton's gaze upward. He saw a man in blue several stories above their heads, waving as he ran through the air itself to disappear into the distance.

"So," Tim said with a guilty smile, "you think Mom kept those steaks warm?"

"Not as warm as your backside's likely to be." Benton pulled Tim's mask down around his throat. "Button up your shirt and let's get out of here." No longer caring if they would be seen, Benton ran from the alley at full speed, Tim racing close behind.

CHAPTER FOURTEEN

"Still Have Those Weird Heaters?"

"I'm a little tired of these phone calls, especially twice in one day, Charlie." Ben Pickern rubbed the bridge of his nose between his thumb and forefinger. "I'm hoping it's good news this time."

"Sorry I'm going to have to disappoint you," Charlie Cronin muttered into the pay phone at the back of The Milestone Club. Fifteen years ago, the monied members of Raceway City society frequented this establishment, confident their dollars ensured that the gin was made in a clean bathtub. But when the luster of outlaw behavior ended with the 21st Amendment, the well-to-do resumed drinking at home or at the new, openly operated clubs built with illegal money.

Just as nature abhorred a vacuum, guys like Charlie Cronin became part of the new clientele. He took a sip from his watered-down scotch as he composed his next thought. "Got a call from someone who just encountered a mystery man."

"Which one?" Pickern took a deep pull on his Havana-rolled stogie. "Was it the one who beat you up? The guy who made you wet your pants in the trainyard?"

Cronin gripped the receiver hard enough to turn his knuckles white. "I didn't wet my pants," he stated with an unintended growl. "This one was mostly in blue." He paused. "Not the guy I saw either time."

"Great. Another one." Pickern searched his memory. "I'll ask around." His voice softened when he spoke again. "Listen, all kidding aside, you've done right by me. There will be a little extra in your pay envelope this next time. Come in after twelve and pick it up, okay?"

Cronin grinned. "I appreciate that, sir." As always, knowing the ears that filled this watering hole, the criminal understood the power in a name. To share it, however casually, could mean compromising his position or getting cut out entirely from the man's favor. There were a lot of goons in the city who'd kill—literally—to have Pickern's home telephone number. "I'll keep my eyes open. I'll call if I pick up anything else."

Without waiting to say goodbye, the phone line went dead for a moment before the dial tone sounded again. Cronin fished in his pocket for a nickel and dropped one into the coin slot atop the telephone. He dialed as quickly as the device would allow. A trio of buzzes sounded in Cronin's ear, signaling the phone ringing at the other end of the line. It never sounded a fourth time as an aged voice said, "Yeah?"

"Thanks again for letting me know," Cronin said. "Come to The Milestone and you'll find a fin on your tab, okay? Talk to you later." Cronin replaced the receiver in its cradle and downed the remainder of his drink in one swallow. He turned to the bartender. "I'll have two fingers neat of what you keep behind the bar, okay?" Cronin grinned. "Pay you tomorrow."

On the west side of town, the last of the steak vanished from Bob Benton's plate. It was surprisingly warm, but not quite as juicy as he hoped. "I'm responsible for tonight," he announced after a lengthy silence. "Sorry."

Benton and Tim managed to get home without being seen, or so he prayed. Upon entering the house, Velma Rowland pointed towards the table and in her most commanding voice said, "Sit. Eat. No one talks until I say so."

Duly intimidated, the men left their shoes by the back door and quickly finished their meal. The trio ate in silence. Velma ate her steak quietly, not looking at either of her tablemates. Benton risked the occasional glance at Tim who kept his head down, chewing carefully, too terrified of what he would hear if he said even one word in his defense.

In fact, the young man still wore his Kid Terror uniform. When Benton practically carried Tim into the house through the back door, Tim reached up to remove his mask. However, his mother awaited them in the kitchen and shot her son a look so murderous, the lad's hands dropped to his sides. Her expression practically shouted that a welcome kiss would be out of the question. Instead, she aimed a slender index finger towards the dinner table.

Benton guided Tim into the modest dining room without saying a word. The fire in Velma's eyes promised the torments of hell, should someone, anyone, speak before she gave them leave to do so. Thus, the men sat down and began to eat once Velma distributed the food onto everyone's plate, including her own.

"Thank you for waiting, boys," Velma announced at the meal's conclusion. She dabbed at the corner of her lips with a cloth napkin. "Bob, I appreciate sharing your food, especially in these trying times. I also appreciate your council." She paused long enough for the silence to fill the dining room. "And I appreciate your retrieving my one and only son from the perilous situation he thrust himself into."

Tim opened his mouth to defend his rash actions but without looking at him, Velma stated, "And if he's smart, he'll accept his punishment like a man."

"Velma," Benton interjected, "I'm the last person to tell you how to raise your child." He aimed his sternest expression towards his junior partner. "And this isn't the first time something like this has occurred." Then his tone softened. "But I appreciate what you tried to do for me, Tim. That means a lot."

"You'd have done the same thing for me," Tim ventured to say, his hands and voice trembling.

"But Bob's an adult." Velma squeezed Tim's hand lovingly. "He's choosing to be responsible for you. And why were you wearing your 'Terror' uniform under your school clothing?"

Tim squirmed in his chair, wishing he was anywhere but at the dinner table at this time. "Umm...well, it makes me feel...heroic."

"You mean special, right?" Benton and Tim traded smiles. "I understand completely. We're two of a kind, pal."

Velma shot Benton a look of concern before saying to Tim, "Son, please clear the table so we can have dessert."

Tim grimaced but obeyed in silence. Once he was in the kitchen, Velma leaned forward. "So, what now? You know what happens if you get caught in the open as the Terror."

"I'm well aware of the consequences." Benton bit his lip as he chose his next words. "It's one thing for me to take the heat. I won't let it happen to Tim or you if I can help it."

With a quick glance to make sure Tim remained in the other room, Velma countered, "But you can only help it if you stop making these midnight strikes against the crime families."

"I can't do that, Velma." Benton rubbed his chin. "A couple of my young customers died. The papers didn't list how, but people talk in my pharmacy. I hear all the neighborhood news." Benton turned his face from Velma. "They were not much older than Tim."

"And this made you want to poke around, find out where it was coming into Raceway City." Velma caught herself smiling. "Just couldn't help yourself, just like the old days."

"Maybe because of the old days," Benton admitted. "Then I got a call that told me to watch Pickern's warehouse. It fit with the deaths, so I cased the joint for a week, studying the comings and goings."

"As the Terror." Velma sighed. "What were you thinking?"

Benton studied the empty spot where his dinner plate had been. "I was thinking the Terror could still do some good. He just couldn't do it from anywhere but the shadows." Benton locked his eyes with Velma's. "And I was right."

"The Terror could get you and Tim in a lot of trouble. Velma paused for a moment. "And why are we talking about the Terror like he's someone else?"

Benton struggled with the correct answer and found none. He noticed the sound of running water from the kitchen, along with the sound of dishes being placed inside a drying rack. "Tim's doing dishes. He's a good kid."

"He was also listening to us with that super-hearing you two share," Velma stated with the certainty that only a mother could deliver about her child. "He knew he was about to get caught so he started the dishes to cover up. But yeah, he's a good kid. By the way, 'kids' are actually baby goats, Dr. Benton."

"I wasn't snooping," Tim announced from the next room, a proclamation that forced a grin on the adults' faces.

"All points taken, Mrs. Rowland." Benton smiled.

"Bring out some pie, please, when you're done with the dishes," Velma whispered towards the kitchen. By way of reply, the sound of clean dishes being set out to dry became louder and more frequent. "And if you break any plates, you get to watch us eat."

"And keep your ears to yourself," Benton added, under his breath. "Well, sounds like our mysterious air-runner will talk to me tomorrow. I'll keep you and Tim posted." He smiled with all the sincerity he could muster. "I promise to be careful."

Velma narrowed her eyes at her guest. She didn't believe Benton's last statement any more than he did. Before she could voice her doubts about Benton's vow, Tim entered the dining room with three plates, each one topped with fresh blueberry pie and some homemade ice cream on the side. He held one dish between his fingers with the other two balanced atop his forearm.

After carefully laying a serving before his mother first, Tim placed the dessert with the extra ice cream in front of Benton, taking a smaller portion for himself.

"You trying to bribe me?" Benton's eyes twinkled with amusement.

Tim picked up a forkful of pie mixed with a large dollop of ice cream. "Only if it works, Bob."

* * * * *

Benton's visit to the Rowland home ended without further discussion of the Terror, nor even a further mention of how Tim's attempt to enter Jean Starr's apartment building was foiled. The attack on the boy was so swift, Tim didn't even get a glimpse of whomever left him unconscious, a feat in itself because of his own amazing strength.

The remainder of Benton's walk to his apartment passed without incident, aside from his keen study of every shadow beside his path. He almost expected to see the red-haired man inside each patch of darkness, ready to pounce. The guy was Benton's prime candidate in Tim's attack and the pharmacist knew he wouldn't mind a small one-sided exchange of fisticuffs.

However, Benton cautioned himself again and again to not imagine what occurred elsewhere, especially once Tim found himself alone with his mother. He grinned as he shuddered at the kind of hell that young man might have endured once Benton left, not that he didn't deserve it.

Then again, Benton reminded himself, *it's not like I've been the master planner in this affair.* His smile faded and he settled in for what he hoped would be a boring night.

* * * * *

"Listen to me, Mr. Pickern," Mayor Brant shouted into his telephone, "I'm now down two shipments and two payments. Find the guy who stole it all, then steal it back."

Didn't take long for this guy to grow a pair, Pickern thought, *did it?* "I'm not sure I like your tone, Mister Mayor."

"You find my tone annoying? Then talk to the people on the street who I supply. They've been yelling at me since we talked last. No product means no income, so find what's mine and find it fast." Pickern gripped the receiver so hard, his knuckles turned ivory. "Mess this up and I'm promoting that preening idiot Cronin to take your place as my go-between."

Ben Pickern held his own earpiece so tightly, he thought he heard the wooden handle groan from the strain. "I'll phone my contact tonight and have the problem solved by tomorrow."

"See that you do." Mayor Brant wrestled with his temper. As soon as his pulse rate stopped mimicking a Gene Krupa drum solo, Brant spoke again. "You know, I'm very proud of our local baseball team, Pickern. Find the stash or the team's using your short-and-curlies for batting practice." With that, Mayor Brant slammed the phone onto its cradle.

Inside his own private study, Pickern laid the receiver of the phone down as if handling nitroglycerine. He pulled out a handkerchief from his rear pocket and dabbed his face gingerly. Two doses up in flames and the money to pay for them missing, Pickern knew he needed to act quickly.

Sure, he thought, *you're getting squeezed by me and by your dealers. Well, I'm getting pressure from above that you couldn't even guess, and from you. It ends now, before you forget your place again.*

A large bar made of highly polished oak filled the rear of the study. Pickern stepped over to it and lifted several file jackets from the gleaming bar top. Sitting down in a plush chair, Pickern took a long pull from his second brandy of the night and opened the first folder. After studying its contents for a couple of minutes, Pickern turned his attention to the second folder, then the third, and so on until he'd refreshed his memories.

Pickern stared into the shadows of the far side of the room, swirling the ice in his drink as if the action helped a plan come together in his mind. He ran his eyes over the shelves of books he had no intention of reading as he tapped his fingers on the bar top. Minutes later, an inspiration hit him. He walked over to a leatherbound copy of Fyodor Dostoevsky's *Crime and Punishment* and pulled it from its resting place. With his hands on both the front and back covers, Pickern opened it wide.

A pocket-sized address book rested inside the hollowed-out pages. Pickern dropped the "book" onto the floor and flipped through the yellowed pages as he strolled back to his telephone.

Picking up the phone again, this time with a lot less trepidation than when it rang a half hour ago, the mob boss dialed for an operator. Once that neutral voice greeted him, Pickern recited a phone number in the Chicago, Illinois area, one that would never show up in any telephone directory. The line went silent for a few seconds before the sound of ringing filled Pickern's ear.

The other phone rang exactly seven times before the other party answered, one who purred like Marlene Dietrich but with an American accent. "Yes?"

"It's Pickern." The mobster paused to collect his thoughts. "I've got a big problem. You still have those weird heaters of yours?"

"Perhaps," the woman stated with no small amount of annoyance. "When do you wish to see me?"

Good woman, Pickern thought. Both operated on the wrong side of the law long enough to know anyone could be tapping the phone line for their own purposes. If Pickern hadn't been so annoyed by the mayor's late night phone call, he might have been more discrete. "How about lunch time tomorrow?"

The lady cleared her throat. "I'm not doing anything right now. How about breakfast, brunch if there's traffic?"

Pickern felt a wave of relief wash over him like the ocean's surf. "If that's all the faster you can get to my place." He relayed his mansion's address before he allowed a smile to cross his lips. "And bring some toys, Mrs. Claus. I have a couple of kids who should be on your naughty list."

CHAPTER FIFTEEN

"You Don't Have a 'Soft Side.'"

The next morning, Dr. Bob Benton opened the drugstore as usual. The temperatures already teased the low end of the forties and the sound of water flowing down the street and into the gutters created a white noise that felt like a balm to the pharmacist as he strolled to work.

Benton woke up a couple of hours earlier, feeling somewhat chagrined when he realized that although his errant cloak had been retrieved, it still wasn't repaired. He thought about asking Velma to perform the task as a favor. Then again, he wasn't sure he was completely on her good side after last night. He grimaced as he contemplated Tim's fate. *I wonder if she let him go unpunished.* Benton thought, *Knowing Velma as I do, I'm sure she's already corrected that oversight.*

No, last night wasn't the one Benton anticipated, but he got his cloak back and he had a splendid, if somewhat cooled, meal afterwards. And best of all, Tim came home to the relative safety of his grateful mother's arms.

Benton didn't anticipate anything occurring over the weekend that would merit the Terror's attention. He believed Pickern would be licking his wounds and trying to come up with another way to bring drugs into the city. While the mobster burned the midnight oil to appease his clients and his nefarious bosses, Benton could take some time off.

So, at a few minutes before nine a.m., Bob Benton put on his other jacket and hat, having left one set in the trainyard during his encounter with the red-haired man. Then he picked up the brown paper bag containing the Terror's shredded cloak and made his brief walk to his drug store.

With the starter change in the cash register and all the lights on overhead and humming softly, Dr. Bob Benton turned the OPEN sign to face the world, ready for another business day.

On the opposite side of Raceway City, a chime sounded once. The sound barely began its inevitable decay in the foyer of a specific mansion before Ben Pickern wrapped his hand around the doorknob and turned it.

A beautiful, dark-haired, woman stood on the top step of Pickern's mansion home. Clad in black from her festive hat down to the brightly polished boots that could be seen under her pleated skirt. An ebony square-shouldered jacket with matching silk shirt and slender silk necktie completed the ensemble. She rested her gloved hand atop a large, wheeled steamer trunk that came to the top of her hip.

Her green eyes latched onto the mobster's. "Ben Pickern." It wasn't a question, but a statement of fact.

Pickern knew this woman by reputation alone. No photographs of her existed in any file, local or Federal. Her determination in carrying out assignments proved to be as strong as her ability to get paid handsomely, and to take no nonsense from any man or woman, according to her reputation.

"You must be Sylvia Devereaux." Pickern flashed his most charming smile until he remembered how futile his courtesy would be. He could expect no concessions from the woman, especially where her price was concerned. "You come highly recommended."

"I'd bloody well better. God knows I worked hard enough for you to hear of me." Sylvia sashayed across Pickern's doorway as she pulled the trunk into the building with minimal effort. A gentle nudge of her toe closed the door firmly. "Where can we sit down and talk?"

Pickern gestured for the woman to follow. "Was that a Nash out there?"

A faint smile tickled Sylvia's bright scarlet lips, that and her alabaster flesh being her only concessions to some other color than black. "The first to roll off the assembly line in '37." Her smile vanished. "Coffee would be appreciated."

"I believe I can do even better than that." Pickern gestured down the hallway before he led her to a large dining room where a large oak table dominated the room. However, there were only two settings. Pickern pulled out one of the chairs and Sylvia eased herself onto the cushion with a dancer's grace.

"The staff has the morning off," Pickern explained as he placed a domed serving plate in front of his guest. "There's no possibility they, or anyone else, will see that you're here. Even my bodyguards are in the opposite end of the building."

"You trust me not to kill you?" Sylvia pushed her coffee cup closer to Pickern. "Showing your vulnerability doesn't get on my soft side."

Pickern smiled as he poured a cup of fresh, hot coffee from a silver carafe. "I'm going to assume you take your joe the way you take your ensemble." He added with a grin, "I'm also going to guess that you don't have a 'soft side.'"

Sylvia picked up the cup and took a small sip. "Your batting average, so far, is good enough for the Major Leagues." She waited for her host to lift the silver dome to reveal a modest breakfast of scrambled eggs, three slices of bacon, and wheat toast. Sylvia leaned towards her plate and inhaled slowly. "I'm not a fan of scrambled, but you did well. It's so easy to overcook them."

As Sylvia dropped her napkin across her left thigh, Pickern sat down and readied his own repast. "Like I said, everyone got the morning off. Otherwise, my chef makes an amazing spinach omelet." He tucked in his napkin along the front of his shirt collar. "Now, are we done dancing, or do you find discussing business over breakfast distasteful?"

"Considering what I do for a living, Mr. Pickern, I'm difficult to offend." Sylvia sliced through her eggs with the delicacy of a surgeon. "Begin."

Pickern greased the wheels of his ambition with the blood of his opponents. He took many a life without losing a second's sleep over it. But something about this ice maiden made his palms sweat and he knew exactly what it was. She too earned her intimidating reputation, and it made him uneasy.

"I have a problem with one of the locals." Pickern picked up a manilla folder from the chair beside him. He held it aloft as he dabbed his mouth with the tip of the napkin. "But this is not a standard contract. This man will prove a challenge, even to you."

Sylvia's eyes narrowed for a second. Then she extended her hand. Pickern stretched out his arm until his guest seized the folder. He turned his attention to his breakfast until he could place the final bite of toast into his mouth.

Pickern looked up and smiled. Sylvia Devereaux drained her coffee cup but was only halfway finished with her breakfast. She turned each page in the file which she studied like a bobby-soxer might read a fan magazine. However, she flipped through the pages of several comic books with a frown. "He seems to be a Caucasian in these children's books."

"Long story," Pickern pointed towards a small stack of unread sheets of paper. "You'll see more about Operation Whitemask as you read."

Sylvia nodded and continued reading the government files. Once she finished, Sylvia held out her cup for a refill, a silent request to which Pickern gladly complied.

"You read too many newspaper strips, Mister Pickern?" She placed the cup to her lips and took a delicate sip before placing it back on its saucer. "I think you've got Flash Gordon on the brain."

"Not at all." Pickern refilled his cup. "I understand that it reads like something out of a Saturday morning serial." He paused for effect. "But this is real. The Terror can do all that you see. I can even get you a couple of witnesses." Pickern took a sip of coffee. "He's already cut into business. If he stayed in his place, we could live with him. But he isn't, thus we can't."

"But now whatever hold you had on him isn't enough to force his ongoing compliance?" Sylvia ran a gloved fingertip over the lip of her coffee cup. "The report hinted there are more of these 'mystery men' across America?"

"It's a global problem, actually." Pickern felt the need for a cigar. He hated being on the weaker end of any business conversation. "And we've got one outsider who's stirring the pot in this 'Black Terror' affair."

"Ah, you realize the Terror's bloody corpse would send a message to any other parahuman you have under your thumb." Sylvia stacked the papers and comic books neatly before placing them inside the folder once again. She smiled in the way a hungry cat might after exhausting a mouse. "I enjoy a real challenge so much, I might just give you a discount."

"I wouldn't have you do that, Miss Devereaux. You'll earn your pay and then some, I'm sure." Pickern leaned back in his chair. "Your thoughts?"

Sylvian Devereaux reopened the dossier and flipped through the report once more. She looked up again, her eyes twinkling with excitement. "I'd love another serving of your splendid eggs, Mr. Pickern. I seem to be working up an appetite."

Pickern nodded with approval. The kill was on. "Would you like them scrambled or over easy?" he asked.

Sylvian Devereaux turned her attention back to the sheet in her hand. "Let's set the mood." She smiled. "Definitely scrambled."

* * * * *

Following the usual lunchtime rush of customers, the rest of the day passed without incident, just the way Bob Benton liked it. He often missed the nights and the adventure as the Terror, to say nothing of helping the neighborhood as a parahuman adventurer. But once he realized he couldn't fight the government, he settled into the work-a-day routine that he enjoyed prior to absorbing the formic ethers.

Now, Benton still served his community in dispensing medications and answering questions that eased their aches, soothed their minds, and extended their lives.

RINNG-RINNG! Benton looked towards the bell over the front door and smiled when he saw Tim Rowland enter.

"Hey, Doc!" the young man waved enthusiastically from across the pharmacy sales floor.

"Greetings, Tim." Benton pointed towards the front of the store where a Coca-Cola cooler rested. "Get us a couple of cold sodas, will ya?"

Tim gave his mentor a huge grin and a swift thumbs-up. He spun in place to face the cooler where the soda bottles were kept.

"No, allow me, gentlemen."

Both men turned towards the woman who entered the building. Light danced over the form-hugging surface of her floor-length ermine coat and matching hat. A pair of pointed boots peeked out from the hem of the expensive garment as the unsmiling woman glided across the floor towards the soda cooler.

She considered the machine for a moment with amusement glowing in her eyes if not on her scarlet lips. Then she looked up at a wide-eyed Tim and whispered, "I must avail myself of your wealth, young man. It seems I'm not in the habit of carrying mere pocket change."

An elderly man moved up towards the cooler. "Ma'am, you don't have to make this boy pay for his own drink. Let me loan you a—"

Before the man could finish his sentence, the woman practically glided across the aisle to meet his gaze. She whispered something to him that Benton strained to hear, even with his enhanced hearing. A glance told him that Tim also eavesdropped on the one-sided conversation. Tim's eyes widened while Benton's narrowed at the woman's words.

"And then I will kill your most treasured loved ones slowly as you listen to them scream. If you breathe a word about this conversation, I will find out and end your life, one friend, one stranger, one pet at a time. Now leave before I do away with you in front of this young boy."

The older man clutched the open front of his jacket and practically sprinted from the building and down the street. Benton and Tim traded a look from across the room before the pharmacist emerged from behind his cash register. He affixed his most likeable smile and pushed his horn-rimmed glasses upwards along the bridge of his nose. Tim placed his back against the lunch counter and took silent inventory of the rest of the sales floor. Only a couple of middle-aged women stood by a display of various cough remedies, gossiping about their neighbors.

Benton stopped and waited for Sylvia Devereaux to face him. Her eyes met his and Benton gazed deeply into the coldest, darkest depths he'd ever seen. Even the most hardened killer or deranged hop head he'd encountered as the Terror showed some semblance of life in their eyes. But not here.

Never allowing himself to flinch or for his smile to drop, Benton said with forced pleasantry, "Good afternoon, Ma'am. We don't receive many strangers to this business. Is there something I could help you with?" Benton stopped with just a couple of feet of space separating the two.

Sylvia tilted her head slightly. "Go back behind your counter, *boy.*" The barely whispered syllable slid over her lips like venom served in honey. "Pretend everything is all right. We shall talk once you close your doors. Raise no alarm or the boy pays for your foolishness." She tilted her head in the direction of the gossiping women. "Or perhaps those two biddies."

Benton glanced at Tim. The boy's eyes blazed with anger, waiting for a signal from his mentor.

The woman added, "The boy stays with us after this apothecary closes for the night. Everyone else leaves." Her eyes narrowed. "That way, they get to live." Sylvia tilted back her hat, exposing more of her perfect features. "Try to exit through your fire door, or make those bitches leave before they make their purchases, and they don't get to see their families tonight."

Sylvia playfully kissed the tip of her gloved finger and tapped Benton's nose like a lover. "I'm going to check out your magazine section. Why don't you go look busy, *Doctor* Benton?"

Benton watched Sylvia stroll casually towards the cooler where Tim stood. She removed one of her gloves and held her hand close to the young man's brow. Benton focused his hearing as Sylvia began snapping her fingers rapidly. The effect wasn't painful to the pharmacist, but it did prevent him from hearing the words she spoke softly into Tim's ear, words that made the boy's eyes widen with surprise and no small amount of fear.

Dammit, Benton thought, *she knows about our powers.*

As soon as Sylvia completed her speech, Tim shot Benton an apologetic look and wandered over towards an area at the rear of the store. Benton watched the assassin for hire slide her slim ebony-nailed fingers into her glove again as she sauntered to the magazine rack. Once there, she playfully wiggled her fingers at Benton, shooing him in the direction of his sales station.

"Hmph." Benton instead chose to approach Tim to compare

notes. He walked as casually as possible towards the corner where Tim stood, poorly imitating someone who might want to purchase a pair of crutches.

Upon seeing his comrade, Tim's mouth formed a narrow line as he subtly shook his head in a quick burst that told the pharmacist to keep his distance.

As Benton halted, Sylvia's throaty whisper filled his ear. "I know you can hear me, Benton. I told the boy to stay away from you but not leave the building. His instructions are similar to yours concerning those old cows. Good God, do they *ever* stop talking? Anyway, I'd advise you to keep your distance from Tiny Timmy or it goes badly for the old bags."

Benton turned towards the front of the store where Sylvia stood, casually flipping through the pages of the latest *Saturday Evening Post*. "Timmy's being obedient. You should do the same, *boy*."

An overwhelming sense of anger competed for Benton's attention against dozens of thoughts about how to take this woman down, none of them workable or without casualties. The dark woman's confidence unnerved Benton, admittedly. It was obvious she knew far more about him than he did her, which gave her the courage to beard him in his own lair.

Taking a deep breath that did nothing to calm his nerves, Benton walked slowly back to his cash register.

Once behind his sales counter, Benton looked up at the large clock hanging above the front doorway. The bright red sweep hand flew over the other two as they registered 4:23…thirty-seven minutes to go before closing. He glanced at the two women who appeared so engrossed in their shared narratives that they completely ignored the time.

Tilting his head, Benton saw Tim feigning interest in a row of gauze bandages. Their eyes met for a moment then turned away. Benton looked at the sharp-dressed woman as she examined a copy of *Jingle Jangle Comics*. She shook her head with disdain as she perused the four-color imagery within its pages.

Still desperate for a plan of action that didn't involve someone dying or him revealing his dual identity, Dr. Bob Benton silently wondered how this situation could get any worse. Immediately, he regretted the thought as the bell rang over the front doorway.

The red-haired man entered with a smile and Benton took to heart a serious lesson in tempting fate.

CHAPTER SIXTEEN

"Impulsive, But Clever."

The red-haired man wiped his feet on the mat just outside the doorway before he entered Benton's Drugs. He waited for the door to close behind him while he took in the rest of the room. His eyes quickly swept the sales floor from one side to the other before he selected the left-most aisle to casually shop.

He also carried a paper bag in one hand, folded at the top.

Bob Benton suppressed a groan. *Which one of the psychopaths is going to hold me down while the other one wails on me?* Benton looked at the woman in black who briefly noted the newcomer's existence, surveyed the room from left to right and back again, shot Benton an emotionless glance, and then placed the comic book back on the shelf.

Tim grimaced as he watched the red-haired man slowly meander towards the end of the first aisle. The newcomer glanced toward the dark-haired woman by the magazine rack, gave her a flirtatious wink, and then strolled in the direction of the two gossipy women.

Finally, one of the elderly ladies said to her friend, "Oh, it's just past four-thirty. Dr. Benton's going to close soon." The other matronly lady grunted in agreement, although neither woman took a step from where they'd stood since Tim arrived.

It took all of Tim's willpower to not sneak a glance at Bob Benton. But the tone of the woman's words still stung his ears. When Tim stood closer to her earlier, she smelled like expensive flowers and had a gentle smile that stirred him in places he dared not talk about. However, her intent sliced into his heart like a scalpel. She detailed her terms for him— *"Do not communicate with the pharmacist in any way, not even eye contact, do not leave, do not warn anyone, and keep your distance should Benton approach you or else I slice up your mommy, Velma."*—before quickly detailing her knowledge of his abilities, where he lived, the school he attended, and even where and the hours his mother worked.

She even claimed to know the size and brand names of Velma Rowland's foundation garments, but Tim stopped listening by then. Then she smacked her lips together in a parody of a kiss before taking her current position at the newsstand.

Benton tidied up his work area, finishing just as the front doorbell rang again. Jean Starr looked around the pharmacy, her eyes wide with uncertainty. For a moment, Benton's pulse accelerated at the sight of this beautiful woman. Then he recalled the other woman by the magazine rack and his heart filled with icy fear.

Best to pretend that nothing was wrong. "Hello, Miss Starr." He smiled brightly and waved her back.

Jean ignored everyone else in the room as she crossed to the cash register. "Hello, Dr. Benton. You've got a nice place here." The pharmacist regretted hearing the lack of verve in her compliment. "I trust you're well today."

"As well as can be expected." *No one's died yet, at least.* "Off from work early, aren't you?"

"Mayor Brant gave me the rest of the afternoon off because I got all my work done."

"That was swell of him." Benton heard the clock over the front door ticking relentlessly inside the spaces between their sentences. He glanced at the timepiece as the minute hand moved to the eight...*4:40.*

Jean bit her lip briefly and studied her shoes for a few seconds. "Dr. Benton, I came to apologize for yesterday."

A feeling of relief washed over Benton as he found himself smiling. "Same here...Jean. I behaved very poorly, I'm afraid. I am truly sorry that I hurt your feelings."

Jean covered her smile as she chuckled. "I'm not blind to Rod's faults, believe me." Her smile faded. "He frequently makes it very difficult to be his friend."

Or more than a friend, Benton reminded himself, but maintained his silence as he nodded politely.

"But I'd like to apologize as well," Jean continued. "You've been nothing but kind since we met, and you didn't deserve what I said either." She averted her gaze. "But I have something else I must discuss with you." She took a deep breath. "I lost your sewing."

Benton, at first, repressed a desire to give out an ironic laugh. Then the mirth died in his throat when he realized that the aforementioned package lay on the seat of a chair in the office behind him. The thought of inviting Jean back there never occurred to him, mostly due to the possible impropriety of the matter. Now, doing so could ruin more than just their slowly mending friendship if she demanded to know what was inside the paper bag, and how it wound up back in Benton's possession.

Even without his enhanced hearing, Benton heard Tim moan. *Be quiet, you little snoop*, he thought.

"Jean." Benton asked, "So, what happened to it?" He believed those would be the most logical words to utter as he realized that this beautiful woman stood in the absolute worst place in his world at the most horrendous time. Benton needed to get Jean out of here before she became another hostage for the woman in black. "How did you...lose it?"

"There was a break-in at my apartment last night," Jean confessed. "Some oddly dressed thug entered my apartment and left with your sewing." Her brow furrowed for a moment. "In fact, now that I think about it, that's all he took. I think that's what he came for."

Benton instinctively glanced over at the red-haired man who momentarily gave a look of embarrassment before he tugged his cap down to hide more of his features. On the opposite side of the room, Tim allowed himself a smirk. "Oddly dressed thug," the boy whispered to himself with no small amount of satisfaction.

It's bad enough that little rat is listening, Benton thought as his eyes swept the room, *but call it a silver lining if my former attacker will ever look me in the eye again...which might be the best thing to come out of today's debacle.*

"Was there something special in that bag?" Jean continued. "That crook went to a lot of trouble to steal some sewing."

"My guess it was someone of diminished mental capacity, if you know what I mean," Benton stated just loudly enough for the red-haired man to hear. Benton could hear him grinding his teeth together, which gave him some sadistic pleasure. "The fool might have thought it was a drug shipment, for all I know."

From the corner of his eye, the pharmacist noticed the red-haired man glaring at him while the mysterious woman at the newsstand looked up from her magazine to eye Benton with undeniable annoyance.

Even the two ladies stopped in front of the greeting card displays and stared at Benton curiously. *Is everyone watching me now? Good Lord...*

"It was very frightening, that's all." Jean raised an eyebrow. "I'd tell you more, but I don't think you'd believe me."

Before Benton could state how willing he'd be to discuss the matter with Jean, perhaps over a casual dinner sometime soon, his reverie was interrupted by four people clearing their throats simultaneously. The mysterious woman in black, the red-haired man, and the two women who stood with their gloved hands filled with greeting cards all stared daggers at Benton. One of the old ladies pursed her lips and motioned with her head for him to kiss Jean.

Only Tim left his impatience unexpressed. However, he looked up at the clock and saw the minute hand's lethargic movement towards the top of the hour.

*Four-forty-nine...*Benton looked over his wire-rimmed glasses at Jean. Even if no one else got out of here alive, including him, he had to ensure Jean's safety. He glanced at the never-ceasing sweep of the second hand over the clock...*four-fifty*...Benton wracked his brain for a solution to this situation.

"MAY I HAVE YOUR ATTENTION!"

Benton, like everyone in the room, turned towards Tim Rowland. The young man held both hands in the air, waving them as if he was trying to guide an airplane onto a landing strip. Benton's heart pounded wildly inside his chest, wondering if Tim just murdered everyone in the drugstore.

"Thank you." Tim's grin stretched wide across his handsome face. "Dr. Bob normally doesn't look at the clock on Friday nights but he's gotta take me home as soon as he can. Not that

I'm looking forward to it, but it seems I stepped out last night and my momma's gonna whup me like an old rug."

"Like that's news?" The second woman laughed at Tim's comment.

"I'm not saying I have it coming, mind you," Tim stated with poorly feigned innocence. "Just the same, I'm figuring if I have a respectable witness like our own Dr. Benton, she might not murder me." He walked to the end of the aisle. "After, all...I have to be in school on Monday morning and being dead might affect my grades."

"Come on." One of the women nudged the other. "Let's get our stuff and head home. I'll put on the kettle when we get there." She gathered her purchases and strode to the cash register where Benton stood, her friend close behind.

"Thanks, ladies," Tim said. "If it was any other night but my last one on earth, it might be different." Both women giggled in reply while Sylvia Devereaux allowed herself a coy smile.

Jean Starr turned to Benton and smiled softly. "Well, I'd best be going. Rod might be outside, ready to start honking his car horn. Sorry again about the theft. Perhaps I can reimburse you for the contents?"

"No harm done, Jean." Benton pulled the first set of greeting cards across the counter towards the cash register. "I hope to talk to you soon. We'll figure things out and settle up then, if need be."

"I'd like that." Jean buttoned up the collar of her coat. "Have a good weekend, Doctor." The sound of an automobile horn sounded outside, and Benton thought he heard Jean whisper a word he wouldn't say to his own parents if they were alive. Jean forced a smile onto her lips. "Good luck keeping your friend alive. Bye, Bob."

"Bye, Jean." Benton turned his attention back to his customers, deflecting their comments about the attractive young blonde and unsuccessfully ignoring the insistent honking outside. A couple of minutes later, Benton escorted the ladies to the front door and wished them a good night before closing it. He quickly flipped the CLOSED sign around before turning to the red-haired man who stood in the fourth aisle by this time.

"I don't know who you are," Benton called out to the man, "but you need to leave." He looked at Sylvia Devereaux, making certain his hands remained in plain sight.

The stranger pushed his cap upwards. He made an effort to soften his expression as he turned towards Sylvia. "Sorry, miss. I have some business I need to discuss with Dr. Benton here."

"No, you don't," Sylvia declared as her gloved hands dove into the pockets of her coat. With the speed of an Old West gunslinger, she pulled out two devices that barely resembled handguns. They each had a barrel, a handle, and a trigger, but the twisting duct work that led from the gunsights to where the ammunition should be looked like something out of a Saturday morning serial.

Sylvia turned her most hateful glare towards Benton and Tim. "You *boys* were told how I expected you to conduct yourselves." Without looking, Sylvia leveled one handgun towards Benton's gut, the other in Tim's direction.

From across the room, Tim called out, "You said not to warn anyone. I just told everyone it was almost closing time, and they took it from there." He raised his hands and approached her from the far aisle. "I don't care what you think. They didn't need to die, lady."

Sylvia contemplated Tim's words. Her lips pulled back as if she was ready to issue a feral snarl. "All right," she decided. "Cleverly played, Timothy. Impulsive, but clever."

"That's Tim to a 't.' Now let this bonehead go." Benton crooked a thumb towards the man in aisle four. "Unless he's here to help you carry the bodies out."

A glimmer of bewilderment crossed Sylvia's face. "I've never seen this man before." Her eyes narrowed as she searched her memories of Pickern's files. "What is your name?"

"If I tell you that," the red-haired man said as he halted several feet from the woman, "you'll probably need to plug me too."

Sylvia turned her gaze back towards Benton. "Tell me who your friend is."

"You tell me. I can't speak for anyone else, but my friends don't try to kill me in railyards." Benton glared at the man for a moment before returning his attention to Sylvia. "Lady, I've got no idea who this clown is except he's got my powers and then some."

The man smiled as he studied the woman's eyes. "Don't be so modest, Benton. You're tougher than I thought you were."

"But I can't run on air, mister," Benton said with a grim chuckle.

"Run on air?" Sylvia's eyes went wide as she moved a hand-gun from Tim to the center of the man's face. "Tell me your name, dammit. NOW!"

The man lifted his hands in surrender. He walked toward her and said softly, "Garret. Garret Daniels."

Without replying, a look of absolute fear filled Sylvia's face. The final letter of the man's name barely escaped his lips when she pulled the trigger on her handgun at near point-blank range.

CHAPTER SEVENTEEN

"It's Not My Real Name, But It's Close Enough."

A stream of white-hot flame erupted from the barrel of Sylvia Devereaux's bizarre weapon. But while her aim rivalled that of William Tell's, the red-haired man who called himself "Garret Daniels" barely moved out of harm's way with a twist of his waist. The shell slammed into, then through, the metal and wooden shelving where Daniels once stood, sending product and shrapnel in every direction.

Without looking at her target, Sylvia pulled the trigger on the other handgun. Benton already stood poised to disarm the woman, but her reflexes proved almost as swift as the artillery she launched at him without looking. But Benton's crouch transformed what would have been a solid gut shot into a graze across his shoulder. Still, it hurt like the blazes, so much so that he didn't hear the projectile strike the wall far behind him.

With no expression on her face and moving with the precision of an automaton, Sylvia gave the merest glance to her left and pulled off a shot at Daniels that barely missed the man as he leapt into aisle eight. The bullet missed the shelving where Tim previously stood but tore into the wall like a drill.

Something whizzed by Benton's ear from behind. Tim hurled a section of racks towards the assassin. The wood exploded at Sylvia's feet, sending splinters in every direction. She took a shot at Tim just as the young man threw himself into the air to land three aisles away.

Benton leaped forward and attempted to seize Sylvia's wrist, but she dodged his hand with an economy of effort. As Benton's momentum propelled him forward, she slammed the butt of her gun against the back of his skull. It might have hurt a normal man like the blazes, but Benton never lost consciousness when he stumbled and slammed, face first, into the news rack.

Tim and Daniels launched themselves from different areas of the store, leaping between the space between the light fixtures and the tops of the shelving. Sylvia swept her glance around the room, stopping at the clock above the front doorway. Without a heartbeat's worth of hesitation, she turned both barrels towards the front door and pulled the triggers simultaneously. The steel and glass frame exploded just as Tim and Daniels landed only a couple of feet from the mysterious, dangerous woman.

With reflexes that rivaled theirs, Sylvia stepped toward the super-heated metal of the doorway and dove through the smoke to the sidewalk. The explosion drew the attention of passersby while those closest to it attempted to put some distance between them and the destruction.

Bob Benton pushed himself from the mountain of magazines, paperback novels, and comic books that covered him like a blanket. Some of them began to smolder as he regained his footing. He looked at the wreckage at the front of his business but knew the woman who caused it was probably far away by now.

While stamping out the small fires in the paper at his feet, Benton quickly looked around the pharmacy. He wasn't sure if he should be surprised that Daniels was nowhere to be found.

But in the next moment, the red-haired man approached from the back of the store with a couple of fire extinguishers. He turned to Tim, "Kid, call the fire department and then the police." As Tim raced to the telephone in Benton's office, Daniels tossed Benton one of the metal canisters filled with foam. "Let's see about putting out any fires while we can."

With a nod, Benton accepted the other fire extinguisher and pulled the hose free of its housing. He turned the canister upside down and a stream of white liquid poured forth. Benton and Daniels aimed their chemicals at the base of the intermittent flames, putting them out rapidly as they surveyed the pharmacy.

Benton checked out the areas of the store where the bullets struck. The special projectiles caused a lot of damage inside the store, but fortunately, they created no major blazes, aside from the wooden shelving they struck.

"I know we move fast," Daniels stated, "but shouldn't the authorities be here by now?"

Benton chuckled bitterly. "Maybe in *your* neighborhood." He set the fire extinguisher on the linoleum floor as he composed his thoughts. "Money for fire protection goes to every side of Raceway City but the west. We have a volunteer fire department, and all of those brave souls already have full-time jobs."

"I can understand that." Daniels smiled gently. "Cops and firemen, they don't have our advantages." He set his extinguisher down also. "I used to be a cop."

With a nod, Benton continued. "If a fire happens during the day, a lot of the men can't get out of their jobs to fight it. Chances are they're rushing to the station house right now."

"If you and I hadn't gone to work," Daniels observed, "this building would have been a pile of ashes."

"And the rest of the block probably would be halfway aflame by the time they got here." Benton weighed his words cautiously. "No offense, but chances are the ashes would be frozen over by the time the police arrived. It's just how things are in this city."

Daniels nodded, his eyes heavy with regret. "No offense taken. Most of my brothers and sisters in blue are stand-up, one hundred percent. It's the ones who make the headlines we're judged by, sorry to say." A smile crept over Daniels' lips again. "Let's start this over, okay?" He extended his hand without hesitation. "Garret Daniels. It's not my real name, but it's close enough. Ex-cop, currently a mystery man."

With a quick nod, Benton met the man's hand and squeezed it firmly. "Dr. Robert Benton. Pharmacist, secret troublemaker. My friends call me 'Bob.' He added with a grin, "You can call me 'Dr. Benton."

"I deserve that." The men shared a brief laugh that was interrupted by the approaching sound of sirens. "So much for your locals not making time." Daniels' expression turned grim. "Listen, I can't stay to answer the local cops' questions. However, I'll gladly get together with you later because it's past time we compared notes." Daniels snapped his fingers. "Hold on. I brought you something."

Swifter than most humans could blink, Daniels raced to the far corner of the pharmacy where he stood before the carnage erupted. He returned to Benton, holding out the paper bag. "You left before you could pick these up the other night."

The pharmacist opened the bag. Inside, his overcoat rested, neatly folded, with his hat resting on top."

"Consider this my peace offering, Doctor. Mind if I use your back door?"

"Go." Benton hurried Daniels to the rear door where he unlocked the three deadbolts and pushed the steel door outward to allow his visitor an exit. Benton stepped into the alley long enough to see the red-haired man take a couple of steps before rising rapidly into the air to disappear over the rooftops.

Once the door was secured, Benton trotted to where Tim emerged from the back office. "That was quick," the young man stated.

"Yeah," Benton led Tim towards the front of the pharmacy. "I'm tempted to say, 'too quick.' Would you mind taking these in back?" He handed the extinguishers to Tim. For an average ten-year-old, the canisters might prove unwieldy. Instead, Tim lifted them effortlessly as if they were empty and made of paper.

Benton looked outside past the onlookers who gathered at the edge of the sidewalk. They gazed at the destruction and offered their own conjectures on the causes of such calamity, sharing misinformation with each other until a pair of uniformed policemen pushed their way through the crowd. One led the way, moving the onlookers to one side with a little more force than needed. His partner followed, muttering his apologies as he passed through the crowd.

"Which one of you is the owner?" the lead policeman called out. The officer's beefy form spoke of too many beers and too few push-ups. His sunken eyes assessed the pharmacist with distaste. He pushed his cap over a crewcut that hugged the man's skull so tightly, it was impossible to tell what color his hair happened to be.

Tim and Benton traded a look before the latter waggled a finger at his smiling young friend. "You stay quiet." The pharmacist walked towards the policemen. "That would be me, sir."

Upon seeing Benton, the policeman gave an overly loud

"Hmph!" He pulled a small notebook from inside his police jacket along with a stub that barely qualified to be called a pencil. "Patrolman Sauer." He thrust a thumb behind him. "Officer Hart. So, what happened?"

"Mmm." Benton scratched his chin. He'd heard about Raceway City Police Department Officer Leonard Sauer. It was said his friends called him "Lenny." However, no one called him that anywhere, not even in his own precinct, because he never worried about becoming more liked. He was a tough cop, almost too tough if you didn't fit his idea of what a proper criminal looked like, whatever that was.

"Aren't you going to separate us for interrogation?" Benton forced a smile onto his lips.

Sauer's face went from slightly annoyed to outright furious in less time than it took to blink. "Look, pal, your local cops got called away so shut it. You don't want me here; I don't want to be here, and I don't know who I browned off at the station, so I got this call. Instead of telling me how to do my job, how about answering some questions so I can leave and make everyone happy?"

"Sounds good." The edge in Benton's voice went straight under der Sauer's skin like a splinter under a fingernail. "Let's get this over with."

As the lead patrolman began his interrogation, Officer Patrick Hart walked around the pharmacy sales floor to assess the damage. He grinned when he saw Tim Rowland first shadowing him and then accompanying Hart in his survey of each aisle. Upon reaching the farthest part of the store from the entrance, Hart stood up to his full six-two height. He removed his cap to expose a full head of blond hair and pushed the hat under his arm. His smile almost glowed under the florescent lighting. "How's it going, young man? I'm Officer Hart and my friends call me 'Rick.'"

Tim regarded the policeman warily. "I'm okay, sir. How the heck are you?"

Hart glanced back at his senior partner who waggled a tiny pencil in the pharmacist's face. However, Benton appeared to be totally unimpressed with anything the policeman did or said. The junior patrolman could almost feel the enmity between the two men and wondered how he thought his partner got any results at all with so much naked hostility in evidence. "I'm okay, mostly."

"Your partner's a bit of a bonehead," Tim opined, "if you don't mind me saying so."

The patrolman made a conscious decision to not nod in agreement but admitted softly, "He has his moments." He smiled at Tim. "I'm glad you didn't get shot, young man."

"Me too," Tim admitted as he brushed some splinters from his trousers. "My momma's mad enough at me as it is."

Officer Hart stared deeply into the darkness of the bullet holes in the back wall. "I suppose you didn't know what made these holes, huh?"

Although it had been the better part of two years since Tim put on his costume and followed Bob Benton into battle against the criminal world, Tim retained his instincts through constant exposure to pulp magazines and radio dramas. "Handguns. Not exactly Smith and Wesson, more like Asimov and Campbell. Didn't even see any sights on them so she had to be a pretty good shot, I'd guess."

Hart checked the scorched wood and metal for signs of blood or fabric. "Not good enough to hit you, though. Where were you standing when this happened?"

Tim pointed a finger to the front of the aisle. "Up around there's where I first saw her. Black hair, bright red lipstick, big black hat and black outfit, pretty but no one I want to date when I get old enough." The patrolman strolled down the length of the aisle with Tim a step behind as the young man continued, "She made me stand as far away from her as possible so I can't really give you a good description of her. Sorry."

"Good observations, though." Hart didn't mind allowing the kid to know how impressed he was for trying. The policeman studied the damage scene at the end of the aisle, not wanting to get any closer to his partner than he needed to be. Ten hours a day was enough of unbridled bigotry and complaining for any man's taste. "Young man, how did that case—" Hart pointed at the gap in the shelving. "—Wind up all the way over there?" He pointed at the remnants of the display case beside the news rack.

"Good question," Tim admitted, suddenly feeling nervous. "You think I'm Samson and I can toss that stuff across the room? I'm just a kid, you know."

"Good answer," Hart countered as he scribbled in his notebook. He pointed towards the damage in aisle four. "So where was your friend standing while the shots were being fired?"

Tim forced a smile onto his face. He admired the cop's interrogation skills, on one hand, but suddenly wished he was home, taking his further punishment for last night's escapades.

CHAPTER EIGHTEEN

"Now What Will They Do?"

"You did WHAT?" Ben Pickern held the telephone receiver so tightly, he wasn't sure what would snap first, the receiver or his knuckles. "Or should I ask, what didn't you do? Aside from removing your target from the world, that is."

Sylvia Devereaux watched the taxi drive away from the phone booth where she stood with her back to the street. With the sun setting on the west side of Raceway City, Sylvia felt completely at home in the shadows. "I wasn't paid to kill children, old ladies, or gingers."

"Gingers?" Pickern's tone softened. "He didn't drop his name, did he?"

"As a matter of fact, yes." Sylvia's reply snapped in Pickern's ear like the crack of a bullwhip. "He had the same, or similar, powers to the black pharmacist. It's the Cobalt Scarab, isn't it? I think my price just went up if you want him dead also." She paused to collect herself. "And while I didn't kill Benton, I managed to wound him." Sylvia added proudly, "It seems my weapons can damage even your parahumans."

Pickern pushed his cocktail across the table in his study. He needed his wits about him to ensure he didn't say the wrong thing to incite the assassin to take her professional frustrations out on him, even though she hadn't collected for the last half of her payment. At least the down payment for the hit on Bob Benton was accomplished by wire less than an hour after breakfast. "Okay, that's a start. Sorry I yelled."

"That's all right," Sylvia replied in a tone that made it clear that she didn't accept Pickern's apology any more than she forgave herself for not fulfilling her contract. "I should tell you that I didn't feel my fee included incinerating the entire block, so I called the fire department to add to the confusion."

Pickern glanced around the study and knew he'd need a second cocktail as soon as this call ended. "That's all well and good, but when will you finish the job?"

"As soon as possible." Sylvia pulled a silver compact from a pocket inside her coat to check her lipstick. "The boy rode home with the police who left once the Fire Department made certain nothing was still aflame."

"How do you know?" Pickern grabbed his drink and took a deep drink from his glass, despite his misgivings. "Are you able to cloud men's minds?"

"I made my way to the roof across the street. Once everyone scattered, I caught a cab to where I'm at now." Sylvia slid the compact back into her pocket. "I will contact you if I need anything. Otherwise, I'll call to let you know the contract's completed." With that, the line went dead before Pickern could ask any further questions.

"At least Mayor Brant isn't phoning," Pickern whispered, but not so loudly that the siren call of the liquor cabinet couldn't be heard. "Not yet at least."

* * * * *

Bob Benton sat in his office, basking in the silence of his wrecked pharmacy. He patted the bandage on his shoulder gently, feeling the flesh rapidly knitting beneath it. The compound that gave him, as well as Tim Rowland, their special abilities didn't extend to giving them steel-hard flesh. Sure, someone might have to work harder to pierce their skin or to knock either of them unconscious, but accomplishing these tasks wasn't anywhere close to impossible.

The pharmacist looked upwards at the light fixtures. He'd already cleaned up as much of the damage from the deadly woman's bizarre attack and carried it to the trash cans behind the building. Now he wondered if allowing the police to take Tim home was a good idea and how much danger the Rowland family might be in. But how would he find this lethal woman? Where would he begin his search?

Oddly enough, the clock above the entrance didn't suffer even a scratch, same as the overhead lights and one of the outside windows. "Must be nice," Benton muttered with a smile as he appreciated the irony of the situation.

"Dr. Benton?"

Benton found himself so lost in his own thoughts that he didn't hear the truck pull up in front of the drugstore. He also didn't notice someone walking through the gap where the front door used to be. However, the shout pulled Benton from his reverie. He rose to his feet, his fists already clenched and ready for battle.

A man stood just inside the doorway. Benton recognized the middle-aged, portly man from his infrequent visits to Westside Hardware and Lumber. He held up a handwritten receipt and smiled as Benton emerged from his sanctuary. "Hi, Dr. Benton. I'm Ralph."

"Ralph Green." Benton smiled. "Good to see you. What brings you to..." He looked around in the darkness. "...whatever's left of the store?"

"Got an order for some wood and a door. I'm gonna pick up the door tomorrow morning. It won't take but a few minutes to install. But the wood can go over the broken windows until you can get them replaced." Ralph picked up a copy of *Collier's* from the floor, smoothed the receipt against its back cover, then held them up for Benton. "Can I get you to sign?"

Benton swallowed hard. "I didn't order anything." The drug store made a decent amount of money, especially given the economic uncertainty created by the new war being fought in Asia and Europe. But as Benton swept up the debris earlier, he calculated how much the repairs to the building would cost and kept coming up short.

The landlord lived on the other side of Raceway City and didn't care how things got fixed, as long as someone else paid for them.

"You didn't have to, Dr. Benton." Ralph pulled a fountain pen from his shirt pocket. "Your buddy did it for you."

"My who?" Benton borrowed the pen long enough to affix his signature.

Outside, the truck door slammed shut and in walked Garret

Daniels. "I think he means me, Benton." The red-haired man strode towards the back of the store. "I already got the goods unloaded onto the sidewalk. Thanks, Ralph. I think we can take it from here."

"That was quick." Ralph folded the paper and slid it inside his jacket. "Free labor and good company? Thank *you*!" He flashed Benton a grin. "Call me when you're ready to rebuild, Doctor. You do so much for the people of this community, the least we can do is help you when you need us." Without waiting for Benton to find the words that filled his heart, Ralph walked back to his truck. Immediately, the engine sputtered to life and the truck pulled away into the night.

"It's after hours," Benton observed. "He didn't have to do this. Neither did you."

"True, on both counts." Daniels grinned. "You've got good friends here and they know what a decent man you are, Benton. We all should be that loved. Now let's get everything fixed so you can go home."

"Let me find a hammer or two, okay?" Benton turned towards his office.

"Sissy," Daniels called out with a grin as he backed towards the front door. "I don't need one. But if your delicate hands can't handle the stress..."

Benton grinned as he stepped out to check the street. With the excitement over, everyone left for home. The pharmacist believed if he kept his body between the few cars passing on the roadway and his work, this could be done quite quickly, and no one would see a thing.

Daniels carried a couple of plywood sheets from where he unloaded the truck. Benton did the same, along with a box of two-inch long iron nails. "Anything you can do, Daniels, I can do better. You start and I'll join in."

The first four-by-eight sheet went over a spot formerly filled by a pane of glass. Fitting the plywood against the bricks that surrounded the window frame, Daniels pulled a nail from his pocket and pressed the sharpened tip against a corner. With little more effort than it would take an ordinary man to insert a thumbtack into a corkboard, the nail pierced the plywood and then the brick. Daniels repeated the movement three more times to fully secure the sheet of wood.

He glanced to his right to see Benton imitating the action, but with a huge grin on his face. The pharmacist turned towards his guest. "I don't get to cut loose like this, Daniels. I guess I've missed being…"

"Special? Tell me about it." Daniels nodded his understanding before resuming his labors. The task took less than five minutes to complete, including securing some wood over the shattered door. With the boards cut to a size slightly larger than the door's width, it wouldn't open until Ralph brought its replacement.

When the task was completed, Benton and Daniels inspected their handiwork with satisfaction.

"Let me pin a note to the door and we can leave through the back." Benton went inside as Daniels gathered the leftover materials. The pharmacist pulled a sheet of paper from the top drawer of his desk. He quickly wrote on the store letterhead, CLOSED UNTIL FURTHER NOTICE, and blew on the paper to hasten the ink's drying.

Daniels carried the leftover plywood and the box of the remaining nails inside and left them in a neat pile beside what used to be a newsstand. His task completed, Daniels walked through the darkened pharmacy with the confidence of a man who could see clearly in the sparse light coming from the back office, which he could.

The red-haired stranger stepped behind the cash register to see Benton staring sadly at the paper in his hands.

"I purchased this store six years ago from the man I interned with after college. His name was Aaron Paris," Benton stated. "It took all my savings to secure this place, but I turned a profit within the first year. I stayed open late, opened early, sometimes came in on Sundays to make sure people got what they needed." He looked up at Daniels. "Now what will they do?"

"We'll figure that out later, okay?" Daniels gently picked up the note and found some thumbtacks in a small jar on the desk. "Get what you need so we can go, okay?"

Benton nodded and smiled his thanks. He rose from his chair

to make certain, one more time, that the safe was locked before putting on his hat and jacket. Almost as an afterthought, Benton picked up the brown paper bag with his damaged cloak inside, as well as the other with his once-abandoned coat and hat. He carried them to the back door where Daniels stood, patiently waiting.

As Benton locked the door, Daniels asked, "You have any plans?"

"Can't say I do," Benton admitted. "I think I'm still in shock."

"Not surprised." Daniels looked upwards and pointed to an iron fire escape that snaked alongside the back wall, two buildings away. "That your place?"

"Yeah, the guy I rent from owns the whole block." Benton walked towards the mouth of the back alley. "You stay here, and I'll let you in from inside." Benton grinned. "I've had to go in the back door a number of times, but I prefer the front one."

"Same here. Not a fan of it either." Daniels zipped up his jacket, but for appearances only. He walked under the fire escape. A few minutes later, Benton opened his back door and whistled for Daniels to come upstairs. One three-story leap upwards later, Daniels landed in front of Benton and entered the apartment quickly.

"So, what's our next move?" But as Benton asked the question, his telephone rang. He exchanged a narrow-eyed glance at Daniels before approaching the device with the same enthusiasm as if he found a hand grenade in his lap that lacked its pin.

Benton placed his hand on the receiver and looked up at Daniels who shrugged and mouthed the words, "Pick it up."

With a nod, Benton lifted the handle and pressed it to his ear. "Hello?"

The female voice on the other end stated, "You know who this is and if you're with who I think you're with, I know he can hear me."

Daniels' eyes went wide, and Benton grimaced as the voice continued, "This isn't the last you've seen of me. I promise, however, that the next time we meet, I will be the last thing you see. I don't like leaving a contract unfulfilled and you won't be the first. Enjoy your last hours."

With that, the phone line went dead. "Well." Benton rose to his feet. "Sounds like we've got an appointment with a lady…and it's not likely to be fun for either of us."

Contaminated by Benton's concern, Daniels walked to the back door towards an inevitable and uncertain meeting, his least favorite kind.

CHAPTER NINETEEN

"Sounds Like You Got a New Partner."

"You two better do as she says," Tim Rowland suggested. The young man took Bob Benton's jacket as soon as he entered the house. Garret Daniels shrugged off his own coat and handed it to Tim who received it with all the joy of getting socks for his birthday.

As Tim carried his burden to his bedroom for safekeeping, Benton walked into the living room. Velma pushed some blazing logs closer together with a cast iron poker. She didn't even look up at Benton as he sat on the sofa.

Once Velma completed her task, she closed the fireplace screen and placed the poker in its stand. She stared deep into the depths of the flames. "My boy told me what happened."

"Good," Benton said. "He might have saved more than one life today."

"Really?" Velma looked directly into Benton's eyes, but she didn't appear ready to agree with the pharmacist's claim. "All I know is he was dropped off by the local police and said something about someone shooting up the drug store."

"Did he mention he came up with a way to save two innocent lives and may have saved mine?"

Velma's expression softened. "No, he didn't. All I heard about was some scientifiction ray guns and having to lie to the nice young cop who escorted him to my door."

Benton quickly related the events of the afternoon, including how they each neglected to mention Daniels to the police and that despite their best efforts, the mysterious assassin got away. Velma listened and occasionally nodded.

Once Benton concluded his tale, Velma turned her attention to Daniels who stood near the front door with his hands behind his back.

"You have something to add?" Velma asked.

"Dr. Benton pretty much got everything right," Daniels admitted. "Your son did us quite a favor. Without risking his own life, of course."

Velma forced herself not to smile. "Now I know you're lying, mister. My boy is a lot of things, but 'cautious' isn't one of them." She nodded towards the sofa. "Why don't you join Dr. Benton on the couch?" She rolled her eyes as she spoke softly. "And I know you're listening, Tim, so come on out. You might as well not strain your ears."

Tim left his bedroom. Benton turned to see the expression on his junior partner's face. True to form, Tim's face mirrored that of every child caught with their hands inside the cookie jar. Unlike Velma, Benton gave himself permission to smile at his friend.

The three men sat in silence as Velma returned to watching the logs in the fireplace ignite anew. Without turning her eyes from the blaze, she asked, "Mr. Daniels, have you eaten yet?"

Daniels looked at Benton, confusion in his eyes. Benton didn't crack a smile as he said, "Answer the lady, Daniels."

"Um, no, ma'am." Daniels stared at the tips of his shoes. "I skipped lunch, too."

"Well, Mister Daniels, no one goes hungry in my home, especially someone who helps protect my only child." She rose and gestured for Tim to set the table. "Go wash your hands, both of you, and let's all talk about the future while we eat."

"Good," Tim muttered to Benton. "I thought I was gonna pass out from hunger."

Within a few minutes, the four sat down to a rather luxurious dinner, as if Velma knew she'd be receiving company tonight. Velma sat at the head of the table with Tim on her left-hand side and Benton on her right with Daniels seated opposite her. As soon as the meatloaf and the mashed potato bowls made their rounds, along with home-baked rolls and gravy thick enough to hold its shape without a container, Velma bowed her head to say grace.

"Thank you, Lord, for bringing Tim and Dr. Benton safely home," Velma said over her folded hands. "And may this evening bring further understanding. Please bless this food, this house, and our company." Velma opened one eye briefly, just long enough to see Daniels respectfully bowing his head, his hands folded on top of his lap. "May all we do please you, Lord, in your powerful name we pray, Amen."

"Amen," agreed all three men. Tim used his enhanced speed to begin eating, much to Benton's amusement. If any unmarried man ever got around to having children, half of them probably hoped for someone as bright and as fearless as Tim. The other half wished for someone less prone to lead with their chins.

"Daniels," Benton began as he sliced a hearty portion of the meatloaf on his plate, "I think the first order of business is to tell us a bit about yourself and how you got your parahuman talents."

"As I said, 'Garret Daniels' is close enough to my real name." He wiped his mouth with a cloth napkin, folding it neatly over his knee. "My father was a good cop. He ran afoul of some gangsters back in New York City, so I became a vigilante in the hopes of bringing them to justice." Daniels stared at the luxuriously loaded plate before him as he spoke. "When working behind the badge as a rookie cop wasn't enough, I turned to Dr. Abe Franz for help. He concocted a special vitamin he called 2-X that gave me the special abilities you've seen."

"I suspect you know this already," Benton said, "but I used to call myself 'the Terror.'" He nodded towards Tim. "He was 'Kid Terror.' What's your handle?"

Daniels chuckled as he swiped his napkin across his lips. "Don't laugh. I was 'the Cobalt Scarab.'"

Velma nodded. "That's certainly imaginative, Mr. Daniels. How did you come up with that name?"

"I had a real yen for all things Egyptian when I was a kid." Velma watched Daniels' face light up. "My dad raised me alone. He wanted me to become an archeologist, I believe." His face dropped. "I don't think he'd have minded that I followed in his footsteps, though."

"Forget all that, Mom. This guy can run on air," Tim told his mother, his voice thick with annoyance and tinged with no small amount of jealousy.

"If you're looking for explanations for my talents, I'm a cop, not a scientist. I'm totally in the dark as to how this all works," Daniels admitted. "In fact, I only took the 2-X a few times before the effects became permanent. Well, permanent so far."

"What do you do about bullets?" Benton asked, his shoulder now aching as it continued to heal.

"Dr. Franz and I created a special metallic mesh that I incorporated into my Scarab uniform," Daniels said. "It looks like chainmail, but it distributes the kinetic energy of small arms fire all over the fabric, so with my special toughness, I barely feel it." Daniels grinned. "Usually."

Benton grinned. "Bulletproof? Must be nice."

"You better get the recipe from him," Velma advised.

"I suppose you want to hear about Tim and me now," Benton volunteered.

"No." Daniels helped himself to another roll.

"I think I'm offended," Tim said. "Who doesn't want to know more about me?"

Any trace of a smile faded from Daniels' face. "Because I already know..." He paused. "I know more about Operation Whitemask than I probably should."

The ticking of the clock on the mantlepiece in the next room sounded like a metronome in the quiet that ensued. Benton broke it with a whisper. "So, you're the reason we can't go out as the Terror Twins."

"No, I'm not." Daniels quickly put up his hands as if ready to deflect an attack. "I was recruited. My choices were to go along or risk someone coming after me." He looked at Velma. "How much do you know about it?"

Velma placed her fork delicately at the edge of her plate as Benton spoke. "She doesn't know much." He rubbed his hands together nervously as he addressed the Rowlands. "Velma, you know that there used to be more of a mob presence downtown. From the day I took ownership of the drug store, Ben Pickern's men regularly shook me down for protection money."

"All I know is you never talked about it." Velma took her son's hand out of instinct. "I know you met Tim when a group of those mob thugs accidentally ran into him."

"They couldn't wait to get their money to their boss. They knocked Tim over and I saw red." Benton smiled at Tim. "I knew Tim from him hanging around and reading every comic on my news rack." His smile vanished. "Anyway, I was too meek to fight for myself, but I was damned—sorry, Velma—if I let anyone pick on a child. That was the last straw for me."

"So, Bob had been giving a few of his customers some vitamins of his own making, something to perk them up." Everyone's eyes landed on Daniels. "It's in your files, Bob."

"I have a file? I shouldn't be surprised." Benton nodded and turned to Velma again. "I had some notes on how to create a vitamin that would really supercharge the muscles, but I didn't know how to combine them effectively. I still don't."

"He'd still be a milksop if it wasn't for me," Tim said softly.

"What your son is saying," Benton told Velma, "is that he accidentally dropped the wrong chemical into my compound. I thought he'd blown the batch. Instead, he found the element that made it work. He also added the correct amount, but that was sheer luck." Benton turned to Daniels. "Formic acid was the key ingredient."

Daniels nodded. "Like from red ants?"

"Yes," Benton verified. "From this came what I call 'formic ethers.' The vapors gave me incredible strength and endurance, just like your 2-X, Daniels." He took a small bite of his now-cooling meatloaf.

Daniels savored the flavor of the meatloaf. "And then Tim got a whiff too."

Benton nodded. "If he hadn't, my career would have been over before it started. He's saved my life more than once."

Velma wiped her mouth delicately with a napkin. "I understood standing up to Pickern's goons back then. I really do. But going out and looking for trouble with Pickern and God knows who else?" She glared at Tim. "And allowing my boy to put his life on the line? You're lucky I speak to you, Bob Benton, much less feed you."

"Anyway, Velma, if I can still call you that." Daniels pushed a forkful of potatoes and gravy against the dinner roll to ensure it stayed atop the tines. "I was a cop for a good long while. Some of us live by more rules than others. Mine meant looking past the regulations that tied Law Enforcement's hands, to say nothing of the black hats in our business." Daniels met her gaze. "When I got the chance to do more to clean up the streets and avenge my dad, I took it. I suspect your son's cut from the same cloth."

"So how did you get involved with Operation Whitemask?" Tim asked.

Daniels chewed thoughtfully, then swallowed. "Somehow, the G-men found me. I guess I wasn't as careful about my comings and goings as I hoped." He cleared his throat. "They offered me a chance to continue operating as the Cobalt Scarab, as long as I became their enforcer. And by 'offered,' I mean they blackmailed me into being their goon." The red-haired man went pale as he recalled his duties. "Turns out I couldn't do it any longer than I did and still be able to look at myself in the mirror."

Velma took a sip of water. "I hope you don't mind my asking, Mr. Daniels, but who did Operation Whitemask threaten to keep you in line?"

"Not at all, ma'am." Daniels wiped his mouth, stalling for time as he gathered his emotions. "Her name was Joan Mason. She was a reporter for the *Daily Blade*." His eyes turned hard. "They got careless, and Joan learned about the organization. To keep us both in line, the Project threatened us with the other's life."

"With you on the run," Velma asked, leaning forward, "what's happened to her?"

Daniels' eyes dropped to his plate. "You tell me, ma'am, then we'll both know."

The clock's ticking filled the room again. Daniels selected his words carefully as he forced himself to meet Benton's unblinking gaze. "There were files that I had access to for a while. But when I bailed out on Operation Whitemask, I had to leave them behind." Daniels wiped the last of the gravy from his plate with a dinner roll. His chewing and the crackling inside the fireplace dispelled the silence of the dining room.

Velma Rowland looked at Benton, her eyes narrowed into slits. "Oh no you don't, Dr. Benton. I can see it in your eyes. I know what you're going to do and I'm not allowing it."

Benton pushed himself from the table. "Tim's staying here, I promise." He caught Tim's eye and raised a finger to prevent any protest. Tim's jaw dropped, but he maintained his silence.

"I'm in," Daniels stated, rising from the table. "Whatever it is."

"Sit down!" Velma placed her palms on either side of her face as she struggled to compose herself. "No more talk about being mystery men or whatnot at this table, in this house." She pushed her chair away from the table and pulled Tim's empty plate towards her. "Tim, help me gather up the dishes and then we'll have dessert."

Tim quietly obeyed as he took Daniels 's plate. Benton handed his own service to Velma who wordlessly carried the dishes into the kitchen. Tim gave Benton a wink before he disappeared into the other room.

Before Daniels could say anything, Benton whispered, "Keep it normal. But I hope you're ready for a late night out. I've got a plan, but let's swing by my place to change, okay?"

With just a glance towards the kitchen, Daniels nodded. "Sounds like you got a new partner, partner."

CHAPTER TWENTY

"Good Ideas Are Rarely Fun."

"Mister Daniels, the least you could do is shiver a little," Velma Rowland stated as she rubbed her arms vigorously to keep them warm. "It's kinda disturbing to see you unaffected by the cold."

A couple of hours' worth of strained conversation later, Bob Benton stood at the end of the Rowland property, waiting for Garret Daniels to say his goodnights. The former policeman stood at the bottom of the front porch steps, looking up at Tim's mother. He put on his warmest smile as he said, "I'll try to remember that, ma'am. Dinner was fantastic and thank you for listening to me."

"I appreciate your company, Mr. Daniels, as well as your honesty." A thought crossed Velma's mind and she raised a hand to her mouth. "Oh! Bob! Your parcel, what's in there? Anything I need to look at?"

Benton stared into infinity as he considered a response. "No, Velma. No need to do anything with it. Just toss it. It's scrap now." He smiled. "I'll talk to you soon. Thanks for a great dinner." Benton thrust his hands into his pockets and turned to start his walk home. He covered a half block before he realized Daniels stood beside him, keeping pace.

"So, Benton," Daniels said, "Tim's out, huh?"

"I promised his mother," Benton replied. "She didn't offer me any other option. You heard me swear to let him grow up to be a normal kid."

Daniels nodded. "I'm sure Tim heard you too. I noticed he never left his room to say goodnight."

"You sure you were a *rookie* cop?" Benton grinned at Daniels. "I'd swear you made Detective." The smile faded as Benton listened to the last of the snow melting from the trees and roofs, each drop of water splashing against the fresh puddles made earlier in the day. "Where are you staying?"

"Wherever I can. Why?"

Benton pointed towards an upcoming alley. "Walk down to the next alley, then do your air-running or whatever-it-is-you-do. Collect your gear and I'll make room for you on the couch."

Daniels studied the serious expression on Benton's face. "You have a plan for your would-be assassin?"

"I hope to by the time you settle in." Benton grinned as Daniels walked purposefully into the alley.

Half an hour later, the Cobalt Scarab dropped onto the roof of the apartment building that Benton called home. He placed a large duffel bag onto the tarpaper roof before taking a quick look over the edge of the structure. A couple of cars slowly made their way to the east as the ex-cop glanced at the front of Benton's Drugs. The boards still stood firm in their housings, much to Daniels' satisfaction. A couple of men at opposite ends of the block stumbled from one light pole to the next, but they didn't, or couldn't, look up so they weren't Daniels' concern.

Picking up his canvas bag, Daniels walked to the rear of the building before he stepped over the roof's edge without hesitation. He dropped lightly onto the iron fire escape twenty feet below before walking to Benton's back door. Daniels tested the doorknob and frowned when it turned to allow him easy access.

Entering the small kitchen, Daniels gazed past that into the living room. Sparsely furnished with a coffee table, a couple of mismatched chairs, along with a sleeper sofa that had seen better days, and an RCA radio that sat on a small table in the corner of the room. A mirror hung on the wall beside the front door beside a well-worn coat rack.

Benton exited the bedroom and nodded at his visitor. "Welcome to my humble home. Sorry if it's not what you're used to."

Daniels dropped the duffel bag on the floor beside the chrome dinette that dominated the kitchen. "I've definitely been in worse." He walked into the front room and shook Benton's hand. "Thanks for putting me up. I've been sleeping in a mission a few blocks from here."

"My pleasure." Benton indicated the sofa. "It pulls out, so

you'll be a little more comfortable than in most flophouses, I'm sure."

"No doubt." Daniels lowered himself onto the couch and his smile said everything about his appreciation. While patting the sofa cushions, Daniels didn't even look at his host to ask, "So are we going to talk about a couple nights ago in the trainyard?"

"You mean why you were out to bash my brains in?" Benton dropped onto the most comfortable-looking chair in the room.

Daniels leaned forward; his hands raised as if imploring for forgiveness. "No, if I wanted to kill you, I wouldn't be here right now. I'd be on the run for your murder." He chuckled ruefully. "But don't worry. I don't kill unless I have no other choice."

"And I always have a choice," Benton stated firmly. "That's why I choose to do no harm. Well, at least no more harm than necessary." The smile returned to the pharmacist's face. "Sorry I don't have anything to drink around here, aside from water and beer." Benton pulled a couple of drinking glasses from a cabinet.

"After today," Daniels stated with genuine enthusiasm, "a tall, cold glass of either one sounds great." He grinned. "And if my choice is beer, then don't dirty a glass just for me."

"What a considerate houseguest you are." Benton pulled out two beers from the icebox. He placed the tip of his thumbnail against the end of the cap and flicked it free of the bottle's mouth before repeating the action on the second bottle. Benton walked over to Daniels and handed him a brew, which the ex-cop hefted in a silent toast before taking a swig. "Now, about our little set-to the other night."

Daniels grinned while he waited for Benton to seat himself again. Then he resumed his narrative. "I came here in the hopes of finding others like us." Daniels chuckled as he studied Benton's features. "Don't look so shocked, Benton. It's not just you and Tim." Daniels downed another measure of beer. "Oh, believe me, there's more parahumans in Raceway City than you realize."

"Stop dancing around the subject." The glass in Benton's hand faintly groaned as the pharmacist applied pressure to it. "What happened the other night?"

"I've been tracking you for almost two weeks," Daniels confessed. "I followed you back here on that night and saw you leave in your black pajamas. I figured you were toeing the line on Operation Whitemask's edicts. Then I followed you to the trainyard."

Daniels chuckled as he turned away from Benton. "I admit I grew too enthusiastic about taking your measure than I thought I would, and I didn't believe it would help either of us if the bad guys thought we worked together. Still, I wanted to stop you from interfering with the transaction."

"Of the heroin or the money?"

Daniels' expression darkened. "Yes, to both. The rest, you were there for it, pretty much. Now, how did you find out about the initial delivery?"

Benton rubbed his face with both hands as he thought. "One of the advantages I have is being able to listen to the people of this neighborhood and their concerns. The local pharmacist is the next best thing to a Father Confessor, regardless of one's faith."

"Minus the penance for the confessor, of course." Daniels leaned over to pull the duffel bag closer to his feet. He untied the thick gray cord that held the end of the satchel closed. "What brought you back into action?"

"I heard about drug use increasing from one of the high schoolers' parents when they came in to pick up some mercurochrome." Benton didn't even try to keep the annoyance out of his voice. "Then I heard from my customers about Ray Maxley, local chemical plant owner, receiving fresh shipments of materials that never made it to any pharmacy. I watched them upload for two weeks and kept track of the deliveries versus the reports of kids winding up in the hospital or desperate spikes in local crime."

Daniels pulled out his spare clothing from the bag, most of which hadn't been laundered in a few days, and placed it on the couch beside him. "And you knew Pickern from—"

"Yeah," Benton interrupted, "from Operation Whitemask. It seems the organization's using organized crime as their eyes and ears" He cleared his throat. "Anyway, I managed to break into the plant and got a look at the delivery logs." Benton paused. "The ones he should keep at home."

"Slick." Daniels pulled out a navy-colored leather jacket from the duffel bag and laid it over the arm of the sofa. "Didn't get caught?"

"I didn't think so." The events of the afternoon flashed through Benton's mind for a moment. "That gives me an idea."

Daniels pulled out his last clean shirt. "Am I going to like it?"

"Probably not," Benton admitted, "but good ideas are rarely fun. I think it's time to push back and hard."

Daniels narrowed his eyes with suspicion, and briefly contemplated a return to the mission.

* * * * *

The early morning sunshine woke Garret Daniels. He sat up with a start and looked frantically in every direction. His heart slammed hard against his ribcage until he realized that for the first time in weeks, he slept in somewhat comfortable conditions. Daniels dragged his fingers through his hair as he listened to the *hissssss* of the radiator on the far side of the room. After a stretch and a yawn, Daniels threw his bare feet over the side of the sofa onto the floor.

Minutes later, Daniels glanced into the kitchen as he buttoned his shirt. A note rested in the center of the chrome-edged table with a note upon which was scrawled "HELP YOURSELF TO ANYTHING IN THE FRIDGE OR THE PANTRY. BOB." Daniels peeked into the bedroom to confirm his host's absence. He contemplated grabbing something to eat for only a moment. Unfortunately, although the ex-cop loved a hearty breakfast, the 2-X chemicals in his bloodstream negated the need to eat. Still, he enjoyed the taste of food and lived for that.

After listening to a local news broadcast on the radio, Daniels threw on his jacket and left via the front door. He made sure the lock engaged before he walked downstairs to the street.

Walking past the pharmacy, Daniels watched a workman install a fresh pane of thick glass inside one of the front window frames. He looked past the construction to see Bob Benton diligently rearranging the products on the remaining sales racks inside. Daniels marched onward, grateful Benton didn't see him.

Daniels continued to move through the West Side business

district. He approached a diner two blocks from Benton's Drugs, the same one where he paid Otis for renting out his job. The sign that swung freely over the sidewalk proclaimed "JACKIE'S EATS" in bright red letters. As Daniels' steps brought him closer to the front door of the establishment, his heightened senses detected the aroma of old grease and sizzling meats, as well as the sound of animated conversation from a variety of voices. He pulled the door handle and stepped inside without hesitation.

Upon crossing the threshold, Daniels saw several faces turn towards him, many of whom stared with open-mouthed astonishment. Those same gawking expressions followed him as he entered the wooden phone booth in the corner. Daniels dropped a nickel into the coin slot and confidently dialed a local, unlisted number. He paused long enough to listen to the ringing on the line for the better part of a minute.

When the person on the other end of the line answered, Daniels didn't wait for the person to say hello. He growled into the mouthpiece, "Don't talk, just listen. I'm living with Benton now so you keep you-know-who away from us or I can't be responsible for what happens, got that?"

Daniels paused long enough to allow the person on the other end of the line to recover from their initial shock before he continued, "You know I can follow through on my threat so stay out of the way until you get the all-clear." Daniels paused for a moment before he continued, "We've worked together well so far, but now things have changed. I'll keep you posted." Without waiting to say farewell, Daniels quickly hung up the phone and emerged from the booth.

Walking quickly to the front door, Daniels filled his lungs one last time with the aroma of good food, evoking memories of the previous night at Velma's, before he stepped out onto the sidewalk.

The rest of the day passed quickly for Daniels as he spent the day in the public library, reading newspapers from the region as well as thumbing through some books on Egyptology as he sequestered himself in a corner of a reading room until well past lunchtime.

Making certain to call no attention to himself by his behavior, Daniels walked back to the apartment. He took the steps at normal human speed and knocked on the door. "Come in," Benton replied.

Upon entering the apartment, the smell of freshly-cooking hamburger swatted Daniels in the face. He took in the aroma like a lover would that of an expensive perfume. "You're going to spoil me, Benton."

"Well, don't get used to it. I usually save my meat rations for dates." Benton smiled.

Daniels grinned in return. "Such as Velma Rowland?"

Benton swallowed hard and averted his gaze. "Get washed up, if you're of a mind to. I've been straightening up the store. I think I'm ready to reopen the doors tomorrow morning."

"Good for you," Daniels said as he walked into the bathroom. He looked around at the modestly sized water closet. "At least you don't have to share a toilet."

"For being downtown, it's not bad at all. This whole block used to be a fancy hotel until right after the influenza swept through about twenty years ago." Benton flipped the burgers. As each pink stretch of meat hit the skillet, a fresh sizzle filled the air. Then the pharmacist dropped a slice of bread into a skillet to toast. "I have some ideas that hit me while I was cleaning today, and you probably won't like them."

"Do they involve finding that woman that winged you yesterday?" Daniels dried his hand on a small towel that rested at the side of the sink. "How are we going to do that and keep a low profile?"

Benton grinned. "By becoming annoyingly visible." Daniels' frown grew when his host added, "And being visibly annoying to someone in a certain food chain. You want in?"

Daniels wanted to shake his head…but he knew he'd be lying if he did.

CHAPTER TWENTY-ONE

"And That's the Way Some of Us Like It."

"Just shut up and don't drop me," the Terror insisted as the ground rushed past, a couple of hundred yards below him.

"Then stop squirming." The Cobalt Scarab's legs pumped energetically as he pushed across the night skies. "And stop asking questions. We're almost there." He tightened his grip on the back of the Terror's belt as they approached Mayor Carlton Brant's mansion.

When he left home to attend medical school, Bob Benton took an airplane ride to New York to attend the Brooklyn College of Pharmacy. He was thrilled to look out the window as the airplane wheels lost contact with the ground. He felt as if the world now moved in slow motion as the clouds grew closer and closer. But that wasn't with the winds slapping him in the face as it was now. Also, he had a few dozen tons of steel surrounding him, to say nothing of the protection that the Laws of Aerodynamics provided.

Once the sun dropped, the temperature did as well. Now in the low 20s, the Terror felt the raw vigor of the elements against the exposed areas of his face and eyes. A normal man might have succumbed to hypothermia by now, but the Terror could hold out just a little bit longer. He forced his lips to move, "Are you clear with the plan?"

"What plan?" the Scarab asked. "I still don't get it."

The Terror moaned. "Okay, *again*, Mayor Brant was rumored to get some campaign money from Ben Pickern who had ties to the Chicago crime scene. Funny how once Brant was elected, Ray Maxley got to build his drug distribution center so quickly, right?"

"As a cop, that would raise my suspicions," the Scarab admitted.

"Good." The Terror took a moment to appreciate the view from their vantage point over Raceway City. From here, everything was bright lights, like stars covering the ground like a blanket. "Anyway, since the criminals have some influence over our dear Mayor, let's let Brant know we're on to him and see if he breaks, especially about the lady killer. That's why you're letting me off here."

The Scarab saw the mansion and he dropped in altitude for his aerial approach. "The plan's kinda thin, Mr. Drugstore. Then Pickern knows you're on to him too, you know."

"He knows, already. You got a better one, pal?" The Terror gave up on trying to look into the Scarab's eyes for fear of making the man lose his grip on his belt. "You ever go into action without a great plan, or any plan at all?"

The Cobalt Scarab grunted his affirmation. Covered in blue leather over most of his body, all lined with the bullet-proof material, the Scarab twisted sharply at the hip to change his angle of attack. He squinted through his crimson goggles. "So, the plan is you drop in on him and scare him into confessing something?"

"And see what he knows about the woman with the weird guns." The Terror took a deep breath. "How soon before drop-off?"

"About thirty seconds left to come to your senses."

"Too late for that now," the Terror declared as the mayoral mansion drew closer. The Scarab slanted his body and the pair descended rapidly towards the peak of the three-story tall building. The Terror's enhanced eyesight picked up a dozen men strolling the grounds, their handguns already out in the open and their gazes sweeping from left to right and back again. "Please don't forget your part of the plan."

"I won't. You just get your part done," the Cobalt Scarab stated with more of an edge in his voice than he intended. Knowing his ally would hear him, even above the whistling of the chilled winds blowing past them, the Scarab said, "Come back alive, pal," as he released the Terror's belt. The Scarab didn't stay around to watch his friend land. Instead, he bent his arms to complete a curve in his trajectory that sent him towards the north side of town.

The Terror plummeted towards the gable of the roof that covered Mayor Carlton Brant's mansion. While he hated going into action without his signature blue and red cloak, the Terror was grateful to not hear it flapping as he descended. No sense making any more noise than he needed to.

Upon landing, the Terror allowed his legs to absorb the impact of his arrival as he gripped the apex of the roof tightly. Fortunately, the snow from almost a week ago melted and the slate roofing tiles were dry, allowing the Terror to hold on with his unnatural strength. He turned to look over his shoulder at the expanse of the property three stories below.

If any of the armed guards walking the grounds heard the Terror's landing, they gave no indication. He waited for the better part of a minute as a smile grew on his lips. While Dr. Bob Benton thrived on being an active and positive member of his community, the Terror thrilled in doing what others couldn't. Once the minute ended, the Terror gripped one of the shingles by its base and lifted it upwards until the nails that held it in place released their grip on the wooden boards below.

With one hand clamped onto the roof, the Terror pressed the other relentlessly against the thick board until it gave way with a sound like fresh celery being snapped in two. The Terror dropped the wood and slate inside before reaching for the next undamaged plank. Once a few more shingles found a new home inside the mansion's attic, and the wood under them pushed out of the way, one chunk at a time, the Terror widened the hole as slowly and silently as he could.

Ten minutes later, delayed by continually ensuring he was being ignored by the security forces below, the Terror's work widened the new opening in the roof sufficiently to allow him to drop inside. A minute later, he found the access door to the third-floor hallway where the Terror moved quietly down the carpeted lobby.

Inside the bathroom adjoining his bedroom, Mayor Carlton Brant inhaled the fragrant steam emanating from his tub as he entered it. Made of cast iron, the white enamel glowed as if plugged into the wall. At each corner of the tub, small eagles' talons clutched a ball that made indentations in the linoleum floor.

Scented Epsom salts created an aroma of lilacs that melted the day's cares away. Mayor Brant tilted his head backwards, savoring the fragrance as his muscles unknotted upon contact with the heated water.

In the midst of his reverie, what felt like a steel band suddenly covered his mouth and nostrils. Jarred to full awareness, a warm whisper filled his ear. "Close your eyes and keep them closed until I say differently. You cry out and I hold you underwater until either you stop kicking or I get bored." The voice paused. "And I have the attention span of a Russian Chess Master."

The mayor couldn't move his head even a centimeter. However, before Brant closed his eyes, he smelled the black leather glove covering his nose, and knew immediately who his assailant was. He did his best to nod, which prompted the hand to move. He sucked in a lungful of sweet, lilac-scented air.

Mayor Brant coughed several times before asking, "So what brings you here, Benton? Forget your place in this world?" He sat up in his bathtub, eyes closed and making no effort to conceal his state of undress. "You realize normal business hours are over."

The Terror closed the bathroom door, then sat on the commode casually as if seating himself at the dinner table. "I stayed quiet because you have my government files, Mayor Brant. I've behaved rather well for two years, don't you think? Given that, what prompted you to send that violent woman to my drug store yesterday?"

"Who said it was me?" Mayor Brant asked casually as he opened his eyes. "Maybe it was your little to-do at the railyard a couple of nights ago. You could have had your choice of important people to annoy." The mayor pointed towards a shelf on the far side of the room. "Fetch me that bubble bath I keep for the whores, Benton. I'm not having you stare at me in the altogether."

The Terror stepped slowly to the shelf and tossed the container of bath soap to the mayor who caught it easily in his outstretched hands. For a second, a thought teased the edge of the costumed adventurer's mind, one where he hurled the glass container to see if the swirling glass pattern might explode on contact with the mayor's face, sending slivered shrapnel into every corner of the bathroom. Or perhaps the bottle would maintain its structural integrity and barrel through the man's skull to bury itself in the wall behind him.

However, the Terror wasn't that type of hero.

Instead, Mayor Brant chuckled. "You were thinking about chucking this like Babe Ruth might pitch a no-hitter, huh? Well, *boy*, you blew a golden opportunity just now." Brant poured a measure of the violet liquid into the water. With his free hand, the mayor rapidly moved his fingers through the bath water until a sizeable layer of white bubbles returned his dignity and the scent of lilacs grew thick in air again. "But that's kind of a recurring theme with you, isn't it?" Brant grinned. "*Boy*."

"Why did you send the woman?" the Terror asked, his fists clenched and resting on his hips.

"And who says I did? Instead, let's ask why you stole my dope and my money?" the mayor countered without hesitation. "Do you know how much you cost me? Pretty stupid, given what I know about you. Just one phone call to D.C. would be all it took to destroy your world."

"Thank you for the information." The Terror gave a sly smile. "I didn't know until now how high up you could reach to mess with me. That's good to know."

"All you had to do was ask." Mayor Brant slid down into the bathtub. He raised his arms, weaved his fingers together, then placed his impromptu hammock at the base of his skull. "Who should I start with? The boy? His mother?" Brant grinned. "Or do I tell my secretary who you are?" The mayor laughed. "Oh yeah, don't think I didn't notice."

Since his dual identity wasn't a secret in this room, the Terror peeled back his mask to expose his true face. "I've done everything Operation Whitemask asked." The Terror's voice steadily rose in volume as did his ire. "I've settled into my day job, and I've kept Tim out of action. Why are you poking at me now?"

"Because you got nosey, that's why." The mayor paused to compose his thoughts. "My people reported you were asking their customers' moms and dads about what was going on at Maxley's and the railyard." He sat up in the tub, sending water and some suds onto the bathroom floor.

"I asked because I'm part of that community," the Terror growled. "I care about them. They're more than just people who buy things from me. They rely on me to keep them healthy, to remove their pain." The Terror gritted his teeth. "You should feel as protective about your constituency."

"Save it for the radio soap operas, Benton. Your situation is more precarious than you realize, and you can only guess how many people now have an interest in you burning that Terror costume." Brant grimaced. "The government wants you and people like you to stay low. The war needs heroes and you're a distraction."

The Terror ground his teeth together. "People like—are you talking about my race or my abilities?"

"Both," Mayor Brant answered evenly. "The government wants every would-be patriot to demonstrate their special abilities in our nation's military."

"As long as they're white." The Terror slipped his mask over his face, barely able to suppress his rage.

"Heroes come in many colors, pharmacist." Mayor Brant shifted in his bathtub. "It's all colors, all genders, with powers you can't even imagine right now. You weren't the focus of the operation until you got uppity." The tone of the mayor's voice dropped in volume. "People don't trust your type. There are parts of the world—hell, parts of America where your kind isn't allowed to drink from the same water fountain as me. And that's the way some of us like it."

"And you plan to keep it that way." The Terror studied Mayor Brant's stony expression. "Give me my Operation Whitemask files and Tim's, unless you'd like me to flatten this mansion into a parking lot." He locked eyes with his opponent. "And tell me who's taken a look at them."

Mayor Brant's eyes narrowed. "First of all, the files are on loan to someone else. Second, you won't have time to put a single dent in my mansion." His eyes darted towards the doorway for a heartbeat's length of time.

The Terror, however, noticed the mayor's tell. He jumped to his feet and turned his entire body towards the bathroom door as it slowly opened.

Sylvia Devereaux stood in the open doorway, one of her peculiar handguns aimed directly at the center of the Terror's chest. Without any expression or warning, she pulled the trigger once. The room filled with thunder as a line of hellfire arced towards the costumed adventurer's chest.

"And here I thought I'd have to hunt you down." Sylvia chuckled. "Instead, you came here for me to kill you. How convenient."

CHAPTER TWENTY-TWO

"What Do You Plan To Do To Earn My Money?"

Hellfire blossomed in the center of the Terror's chest. His eyes stung and everything went black for a moment from the pain. He slammed against the wall near the head of the bathtub from the weapon's force. As he slid down the tiles, the Terror wiped a leather gauntlet across his eyes and looked down to see blood covering his insignia.

"Finish him," Mayor Carlton Brant commanded calmly.

Sylvia Devereaux lifted her pistol for a head shot. The Terror was too dangerous to take undue chances with and a blast between his eyes would be the most expedient way to drop the costumed man.

As Sylvia's finger slowly squeezed the trigger, the Terror glanced at the mayor as he happily watched the action from his bathtub.

Pressing one hand tightly against his wound, the Terror stepped forward and seized the bottle of bath oil from Brant's hand. Before Brant could cry out, the Terror hurled it at the floor where it turned into razor-sharp shrapnel that flew in every direction. The Terror barely registered where the shards struck his powerful body and Sylvia managed to raise one of her arms to protect her face.

Mayor Brant cried out in pain. "MY EYES!" before he felt himself being lifted from the bathtub by his arm. He opened one eye to see the Terror holding him high above the floor as if he was weightless.

The Terror flung the naked man at Sylvia, striking her solidly. The two bodies tumbled into the hallway, each rolling over the other until they struck the far wall with painful force.

Sylvia attempted to get to her feet to save a modicum of her dignity, but the stunned mayor covered her body like a lead blanket. Sylvia pushed frantically at his limp form to limited avail as she noticed her futuristic handgun lay several yards down the hallway from where she now lay trapped.

As Sylvia tried to move her employer's bulk, the Terror delivered a solid kick to the base of the bathtub. The cast iron gave way instantly and water rushed from the tub's gaping wound. The Terror pushed the lather towards every corner of the bathroom with his boots. Then he knelt and filled his hands with more of the water which he flung at the areas where his blood covered the sink, the walls, and the toilet before he leaped into the hallway.

Once he landed a couple of feet from his attacker and the mayor, the Terror heard footsteps and shouts approaching from either end of the floor. He glanced one way, then the other, before dropping his gaze to where Sylvia's handgun lay unattended. The Terror sprinted towards the weapon, bent down, swooped it up, and pushed it under the back of his belt as he raced down the hallway to his right.

Half a dozen men reached the floor as the Terror claimed Sylvia's pistol. In unison, their hands dove into their suit jackets to withdraw their handguns.

The Terror mentally noted that at least these were normal firearms and not something from a Republic Movie Serial. He ran toward the access panel to the attic and launched himself upwards to enter the open passageway easily.

Landing on the frame of the entryway, the Terror moved swiftly along the ceiling supports towards the hole he'd left in the roof only minutes before. Before he could reach the hole he created, a wave of dizziness enveloped the Terror and he stumbled, barely able to maintain his balance. He stopped and realized he still clutched his chest in an unsuccessful attempt to stop his bleeding.

Don't think it hit my heart, the Terror thought, *because I'm still moving, thank goodness. Still hurts like the blazes, though.*

Exposure to the formic ethers enhanced the Terror's healing abilities, but he didn't have the time to stop, rest, and allow his wound to knit properly. Each fresh breath reignited the blaze in The Terror's chest.

Despite the worst pain he'd ever felt in his life, the Terror leaped upwards through the gap in the roof, barely clearing the remaining tiles. But once his ebony boots made contact with the roof, his feet slipped out from under him, sending him sliding down the shingles towards the ground.

The Terror arrested his downward movement by stretching out an arm to grab the edge of the hole. But the sudden stop yanked at every muscle in his chest, and he let out a short cry of pain.

He lifted his head, hoping to see if there was a tree nearby that might absorb some of his velocity. Otherwise, he expected to break both of his legs when he landed on the lawn, just before the guards opened fire on him. The Terror felt the jagged edge of the hole digging into his leather gloves and wondered if the wound affected his limited invulnerability.

I'd say this wasn't going as planned, the Terror thought, *but then again, I didn't come here with much of a strategy.*

As the Terror spotted the apex of a large pine tree within leaping distance, the roof exploded to his immediate right, sending shingles and wood flying into the night air. The familiar retort of Sylvia Devereaux's bizarre handgun sounded again and again, destroying the surface next to where the Terror laid. More out of instinct than deliberation, he rolled to his left, barely avoiding a fresh explosion that laid waste to more of the roof.

Dammit, he thought, *I forgot her gun came with a twin.*

As the Terror twisted, another sharp, sudden pain in his chest forced him to lose control of what little grip he had. Gravity took over and the Terror again slid downward. With the agony of his wound flaring once again, he couldn't summon enough muscular control to dig into the roof as he slid towards its edge. He clutched his chest tightly, barely able to feel himself going into freefall.

The Terror barely registered the guards as they shouted to one another. He knew they wouldn't take a shot at him, considering the fall would more likely kill him for free rather than waste the expense of bullets, to say nothing of the attention their gunshots might attract.

Overhead, the clouds parted, exposing the fullest moon a man could hope to see in his final moments. Before he could summon the willpower for a final prayer, something dark crossed the Terror's field of vision for the merest of instants.

A heartbeat later, a gloved hand seized the back of his dark uniform and lifted him upwards. The Terror felt himself rising into the sky. Distant gunfire rang in his ears as bullets whizzed by him. The night winds whipped against the Terror's body, and he wished, oddly enough, that he still had his cloak. He glanced at the moon once again and allowed unconsciousness to claim him.

When the Terror opened his eyes again, he found himself inside his apartment once more. He attempted to sit up, but the now-familiar pain in his chest halted him. The Terror noticed warm air touching his unmasked face and the absence of his skull-adorned shirt and boots, leaving only his tights. As he tried to sit up one more time, a pair of strong hands pushed Bob Benton back onto the sofa cushions.

"You take it easy, okay?" Garret Daniels said. "I've cleaned that wound as best I can and now, I'm trying to find something to close it up with." He prodded the still-bleeding area with surprising gentility. "What kind of cannon did you get nailed with? Was it that?" Daniels gestured over his shoulder.

Benton focused his eyes on a shiny object across the room, in his favorite chair. Within seconds, the blur became Sylvia Devereaux's futuristic hand cannon. "I brought one home to play with. Whatever that slug is, it pierced a ceiling and a slate roof to get me."

"Haven't used a gun in months," Daniels mused. "Damn things make you lazy. Got any needle and thread?"

"If you think you're going to practice your seamstress skills on my chest, forget it. I don't keep needles or thread around anyway." Benton eased himself up to a sitting position. "The wound's closing up, so stand back, Dr. Kildare."

Daniels brought a mug of hot tea from the kitchen and offered it to Benton. As Benton took his first sip, the ex-cop examined the wound. "Nice. I can heal pretty fast. Glad to see you can too."

"Sounds like your 2-X is the oral form of my formic ethers." Benton took another short drink of the tea. "Great tea. You'll make someone a fine wife someday."

Daniels grinned. "You won't. What kind of bachelor doesn't have a needle and thread handy? I mean what if your wife comes home with a sucking chest wound?"

Benton closed his eyes, allowing the tea steam to fill his sinuses. "I have a friend who does these things for me." He grinned. "Now be a good wifey and fetch me a couple of aspirins, please?"

As the pain subsided in Benton's chest, across town, Mayor Carlton Brant felt another kind of pain building.

"You're supposed to be the best hitman—sorry, hit lady on the North American continent." Mayor Brant adjusted the towel around his midsection once again. "You've blown two—TWO different chances to kill that—"

Sylvia Devereaux raised a hand to interrupt her employer. "Use that word and I'll forget you owe me a lot of money." She leaned against the far wall of the bathroom as the security men behind the mayor scrambled to clean up debris and consolidate their information on the mysterious stranger. Her eyes narrowed as she spoke, "Apparently, those files didn't tell me everything I needed to know about this so-called 'Terror.' He's apparently grown in his power since you last spoke to him two years ago."

Mayor Brant muttered something under his breath before adding, "You're probably right. Or else he lied during his debriefing. But who was that with him?"

"If that wasn't Garret Daniels," Sylvia's eyes focused on the foaming scarlet mess at her feet, "then we have no idea what we're dealing with. That 2-X is compounding his abilities exponentially to the point where he can now defy gravity." She dragged the tip of her shoe across the foam, creating a scar in the froth that exposed the tiles below. "Can you take a sample of the plasma and figure out what's in the Terror's blood?"

Brant shook his head. "I've sent off a sample to Maxley's lab. He'll report back if he can pull any information from this mess, but I'm not optimistic. I think Benton deliberately messed up the blood. He's clever like that, being a chemist, after all."

"So noted." Sylvia checked her fingernails. "What's your next move?"

After a moment's thought, Mayor Brant snapped his fingers.

"Gotta call my Chief of Police. I think we can make things a little warmer for that black clown, maybe send a message to that—"

The mayor caught himself before he could utter another racial epithet. "We'll keep those so-called 'mystery men' in their places." Brant hiked up his towel again to maintain what little modesty he owned. "So, what do you plan to do to earn my money?"

"You'll see." Sylvia pushed herself away from the wall. "I have a job to do. Excuse me." She stepped to the doorway and added, "And don't worry about covering up. I've seen it before, and better." With that, Sylvia left, her footsteps muffled by the hallway carpeting.

Sylvia passed the security and other help as she walked to her jet black 1937 Nash Ambassador. After entering the vehicle and locking the door, she pulled a small notebook from her jacket pocket and flipped through the pages with intent.

After finding the appropriate name and address, Sylvia put the vehicle in gear and sped into the night, leaving exhaust and gray snow flying in her wake.

Thirty minutes later, Velma Rowland sat in her favorite chair in front of the fireplace. She snipped a length of black thread from the pile of fabric on her lap. An RCA Radiola 106 emitted the soft sounds of Tommy Dorsey and His Orchestra from atop her fireplace. However, Frank Sinatra's vocals suddenly gave way to a several second burst of static before a staff announcer broke in.

"Ladies and gentlemen, we interrupt tonight's selection of music to bring you a special news bulletin."

"Better not be another Martian invasion," Velma muttered.

The announcer continued, "Reports are coming in of an assassination attempt against Raceway City Mayor, Carlton Brant. Only an hour ago, witnesses reported several explosions coming from the top floor of the mansion." The air went dead for a second, followed by the sound of rustling papers. "This just in: Raceway City Police Chief Samuel Alder has just issued a statement concerning tonight's attempt on our mayor's life.

"Police are wanting to interview a man..." The speaker

paused. He ruffled the paper in his hand and his tone of voice was filled with a certain amount of disbelief, as if the words "APRIL FOOLS" should appear at the end.

Velma felt her heart racing in her chest as the news reader delivered an all-too-accurate description of the Terror, from the skull that served as his chest emblem to the color of his flesh. A chill traveled along her spine.

"Son," Velma whispered as she turned to face the hallway, "I know you can hear me. If you leave that bedroom, I don't care how many powers you have—" She left the threat unspoken as she tossed her needlework onto the floor and sprinted down the hall.

A blast of cold air smacked Velma in the face as she entered her son's bedroom. Her jaw dropped as she saw Tim's street clothing strewn across his bed and the night air pushing the curtains away from the half-open window on the far side of the room.

Due to the formic ether that gave him his own special abilities, Tim Rowland could be halfway across town, and probably was, by the time Velma closed his bedroom window. She moved quickly towards the phone in her living room, picked up the receiver, and began dialing with a shaking hand.

CHAPTER TWENTY-THREE

"Will You Stop Screaming?"

Bob Benton barely lifted the receiver before he and Garret Daniels, via his enhanced senses, heard Velma Rowland's frantic voice. "I don't know where he is," she said, her voice punctuated by fits of sobbing. "Please find my baby boy."

"We'll find him, Velma." Benton stated with conviction before he hung up the phone.

Daniels reached into the pile of laundry that accumulated at the foot of the sofa and removed the pieces of his Cobalt Scarab uniform. "Where do I start looking?"

Benton struggled to a sitting position, ignoring Daniels' glare. "You can pretty much fly and your vision's probably as good as my own." Benton gasped, but grateful his wounds didn't reopen, at least not yet. "Look for someone about half our size, in a costume identical to my own, running as fast as a racecar, probably down the alleyways, I don't know." Benton buried his face in his hands for a moment. "I'm out of practice at this mystery man thing."

"Like riding a bicycle," Daniels stated as he swiftly removed his civilian clothing and dropped them onto the floor. "You stay here and finish knitting up, okay? Leave the heavy work for me." He added solemnly, "I promise. No harm shall come to Tim."

"Sure." Benton leaned back against the sofa cushions and closed his eyes, lapsing into unconsciousness. He didn't hear Daniels complete his change into the costume of the Cobalt Scarab. Nor did Benton hear the back door to his apartment close, nor did he hear his roommate's footsteps as he stepped onto the fire escape to fly away into the night.

After a few minutes, Benton opened his eyes. He groaned as he rose to his feet. With one hand on the wall to steady him, Benton hobbled towards his bedroom, intent on a change of clothing.

Unaware of Benton's defiance of his admonitions to rest, the

Cobalt Scarab raced across the sky, gaining altitude with every pump of his powerful legs. His eyes swept the neighborhood below. Smoke wafted from almost every fireplace and Daniels could see the occasional patches of compacted snow at the edges of the sidewalks and driveways.

As he rose higher into the cloudless skies, the Scarab searched his mind for where Tim could have gone. In his brief time in Raceway City, the mystery man learned about the structure of the city's influences, legal and otherwise, from information purchased as cheaply as a glass of whiskey or as expensively as several twenty-dollar bills. He heard of a place that maintained a thin veneer of respectability on the north side where the more monied ne'er-do-wells would meet.

From his days on the streets of New York, Daniels knew how to encourage those who made their coin in information. He encountered several men who couldn't be bribed to share their knowledge…but there were other means to persuade tongues to loosen.

Below, from his vantage point from between three rusted trash cans at the edge of an alley, a pair of dark brown eyes watched the blue-clad mystery man hurl himself towards the north. Tim Rowland grinned as he followed the figure's move across the heavens. Once the flyer vanished into the lights of Raceway City's northern business district, Tim rose to his full height.

No, not Tim Rowland, the young man reminded himself, *Kid Terror*. Kid Terror counted to five before sprinting from his place of concealment toward the next alleyway. He straightened his ebony mask over his eyes and allowed his blue and red cloak to ride in his wake upon the icy night winds. He thanked his lucky stars that he made his way across town with a caution that would do his mentor proud as he thought to look up just as much as around.

Several minutes later, now closer to the downtown area of the city's north end, Kid Terror stood at the mouth of another alley, pressing himself against the side of a dry goods store, hoping to not be seen by the few people wandering the street. On a Sunday morning, long before decent people woke up to ready themselves for church, a few couples strolled the street, most of them intoxicated and seeking nothing more than a safe path home.

Kid Terror peered around the corner of the building to scout out his surroundings. Across the street, he could see the marquis-style sign over the local bar. He watched the name "The Milestone Club" flare into electric whiteness before fading again. He knew from his mother that this place was once a haven for the well-to-do to escape the pressures of pursuing excessive wealth, especially at a time when banks closed, and fortunes became as temporary as a dream.

Now, it was a place that mothers warned their children not to enter, as if corruption of the soul was a virus that spread faster than the Spanish Flu of two decades before, with far worse results.

Kid Terror watched the name shine brightly, dim, then glow again as he thought to himself, *Okay, I'm here. Now what do I do? What would the Terror do?*

Then, as many children and any number of adults tended to do, Kid Terror decided on a course of action he'd seen in too many movies and heard on far too many radio programs.

Inside The Milestone Club, Charlie Cronin lounged at his usual corner table. He stared at a single lightbulb that illuminated the men's room entrance. For several years, Cronin found an odd contentment in contemplating that one naked bulb long enough to imprint numerous spots in the center of his vision. He also enjoyed the sound of church bells outside his apartment when he woke up at his table, following a bender. He smiled at the multicolored blotches inside his eyes and contemplated the cold walk home.

Cronin adopted The Milestone as his watering hole of choice years earlier. While he knew many of the regular patrons of this establishment, he realized that he never bothered to learn the usual bartender's name. Unfortunately, Cronin's desire to expand his store of knowledge vanished once the front door opened and he felt a cold breeze hit his face.

"Get out of here, kid," the unnamed bartender shouted as he sprinted around the bar and towards the door. "Halloween was months ago." Just as he completed his sentence, the barkeep pushed the front door with all his might, waiting for the satisfying

SLAM that only an oak door reinforced with steel could deliver.

But instead of the expected clatter, the door exploded in the bartender's face. He dropped to the floor as his hands pressed against his skin and a terrified scream issued from his throat.

All eyes in the bar turned towards the open doorway and the young man standing there. Kid Terror stepped into the building, his blue and red cloak flapping in the night winds.

The bartender scrambled to a sitting position. "Get out! Get out! We don't need your kind in here."

"MY *WHAT?*" Kid Terror took one step, then executed a short leap that propelled him across the room to land behind the bar. Before the bartender could register his astonishment, the Kid seized the man's shirtfront and pulled the older man into the air with just one hand. *"MY KIND???"*

The bartender stammered, "M-m-mystery men. *Whuh*-what else?" before passing out from fright.

Kid Terror released the barkeep, allowing him to drop, limp, to the floor. The Kid swept his gaze across the room, unsure of what to do now.

Charlie Cronin downed the last of his drink when the kid's violent entrance drew his attention. However, to his alcohol-tainted eyesight, Cronin saw what had to be the person who attacked him at the warehouse, then again at the trainyard...only much shorter. Without intending to, Cronin dropped his glass with a short *"EEEK!"* at the sight of a diminutive version of the costumed adventurer who haunted his dreams.

When Cronin's glass shattered on the floor, Kid Terror turned towards the sound. His eyes narrowed in inverse proportion to how Cronin's eyes widened. Although the Kid's experience in crime fighting proved limited, he knew a guilty look when he saw one. Cronin turned to flee but two distance-killing steps later, Kid Terror stood by his side with his fingers firmly gripping the back of Cronin's jacket.

Before Kid Terror could ask his first question, Cronin instinctively grabbed his unoccupied chair, closed his eyes, and swung it at the youth. Surprised more than injured, to say nothing of unbalanced from his landing, Kid Terror dropped to one knee and instinctively covered his face. The chair shattered against the young man's forearms, sending pieces of wood flying in every direction.

Cronin opened his eyes to find his enemy down. He reached inside his coat for a weapon, unable to recall which one he carried on this evening. He growled with drunken bravado, "Don't know how you do what you do, but you ain't tougher than—"

But whatever the man believed was mightier than Kid Terror's formic ether-inspired strength would be lost to the ages. Still on one knee, the Kid swung a fist towards Cronin's left leg. The unrestrained force of his blow shattered Cronin's left tibia and fibulae and the crook dropped onto his side, wailing in pain.

Kid Terror rose to a standing position as one set of fingers dug deep into the nearest table. "Will you please stop screaming?" Kid Terror muttered as he looked around the bar. "I'm trying to find where—"

The young hero's statement died in his throat when he saw several men pull pistols from their holsters and carefully aim them at the center of his chest.

On the west side of town, Bob Benton used every iota of concentration to not burst into a running gait that would leave most automobiles far behind him. As it was, the sight of a black man jogging through even the west side of town would attract unwanted, fearful attention. It wouldn't help matters if his witnesses learned that normally, this activity left him no more winded than if he'd lifted a cup of coffee.

Benton's chest burned where he'd been shot. He hoped he didn't have to open his jacket to check his wounds for fear of their reopening.

A more sensible man would have stayed home and healed up. A more patient adult would have gathered his allies and planned a counter-offensive based on what they knew about their enemy.

Then again, Benton survived a point-blank gunshot to the chest, something that most people couldn't do.

But even more importantly, Bob Benton believed at this moment that he should never have inhaled those formic ethers and become the Terror. Sure, he and Tim saved quite a number of lives during their brief time as mystery men, but nights like this—well, the Terror never had a night like this before.

He also knew that if he didn't stop this killer woman, either these nights might never end, or he would cease to be, along with everyone close to him.

No, not if I have anything to say about it, Benton thought with renewed reserve as he picked up his pace, *and I do*.

After finding too many water puddles on the sidewalk as he ran, Benton gave up on trying to dodge them. With only a couple more blocks until he reached Velma Rowland's home, his trousers, shoes, and socks now thoroughly drenched, Benton allowed himself a short smile as Velma's house came within view.

Upon reaching Velma's property, the front door of the Rowland home opened slowly. Benton slid to a halt at the edge of her walkway, his keen eyes taking in the sight of Velma Rowland walking onto her porch without a coat or any expression whatsoever. As Benton cautiously climbed the front steps, he looked past Velma to the barrel pressed against the back of her neck, and then at the person holding the gun.

Sylvia Devereaux crossed the front threshold, her body pressed tightly against her hostage's. "Come inside, Benton. Let's all get warm together."

CHAPTER TWENTY-FOUR

"And What's That Bug On Your Belt?"

A hand landed firmly on Kid Terror's shoulder. The young man shrugged with enough force to either send the man staggering backwards across the barroom, or to shatter every bone in his hand. Instead, the hand dug more firmly into the Kid's flesh, much to the young man's surprise.

"And who the hell are you?" the bouncer asked as he emerged from the gentlemen's room. He wiped his freshly washed hands on his trousers.

The Cobalt Scarab patted the Kid's shoulder. "Hi, Kid. Let me handle this." He turned to face the approaching bouncer with the intention of de-escalating the situation. As the distance closed between them, the Scarab tilted his lens-covered eyes up, up, and up some more in order to meet the taller man's gaze.

"I asked you a question, shorty!" The bouncer's left eye didn't open quite as wide as his right and he lacked most of his ring finger. He stopped a foot away from the Scarab. "What's with the blue leather? Those goggles make you look like some kind of bug." The thug grinned evilly. "You a cockroach? A beetle? And what's that bug on your belt?"

After sighing and shaking his head, Garret Daniels muttered, "No one gets it, man. It's a scarab. A *scarab*, okay? It's supposed to inspire fear in—oh, why do I bother?" As soon as the question escaped his lips, the Scarab pulled back his fist with the speed of a jaguar and popped the bouncer on the chin.

The thug's head snapped back, and his feet left the floor as he flew several feet backwards to land in a heap against the bar.

Upon seeing that, the wide-eyed customers holstered their weapons and held their hands in the air.

"I'm taking this boy out of here," the Scarab announced. "Anyone got a problem with that?" He muttered so only Kid Terror could hear him, "That includes you so shut up until we're outside."

Without waiting for an objection from the bar patrons, the Scarab dragged Kid Terror towards the door and then outside.

Once the cold night air filled his lungs, Kid Terror turned to face the man he saw outside of Jean Starr's apartment the other night.

"Yeah, it's me, Kid. It's Garret." The man threw his arm around Kid Terror's shoulders and led him across the street, ignoring any stares they received from passersby. "You feeling any better?" Once on the opposite side of the roadway, the Scarab paused to examine the Kid's skull. "Looks like you got clocked pretty good. I'm glad you've got a hard head, Kid." The Scarab gestured towards a nearby alley.

"That's what my mom tells me." Kid Terror kept pace with the Scarab as they entered the alleyway. "Thanks for getting me, but I think I could have taken them."

"I know you could," the Scarab lied. "But that's no way to gather information, if that was your intent. You'll learn." He stopped in his tracks as did Kid Terror who remained silent as the older man closed his eyes, dropped his head, and concentrated deeply. After a few seconds, the Scarab tilted his head in the direction of The Milestone Club. "I was trying to listen, but there's too much chatter in there." The Cobalt Scarab's eyes met Kid Terror's. "But I suspect someone's getting a call about us."

"Did I mess up?" The Kid gripped the Scarab's arm tightly. His fingers dug into the adult's flesh and muscle. "Tell me the truth. I screwed everything up, didn't I?"

The Scarab chuckled as a sensation of pain ran up and down his arms, something few people could give him. "No more than your senior partner did. At least you didn't get shot." As soon as the words left his lips, the Scarab regretted uttering them as Kid Terror's eyes widened.

"Get shot?" Kid Terror seized the Scarab's shoulders and squeezed hard enough to make the man wince. "Did Bob get hurt? Tell me." The boy's face furrowed with concern. "And what's wrong with your face?"

"It—it—it hurts." The Cobalt Scarab shrugged once, twice,

then a third time but with all his strength on the last desperate attempt. "Let—go!"

Kid Terror released his grip on the Scarab. "Gosh, I'm sorry. You okay?"

The Scarab rubbed his upper arms gingerly, first his left then his right. "Kid, that's the first time I've felt real pain in almost two years. What's in your system, anyway?"

Rather than reveal the secret of his strength, Kid Terror said, "Let's get back to Bob." He turned towards the far end of the alley before he said, "And what's this about getting shot?"

"Don't worry about that, I say." A smile crossed the Scarab's lips and the change of topic made Kid Terror uncomfortable. "We have something else to discuss." He grinned. "Call it a change in whatever plans you made."

Many blocks away, Sylvia Devereaux motioned with her futuristic handgun for Bob Benton to enter Velma Rowland's living room. She moved behind him quickly and pushed the front door shut with the pointed toe of her expensive boot. "On the couch, Benton."

Benton walked slowly towards the sofa, removed his coat, then draped it over its back. He sat down gingerly, his gaze locked on Sylvia.

"Stop glaring at me, Benton." Sylvia laced her fingers through Velma's hair and pulled hard. Velma gritted her teeth but refused to gratify her captor with a yelp of pain, even when Sylvia shoved her onto the couch. "And I see you heal quickly, pharmacist."

"You don't sound disappointed," Benton stated. He looked down at what used to be his cleanest white shirt. A small patch of moist scarlet slowly expanded over his heart. "Oh, you were being sarcastic. Sorry."

Sylvia grinned. "I'm not disappointed at all. That was a clever trick you pulled in the mayor's executive bathroom, Benton. You thoroughly contaminated any would-be blood samples. No lab analysis of what makes you special." The assassin drew a finger firmly across the scarlet stain on Benton's chest. She briefly checked the bright red stain that coated her digit. "It's about time I had a target worth my effort."

Benton shrugged as the pressure of her touch sent his nerve endings into screaming agony, which he refused to acknowledge. "Forgive me for not trusting Mayor Brant. Truth is, I didn't even vote for him."

"Raceway City is disappointingly progressive, what with encouraging your type to vote." Sylvia's eyes shot towards Velma for a second. "And I understand your dislike of the mayor." She regarded the crimson stain on the tip of her index finger with a smile. "Did you know he's worked tirelessly with your government to keep the so-called heroes of Raceway City in their places?"

"Yeah, I figured." Benton tried to keep his eyes from searching the room in the hopes of finding a way to get Velma out of the house. With any luck, he wouldn't have to kill this beautiful assassin, but he knew that he would have to create his own luck. "So, what are you waiting for?"

Sylvia leered at Benton. "Isn't it obvious, Benton? I'm waiting for your youthful assistant to come home." The killer smiled coldly as Velma's eyes went wide. "Sure, it's not a school night, but what kind of awful mother are you to allow the lad to roam about this late?"

"Kill me instead." Velma's voice quavered. "He's just a boy."

"His age means nothing to me," Sylvia snarled through her icy smile. That evil grin vanished as Sylvia regarded Benton again. "I assume you know your exploits now inspire many American youths."

"Yeah, I know." Benton turned towards Velma again. "To add insult to injury, Washington has been feeding information on my earlier cases to the company that's making new comic book adventures of someone they call 'The *Black* Terror.' Just one insult following another."

"It's hilarious." Sylvia's high-pitched laughter filled the room, grating on Benton's ears like nails on a chalkboard. "I assume that's why you don't carry many of those long underwear funny-books?"

Benton unclenched his fists and rested his hands on his knees. "You didn't come here just to remind me how heavy Uncle

Sam's thumb weighs on me. What the hell do you really want?"

"Language, pharmacist." Sylvia lifted her futuristic pistol for Velma and Benton to see. He noticed a series of holes drilled into the handle, but for what reason, he couldn't discern. "I was hired to kill you, Benton. You and your friends ruined my perfect reputation in just one day. And then you had the nerve to do it twice." Sylvia turned her gaze towards Velma once more. "Now I've got to erase everyone involved before I have to start charging less for my services."

Velma gasped. "Do you want me to beg? Tim's got an aunt who can raise him." She paused to wipe the tears from her eyes. "I don't have a lot of money, but—"

"Oh, please, woman." Sylvia sneered. "Don't pander to a good side that isn't there. I'm in this for my boss's money and only for his money." She aimed the pistol at Benton. "Word travels quickly in this business. One failure and you're as good as unemployed." Sylvia smiled as she whispered, "But I know how to remain quite profitable once I get a sample of blood from your corpse. There are many people, many countries, who'd love to have a battalion of supermen just like you. And I'm not talking about America." Sylvia grinned as she slowly licked her index finger clean. "Only white, though," she added. "A girl's got to have some standards, you know."

Sylvia's expression darkened as she shuddered briefly. "That little stain on your chest isn't as little as when you came in here." She frowned. "Either you're losing your powers, or I tagged you better than I believed. Chances are you'll run out of go-juice before I can drag your butt to a laboratory." Sylvia grinned. "No, I made a phone call to my employer. I have a backup plan."

Benton winced as Sylvia pressed her finger against the crimson stain again, harder this time. Her eyes twinkled as he gritted his teeth, and again when she made a show of cleaning her finger with her long, wet tongue.

"The mayor—" Benton began.

"Believe what you will," Sylvia interrupted. "I have become weary of explaining myself to the likes of you." She sighed. "But if it'll shut you up for now, my contact suggested I lurk about in the mayor's mansion because he was certain you'd show up sooner or later. And sure enough, there you were." Sylvia aimed the pistol at Benton's chest. "Now be silent, *boy*, or I'll take away your options, along with your lady friend's."

A knock sounded at the door. Benton whirled around, instinctively ready to leap into action. However, as he shifted his weight on his feet, Benton felt a fresh wave of fire across his chest, stealing his strength and forcing him to stagger back against the sofa.

Sylvia moved toward the door, her handgun never wavering from Velma and Benton's direction. She gripped the doorknob, turned it quickly, and peered outside. "What the hell?" Sylvia's head swiveled quickly between her hostages on the davenport and the visitor at the edge of the threshold.

"You going to make us stand out here all night?" The Cobalt Scarab hefted Kid Terror's limp body high on his shoulder. "Or is freezing someone to death your new M.O.?"

CHAPTER TWENTY-FIVE

"I'm Full of Surprises, Benton."

Sylvia Devereaux's cool shattered like an Edison Cylinder striking a hardwood floor. "What in the hell are you doing?"

The blue-clad man stepped across the doorway and into the Rowland home. "Call me Scarab, okay? He turned to see the horrified expression of Velma Rowland as she saw the limp form of her only son across his shoulder. He raised a red-gloved finger and commanded Tim's mother, "Stay seated and don't say a word, got it?"

Bob Benton placed his hand on Velma's shoulder. She glanced back at the pharmacist to receive a curt nod. He narrowed his eyes at the Scarab. "I never saw this coming, Scarab."

"I'm full of surprises, Benton." The Scarab snarled at Sylvia, "As for you, your employer is very unhappy with you. Now lower that gun and let's get out of here. The boss wants to ream you out in person."

"You want to see some reaming out?" Sylvia stepped forward and aimed her weapon at a point between the Scarab's eyes. "If you knew who I worked for, why don't you identify him by name?" She smiled slyly as the seconds ticked by. "I recognize your chin. The drugstore. You're that red-haired man, and a parahuman too." The pistol hummed ominously in her hand. "Nice try, blue boy. Now who's full of surprises?"

"ME!"

As soon as Kid Terror replied, he brought both legs up swiftly and knocked the handgun out of Sylvia's grasp. By the time she recovered from the surprise, Sylvia looked up to see her weapon embedded in the ceiling. With a brief bend at the knee, Sylvia launched herself upwards to retrieve her handgun. But the weapon remained just beyond the reach of her fingertips.

Kid Terror dropped from the Scarab's shoulder and in a bound, the young man reached his mother's side. "Come with me," he stated with adult firmness and for once, she didn't object. The Kid swept Velma up in his arms and leaped towards her bedroom. A second later, the door slammed shut and Kid Terror pressed his palms tightly against the door from the inside, ensuring it would not move.

Bob Benton jumped to his feet, his fists raised. "All right, lady. Time to stand down."

Sylvia growled like a wounded tigress, "I'm going to finish what I started two days ago." She turned her angry gaze toward Benton.

The Cobalt Scarab took a swing at the killer. Unfortunately, Sylvia anticipated an attack and dropped to a kneeling position. Off-balance as he followed through on his blow, she executed a perfect leg sweep that took out the Scarab's legs. He fell hard onto his back.

"Get my gun, Benton!" Sylvia demanded. "You don't know what kind of trouble you're in, boy."

"You want me to get the pistol that opened a hole in my chest?" Benton asked with a confident grin. "I don't think that'll be happening." To prove his point, Benton reached a hand towards the back of his belt. "Not when I have this."

Benton held up the twin to the weapon imbedded in the ceiling, the handgun he took from Sylvia back in the mayor's mansion.

Sylvia's eyes widened with surprise and longing. "Give it here." Her face twisted into an ugly mask of fury, "I said give it here, boy!"

"I'm really tired of you calling me that." To punctuate his declaration, Benton squeezed hard. Immediately, the metal of the handgun turned malleable like putty in his mighty grasp. Before Sylvia could do little more than gasp, Benton wiggled his fingers, transforming the pistol into an unrecognizable ball of scrap metal.

Sylvia's eyes widened in horror. Several months ago, a young woman suffered a miscarriage in the hospital where Velma worked. Benton's heart broke every time she walked past his store's selection of greeting cards and bawled upon seeing the baby announcements. His customer's cries never achieved the intensity of what erupted from Sylvia's throat.

With a flick of his wrist, Benton tossed the misshapen ball of metal to one side. "And if I reach up, I'm turning your other toy into part of a matching set."

"You bastard!" Sylvia snarled. She shuddered and smiled briefly as the Cobalt Scarab's arms encircled her upper body, pinning her arms to her sides. He latched his fingers together to reinforce her impromptu incarceration.

"Settle down, lady," the Scarab ordered. "Or else I'll have to—"

"Have to what?" Sylvia asked. "Reveal your identity to the local police? Beat me to death because that's the only way I'll stop trying to kill you two?" She crooked her head in the direction of Velma's bedroom and said to Benton, "Sorry, you *four*."

Sylvia licked her lips, shook her head, planted her feet, and then attempted to move her arms away from her body. She felt the Scarab's hot breath on her ear while his chuckle dropped softly in volume when he realized his fingers no longer laced with each other. He redoubled his efforts, but to no avail. With a powerful flex that surprised everyone in the room, including her, Sylvia broke the Scarab's grip and then followed with a reverse kick that drove her heel deep into his stomach.

"Get a load of me," Sylvia hissed like a snake. "The blood is the power, boy. So, this is what it feels like to have the strength of a god." She threw herself at the pharmacist with a speed to rival the fastest baseball pitch recorded.

Benton leaped from the sofa toward Sylvia, but she sidestepped his outstretched arms easily. As he passed her, she delivered a powerful elbow to the back of his skull. For a moment, the world went dark, leaving him with the impression that his limp fingers dropped the woman's pistol.

The Scarab caught Benton in mid-flight, ensuring his ally wouldn't land in a heap on his face. As Benton found his footing again, Sylvia bent down just long enough to pick up what had once been her handgun. She hefted it a couple of times like a bowler measuring the weight of her ball before she hurled it toward Velma's bedroom.

The aged timbers of Sylvia's door frame exploded like a

bomb, followed by a young man's painful cry.

"TIM!" Benton released himself from the Scarab's embrace, clearing the sofa effortlessly. Another leap carried him easily to the end of the hallway.

The Scarab barely registered a dark movement in the corner of his eye when Sylvia caught him on the chin with a perfectly aimed kick. His head snapped back, and the world turned blurry for several seconds. Sylvia gazed down the hallway where she could hear Velma's sobbing as clearly as if the woman stood beside her.

"Hey, Benton. Stick with your own kind." Sylvia's scarlet lips pulled back into the grimmest parody of a smile imaginable. "In fact, first, I think I'm gonna take care of that pretty white girlfriend of yours, so you'll remember which end of town to stay in." Sylvia looked down at the slowly reviving Scarab before she raced to the front door. "And then I'm going to rectify my four other mistakes. So don't go anywhere."

In short order, the front door slammed shut, followed by the roar of Sylvia's automobile's powerful engine and the immediate squeal of expensive tires on the cobblestone street.

The Cobalt Scarab's vision cleared just as Benton emerged from Velma's bedroom. The pharmacist made no effort to conceal his inner turmoil. The Scarab used the arm of the sofa to reach a standing position as Benton watched from the other end of the davenport.

"Thanks for trying to help, Daniels." Benton bit his lip. "But she got away, right?"

"Yeah." The Scarab flopped onto the sofa. "I don't recall being stuck that hard since my first dose of 2-X." He shook his head with the intent of clearing it. Instead, a fresh wave of agony filled his skull. "How's Tim doing?"

Benton chuckled. "The kid was at the door and took most of the brunt of the attack. He's gonna hurt like he just gave birth for a few days."

"At least he's alive," The Cobalt Scarab concluded. "And Velma?"

"Madder than hell." Benton's eyebrows furrowed. "I think

I've created a monster." As the Scarab attempted to formulate his next question, Benton continued. "My blood. That bitch tasted my blood."

"Probably not the first blood she's ever tasted, pal." Daniels pulled back his hood and slid his ruby goggles from his forehead. "Not given her profession."

Benton laid a hand on Daniels' shoulder. "No, I meant she sampled the blood from my shirt." He looked down to see the wound had opened up again. "She's got a bit of the formic formula in her bloodstream now. I have to stop her." Benton's attempt to cross the living room was halted when Daniels put out his arm, blocking his friend's way.

"You caught that about a 'white girlfriend?' What did she mean?" Daniels took a deep breath and snapped his fingers. "In the drugstore. That woman who came in around closing time?"

"Her name's Jean Starr." Benton straightened up. "Listen, I need to get back to my pharmacy for something. As for you, remember where you ran into Tim a couple of nights ago?"

"I know where to go." Daniels tugged his cowl and goggles back into position. "I can get there before that car if I leave now. What about you and Tim?"

"Tim's going nowhere for the moment." Benton reached for his top shirt button before he recalled a costume he couldn't wear. "And if we stop that woman tonight, Velma and Jean are both safe."

"So, we take the battle to Pickern and Brant?"

Benton smiled softly. "Soon. Just try and stop me. Now go."

The Cobalt Scarab nodded and practically sprinted to the kitchen. Without another word, he opened the door and disappeared into the night.

An easy jump later, Benton pulled the imbedded weapon from the ceiling. *Dealing with her new abilities,* he thought, *distracted her from retrieving her weapon, thank goodness. My strength and her weapon? She'd be even more unbeatable than she is right now.*

Benton entered the kitchen to close the back door. "Bob?" At the sound of that voice, Benton hurried back into the living room.

Velma stood at the mouth of the hallway, her head bowed, and one of her hands behind her back. "Bob, Tim's resting."

"He's gonna be okay," Benton said without conviction. "He's a strong kid and Garret will make sure she—"

"No," Velma interrupted. "He's a cop. That woman sees no other solution to whatever stands in her way but someone dying. By the time she reaches the point where Garret can justify harming her, who knows how many people could be dead by then?" Tears played at the corner of Velma's eyes. "You don't know what she said before you got here, the things she'd do to Tim and to me."

Benton nodded before he wrapped his powerful arms around Velma. "I know. It ends tonight. I promise. No more hiding, no more fear." Benton lifted her chin and softly dried her eyes with his thumb. "I'll figure out the consequences after I'm done."

Velma pushed herself away from Benton with her free hand. "No, you aren't going out there." She sniffed loudly and the steel returned to her eyes as she met Benton's gaze. Velma drew her concealed hand forward, revealing a folded bundle of black, blue, and red fabrics. Holding the cloths with both hands, she shook out the folds, revealing a fresh Terror uniform.

"I knew one day, you'd need a spare," Velma stated solemnly. "Tonight, Doctor Robert Benton has done all he can. Now, it's up to the Terror to make things right."

The Terror could punch a hole in the side of a boxcar or leap up to a third-story window. But in the face of this much confidence and respect, Bob Benton's hands trembled as he accepted the uniform. "Thank you, Velma," was all he could think to say.

Velma smiled as fresh tears flowed down her cheeks. "Now get your butt into the bathroom and get changed. You've got a killer to catch."

CHAPTER TWENTY-SIX

"Do What You Must."

In her ears, Sylvia Devereaux's heartbeat drowned out the roar of her automobile's engine. A tightness spread across her chest as she took still another corner on two wheels. Sweat beaded on her face as she pressed the accelerator to the floor. Sylvia's mind raced, sorting through her dwindling options, as she gripped the steering wheel even more tightly.

As she did so, she felt the steering wheel in her hands crack.

Sylvia glanced at the floorboards on the passenger's side of the vehicle where the file folders lay. She'd practically memorized every page about the Terror and Kid Terror. However, Sylvia never anticipated meeting the Cobalt Scarab, so she merely skimmed his dossier.

Now, Sylvia wished she'd taken the time.

As the vehicle approached an intersection, the traffic light turned a vibrant red. Sylvia pressed hard on the brake and the clutch, almost sending the car into a skid. As it came to a halt, Sylvia took in a lungful of chilly night air, forcing herself into something more resembling her usual state of icy calm. She rolled down her window and extended her hand to signify her intention to turn left at the light.

"It's his chemically altered blood," Sylvia whispered. "It must be." She fought down a wave of nausea. She licked her fingers for effect back at the Rowland house, to intimidate her intended victims. But how could anyone know the power housed in his plasma?

He must have known, Sylvia reasoned. *Why else would he have contaminated the splatter in the mayor's bathroom? Has someone else tried to take his blood before? Or did he do so because he's a pharmacist and knows chemistry? Who knows?*

Syvia squeezed the steering wheel. A very satisfying CRACK filled the air. *Who knows? Who cares?*

Another notion entered Sylvia's mind as she watched the sporadic early morning traffic cross her path. *No doubt, the factories have changed shifts and these simple, classless fools are heading home to their mundane lives.* Her lips pulled back into an evil grin as she raised her left hand straight up in the air to signal not only a change in destination, but a change in her life.

Back at the Rowland house, Velma leaned against the wall next to her bathroom. "I know it hurts you to talk about it, same with Tim." She wished she had a pack of Chesterfields right now, but Tim nagged her into throwing the cigarettes away a year ago. It was easier to go through withdrawal than to listen to him complain. "You never told me about why you and Tim stopped fighting crime completely. I mean you could have operated in secret from the government too, right?"

A rueful chuckle came from inside the bathroom as Benton thoughtfully removed his glasses. "I thought we already were." He stopped changing for a moment, to recall the good deeds of The Terror Twins, as they called themselves.

"Tim and I had stopped a number of criminal schemes, here in Raceway City and a few more at destinations that won't make you terribly happy with either of us." Velma heard the pharmacist's trousers strike the floor. "As for stopping our activities, it certainly wasn't my idea."

Velma waited for Benton to continue. She imagined him carefully folding his street clothing and placing it gently upon the toilet tank. His voice grew somber, "I know you didn't want Tim to help me as Kid Terror in the first place. But he's done so much good, Velma. One day, I'll tell you what he's done, and you'll be so proud of him. Just like I am."

"I know," Velma said. She recalled the defeat in her son's eyes when he announced that he was giving up being Kid Terror two years ago. It scared her to know he fought crime with abilities straight out of a comic book, but nothing prepared her for having to deal with her son no longer wanting a life of adventure.

The boy was smart, so very smart, but couldn't find the words to articulate his fears. Velma saw how the encounter with the members of Operation Whitemask upset him so she let it drop and hoped the time would come when he could share his burden with her. Before Bob could apologize, as he was likely do to, Velma continued, "Please, Bob. Go on."

The sound of Benton sliding his muscular legs into the ebony leggings reached Velma's ears. He removed the blood-stained t-shirt and slipped the fresh tunic over his bare chest. "They wanted heroes for the boys overseas. However, most of them were going to be white and from areas where proud Black men weren't exactly welcome." Benton sighed. "You know…two water fountains, two sets of standards."

Velma heard the creak of the yellow leather belt as Benton fastened it to his midsection. "So, they told us to lay low, to stop what we were doing. Otherwise…" He paused. "I couldn't let Tim grow up without a mother, Velma. I just couldn't." He took a deep breath. "I'm sorry."

"I appreciate that," Velma managed to say through her tears. "Thank you, Bob. I can only guess what that agreement took out of you."

"No, you can't." Benton said softly through the door. He unfurled his blue and scarlet cloak and tucked the ends into the special pockets at his collar that would hold the cape tight against his body. "In exchange for a safe and uneventful life, we had to relate our cases to the government in detail. As it happens, our tales wound up in comic books. The stories were changed so the heroes were white." Benton paused for several seconds. "The editors of those rags didn't even bother to change our names."

Benton's sigh reached Velma's ears through the wall. "And that hurt. They whitewashed our adventures, literally. They stole from us all the good we've done for this community, even the world."

Velma realized she'd been grinding her teeth. "That's awful."

"Yeah," Benton agreed, then chuckled. "That's one of many reasons I don't carry long underwear titles in my store. It's a futile gesture, but it helps me sleep at night." Benton chuckled. "Also, I didn't tell them everything, such as the extent of my abilities and Tim's." He laughed ruefully. "Imagine, someone believing our strength diminishing over time and being so easily knocked out. But that's our secret."

"No worries, Bob." Velma smiled. "So, are your powers changing?"

Benton considered Velma's question. "Not so far. Time will tell." All humor vanished from Benton's voice. "It was our own government that did this to us, Velma. They levied the entire power of the federal government against Tim and me. There was nothing we could do but say yes."

Velma nodded and dabbed at her eyes with a laced handkerchief. "Until now?"

"Until I couldn't stand by anymore and watch kids not much older than Tim get hooked on drugs that came in because the city fathers make good money to look the other way." Benton paused. "I listened to conversations in the store, researched the relationships between the politicians and the career criminals who truly run this city."

Benton paused, choosing his next words with deliberation. "It's a vicious symbiotic relationship between Washinton, D.C., the crooks, and the people who are supposed to be looking out for everyone's welfare." Suddenly, Benton's voice sounded with a newfound resolve. "I firmly believe I was given these powers for a reason. Thus, I had to take action."

Velma added, "Or rather, the Terror did."

The bathroom door opened, and Dr. Bob Benton emerged in the uniform of the Terror. Velma noticed how he seemed to stand up straighter and his gaze gained greater focus than when he was Dr. Bob Benton. Her heart swelled as she studied the lines of his garb. Except for looking onto Bob Benton's unmasked face, Velma would swear she now saw a completely different man standing in his place.

Velma smiled and straightened the pleats in the Terror's cape. "You look good, Dr. Benton. Now go out there and save Raceway City." She gently pulled the mask up and onto the Terror's face, completing the transformation. "And don't worry about us being held over your head like blackmail." Before the Terror could say anything, Velma shushed him as she pressed her index finger onto the man's lips. "I'll take care of Tim. You just make sure she doesn't come back here."

"Yes, ma'am." Whether he intended to or not, Velma noticed the Terror's voice dropping an octave. "I think I need to say goodbye to Tim."

"No, you don't."

Tim Rowland leaned against the doorframe. The blast that tore the bedroom door apart shredded the young man's street clothing, exposing the Kid Terror uniform underneath. Pain colored Tim's voice as he spoke in a tone that belied his meager years, "I'll keep Mom safe, Bob. You go stop that woman, okay?"

"Will do, partner." With a quick nod, the Terror stepped back into the bathroom where he left Sylvia Devereaux's handgun.

He returned to the hallway and dropped the pistol in Tim's hands. "Hold on to this." The Terror fought the urge to tell his young friend, *If I fail, you use that.* Instead, he forced a confident smile onto his lips. "I'll fix your ceiling when I get back, Velma. Walk me to the door?" She started to protest, but the Terror stated firmly, "Right now, I don't give a damn who sees me here."

Less than a minute later, the adults stood on the front porch of the Rowland household. Velma and the Terror looked into each other's eyes, unable to say everything they wanted to, knowing how little time they had. They stared at the other for what felt like too long before the Terror spoke. "Velma—"

"I know," Velma said, the quiver in her voice not solely from the cold, "do what you must."

The Terror took a deep breath before he leaped from the front porch to land in the center of the street half a block away. Without a backward glance, the Terror broke into a run. By the time he reached the nearest cross street, his speed rivaled that of a racecar. Soon, the Terror was out of sight and Velma locked herself and Tim inside their home.

On the other side of Raceway City, the Cobalt Scarab raced several hundred feet above the city. Clouds rolled in slowly from the west, perhaps bringing a fresh layer of snow. Below him a lone car headed towards the south side as he kicked his legs harder, rising upwards, moving towards the apartment building where Jean Starr lived.

The Scarab wondered if the car might belong to the woman who took shots at him in Benton's pharmacy. However, he couldn't see her vehicle currently moving at a normal rate of speed, especially after all the crimes she'd committed in the last 48 hours. The Scarab believed she would be professional enough in her vile profession to leave town after a final attempt on Benton's life.

On the other hand, the Cobalt Scarab made a promise to the pharmacist. So rather than chase down who he believed could be Sylvia Devereaux, but also might not be, the Scarab hoped the pharmacist could keep himself and the Rowlands safe.

Extending both of his arms ahead of him, the Scarab rose almost straight up towards the stars until he saw his destination.

The Cobalt Scarab circled the building, looking for any movement inside. But aside from a couple of what he assumed were bathroom lights, the building lay dark as the occupants slept through the excitement on the west side of town, not that it would get much coverage from the local press.

When Garrett Daniels was a New York City cop, he knew the more skilled burglars pried open windows just enough to get in and out safely. By creating minimal damage to the window, they could revisit their more successful robberies and take what they missed before.

Yeah, besides, crooks usually returned to the scene of the crime. The irony of the thought crossed the Scarab's mind, painting a small smile on his face as he approached Jean Starr's bedroom window. He ran close to the sill and thrust out his hand. His fingers found a gap between the exterior bricks as he pulled up his legs and kicked violently, bringing his flight to a halt. Holding himself in place with one hand, the Scarab gently raised the window, positioning himself to leap inside and cut short any cry of fright once the frigid night air touched the occupant.

As the Scarab entered the bedroom, a handgun appeared, mere inches from the invader's face. The owner of the firearm said softly, "You're letting the heat out. Either come inside and get shot or I'll shoot you as you fall to the ground, your choice."

CHAPTER TWENTY-SEVEN

"I Said, 'I Insist.'"

"Keep your hands in the open," Rodney Clark commanded. He took a step closer to the bedroom door, the .38 in his hand never wavering from the center of the Cobalt Scarab's chest.

Daniels pulled himself easily into the room. "Mind if I close the window?"

Clark waved his pistol in agreement. "Don't get any funny ideas, pal. I don't want to have to clean up the broken glass and blood before she gets home again." The city comptroller paused as the Cobalt Scarab pushed the window closed. "Surprised you didn't see Jean on the way in. And take off that damn hood and glasses."

"I might have seen her driving around, come to think of it," Daniels admitted as he pulled his blue hood down and removed his scarlet goggles for good measure. "Didn't think anything of it. Pretty careless of me." The red-haired man grinned. "You two have another squabble? That seems to be happening a lot lately."

"Shut up." Clark motioned for Daniels to walk towards the far wall, putting Jean Starr's bed between them. "So, what brings you back here, Daniels?"

"I'm not surprised you know me." Daniels silently admired Clark placing an obstacle between them, probably in case the other man felt the need to escape. "Being part of the mayor's office probably gave you a chance to look at the government documentation on all of us."

"Nope." Clark's thin-lipped smile stretched across his face. "The current curator of those documents could stand to have some better security. So yeah, I know about you and Benton and that kid and a whole lot more of you freaks." He grinned. "I don't have those files in my possession, but I'm a quick reader and I've got a decent memory."

Daniels folded the strap of his goggles as he spoke. "Trying to advance yourself? Being city comptroller isn't good enough for you?"

Clark chuckled. "No, I'm happy where I am. I can pull strings for my people and let Brant and Pickern draw all the attention and the heat that goes along with it."

"Your people?" Daniels' brow furrowed. "What people?" he asked with narrowed eyes, "The government?"

"Bigger than Washington, London, Paris, Tokyo, Berlin, and Moscow combined." Clark grinned like he was fighting the urge to laugh like the villain in a radio drama. "You didn't answer my question, Daniels. What are you doing in Jean's bedroom?"

"What I always do, Clark. Serve and protect." As Daniels said, "Mainly serve." With that, he flung the goggles at Rodney Clark with his X-2 amplified strength and speed.

Daniels' eyewear struck Clark's hand, but the comptroller retained a grip on the handgun, even as he stumbled back. Before Clark struck the wall behind him, Daniels leaped over the bed and wrapped his powerful fingers around the comptroller's throat.

"Talk, Clark," Daniels commanded. "What's this organization? Who are you talking about?"

Clark gurgled a reply which compelled Daniels into releasing the man. Rodney Clark doubled over, clutching his injured throat, painfully pulling in one labored breath after another. Daniels took a step back, waiting for Clark to regain his power of speech.

After several attempts to draw in a full lungful of oxygen, Daniels approached Clark who doubled up, coughing. "You okay?" He leaned downwards, listening intently.

Suddenly, the world vanished in a wet, ebony cloud. Daniels clawed at his eyes frantically with both hands. He cleared his vision enough to look down at the back of his gloves and see a dark blemish spreading across them. His eyes started watering, obliterating the sight of Clark's fountain pen as it rolled to a stop beside the Scarab's goggles on the carpeted floor.

Daniels looked up to see Rodney Clark standing several feet farther away. One ink-stained hand held a pillow at waist level, stolen from Jean's bed. Daniels heard the *CLICK* of a gun's hammer a fraction of a second before a yellowish, flaming rose sprouted in the center of the cushion that muffled the pistol's roar.

Feathers rained in the small room. The man in blue dropped to his knees and gave a throaty moan upon fully striking the floor. Daniels listened intently, opening his senses to their fullest, but only heard the outer apartment door opening.

"Well, hell." Daniels pushed himself up from the floor. "So much for visiting the well once too often." He picked up his goggles and slid the scarlet lens over his eyes with one hand, and his hood upwards with the other.

As the Scarab entered the living room, he saw Clark leaning against the opened bedroom door, a sofa cushion having served as an ersatz silencer. Daniels stopped in his tracks just as the handgun fired again. The blue-clad man tried to twist out of the bullet's path but felt an explosion of fire in his left temple for a brief moment. However, he didn't feel the impact of striking the floor, unconscious.

"Fooled you," Clark gloated. He cautiously approached the former policeman, his handgun pointed unwaveringly at Daniels' skull.

"I read your files, Daniels. I know your clothing repels bullets, but your flesh and bone cannot. You really shouldn't have removed your hood." Clark aimed his weapon squarely at the wellspring of blood issuing from Daniels' temple as his finger tightened on the trigger.

* * * * *

Jean Starr gripped the steering wheel tightly. She blinked back her tears, following another evening and most of the night wasted in another argument with Rodney. Once the disagreement reached its crescendo, Jean fled her apartment and took to her automobile, seeking solace in the night's quiet.

At one point, Jean briefly heard the roar of another automobile as it tore through the darkness, but the din faded rapidly as the vehicle moved to another part of Raceway City. Unused to being up this late, Jean yawned loudly. The argument-inspired adrenalin fled her body, leaving her fatigued and in need of sleep. She contemplated calling in to work the next day as she listened to the sound of her car's tires on the pavement.

Rodney Clark offered nights on the town and the prestige of being on the arm of an important member of the city's government. With his leading man looks and enough ambition for a dozen men, the city comptroller could one day find himself in the governor's office, perhaps even higher. Unfortunately, the man carried a wide streak of darkness in his heart that he seemed to only show to Jean when she least needed to see it.

In the past, Jean could overlook Rodney Clark's prejudices. She even entertained the thoughts that if she fell in love with the man completely, she might be able to change him. On the other hand, her late mother was very clear about not taking a husband in the hopes of transforming him. Instead, one should find a compatible man who would find ways to improve himself through the power of love.

Jean considered a return to her apartment in the hopes her would-be beau got tired of waiting for her and stormed out. Ever since Bob Benton came to visit her earlier this week, Clark seemed more on edge than normal. She made sure when Benton's name came up, it was Clark who did so while she refused to betray her thoughts.

Dr. Benton was always courteous when he came to visit, even if he showed the occasional sign of nervousness every now and then, which was rather cute for a guy his age. But for a moment, the other day, Benton showed a glorious spark of righteous anger. Jean spent every workday with men who hid their emotions behind a wall of forced congeniality. It was almost beguiling in its rarity to see an adult man express himself honestly, and not in a bigoted or negative way.

Then Jean recalled how the physician backed down when Rodney Clark challenged him earlier. Her warmth for Dr. Bob Benton cooled substantially at the memory.

Jean's reverie broke when she realized where she'd driven. This was the so-called "bad part of town," the west side business district where Benton's pharmacy happened to be. She had no problem roaming through there during daylight hours. But the city scuttlebutt long said this was no place for an attractive young woman to be once the sun set.

Instead of turning her vehicle around, Jean drove towards the heart of the district.

The business signs appeared almost glamorous in their new-ness to Jean. She'd been through here before, and often, but she saw her surroundings in a new light this morning. Jean swiveled her gaze from one side of the street to the other. Diners, shoe re-pairmen, clothing stores, nothing seemed threatening in this strange world.

But with no one on the streets but her, surely this part of town was as safe as it would ever be, right?

Upon seeing the sign for Benton's Pharmacy, Jean instinctive-ly slowed down. She nodded with approval at the outward cleanliness of the building, even with the plywood covering some of the windows. But as Jean looked through one intact window, into the shadows of the drugstore, she saw a light coming from the rear. Whether it was for security reasons or not, Jean had no way of knowing.

Curiosity compelled Jean to park her vehicle directly in front of the pharmacy. She exited the automobile to see someone mov-ing inside, a fleeting shadow in the rear of the store. Jean walked to the front door, formulating the words she'd say to Benton in the hopes of keeping the lines of communication going between them, despite what Clark wanted.

Jean's footsteps echoed across the street and a chill wind slapped against her, tossing up the hem of her coat. She pulled her collar tight against her throat. What would she say to Benton? She already had a boyfriend, perhaps. Rodney Clark seemed to think so anyway. Jean's mind argued with itself as she reached for the door handle.

She pulled on the door and it opened easily. Jean's brow fur-rowed as she wondered why Dr. Benton would leave the front door unlocked at this hour, even if he intended to be inside for just a minute or two. She stepped into the darkness, her heels grinding against something loudly. "Doctor Benton?"

A loud *THUD* sounded behind Jean. Before she could turn to

investigate the noise, a slender hand wrapped around Jean's throat, cutting off just enough of her wind to make a scream all but impossible. The attacker's other arm wrapped around Jean's midsection and lifted her easily off her feet.

The temperature outside the pharmacy was still cold, but Sylvia Devereaux's whisper was even more so. "Hello, little lady. The doctor is out. I insist we wait inside for him." She paused, savoring her captive's trembling. "I said I insist, and I always get my way."

* * * * *

On the west side of Raceway City, the Terror sprinted down the deserted street at a speed that would make an express train jealous. He couldn't care less who saw him now, his blue and red cloak flapping loudly in his wake. Despite the man's exertions, he breathed as normally as any man at rest might.

The Terror rarely felt the exhilaration of cutting loose, of opening up the throttle and using his amazing speed and strength to their fullest. But tonight felt different as a week's worth of intrigue came to a head. The Terror increased his pace, not knowing if he'd get another chance to exercise his super-charged muscles like this again.

In a couple of minutes, the Terror approached his pharmacy and decelerated until he came to a stop at the front door. Aside from a wind bringing in moist northern air that whistled down the roadway, he could hear no sounds of life in this largely ignored part of town.

With a smile, the Terror realized how much he loved this community, how the locals embraced Dr. Bob Benton's ownership of this long-standing business. In return, he vowed to use every skill in his healing arsenal to keep his people not just alive but enjoying their existence as thoroughly as he could, even if tonight meant the end of the Terror's heroic activities.

The Terror's smile faded rapidly as he looked at Jean Starr's automobile, parked at the front door of his pharmacy. He also glanced at the significant gap between the establishment's front door and the metal frame where the lock used to be. He placed a gloved hand on the handle and pulled gently. The door slid open silently and the Terror stepped inside, closing the gate behind him, at least as much as he could.

"I see Jean's car outside," the Terror stated softly as he cautiously approached his business office. He usually kept his thoughts to himself, but his instincts screamed at him. "She better be okay."

When Bob Benton's floor safe whizzed toward the Terror's head, the man knew that Jean's safety was just one of his many concerns at this moment.

CHAPTER TWENTY-EIGHT

"There's a Reason I Only Breathed the Formic Vapors."

The Terror spun and slammed the flat of his hand against the cold steel exterior of the safe. Its momentum interrupted, the safe dropped onto the tiled floor with a crash that anyone could have heard two blocks away. The Terror fully expected his neighbors to phone the police soon.

But the Terror also expected this confrontation to be over before the law arrived. A dark thought crossed his mind: *She's got my strength. She's got to be stopped now.*

"You have my attention," the Terror stated softly.

Sylvia Devereaux stepped out from Benton's office slowly, backlit by its fluorescent lights, both hands held behind her back. "I have much more that I want, rather than merely tossing a safe at you, pharmacist."

The Terror walked cautiously toward the rear of the pharmacy. "If you're talking about Jean Starr, I saw her car outside. You should let her walk free. I'm here, so you don't need her."

"Agreed," Sylvia said with a smile, "she's long outlived her usefulness as bait." Sylvia's smile vanished. "So, she's now collateral and free for me to damage." Sylvia's lips slowly pulled back into a Cheshire grin. "Is this where you tell me what you'll do to me if I hurt her?"

"This isn't one of your boss's comic books." The Terror pulled his fingers into fists, so tightly his knuckles cracked. "I don't make threats. I keep promises."

"My boss?" Sylvia's laugh arrived in a chilling minor key. "I don't have a boss, not like you might. I'm strictly freelance."

The Terror cracked his knuckles again. The noise sounded like a tree limb being shattered by lightning. "I want to see both your hands. Get them where I can see them."

"I'm sure you do, Benton." Sylvia revealed a familiar section of flooring in one previously concealed hand. "Interesting place to hide the source of your power, underneath these floorboards. Do you have to renew your dosage periodically?"

Sylvia paused as the Terror came to a halt, just a few feet away. She continued, "Your dossier had a list of all known acquaintances, probably several dozen you've forgotten. That's how I knew about your girlfriends." Sylvia spoke the last word as if it came coated in snake venom. "But the technical aspects of your abilities were never revealed. You were a bad boy and neglected to reveal some details, I suspect."

"Got to keep some secrets, right?" The Terror narrowed his eyes under his ebony mask. "I wouldn't tell an Army Colonel. Why tell you?"

Sylvia laughed. "No need, boy." She delivered her slur for the pharmacist as if it was dessert. "Very clever to hide your Formic formula underneath your safe in a secret compartment. No one could lift the box to get beneath this wood panel. Except you and your brat, and now me." Sylvia's tone instantly turned arctic. "Did you bring my gun?"

"You and your gun." The Terror stood close enough to the assassin that he could see the crinkles around her eyes as she glared at him, even without his enhanced senses. "Who made it for you? What all does it do?"

"Shut up, boy! You ask all the wrong questions." Sylvia threw the wood flooring downward with an almost casual flick of her wrist. It struck the floor with a noise like a cannonball piercing the side of a large battleship in the early morning quiet. "Instead, allow me to give you more useful answers."

"Fine." The Terror tensed his muscles, ready to react. "I'm listening."

Sylvia grinned, which did nothing to end the chills racing up and down the Terror's spine. "Your tramp is in the back of your office. I emptied the contents of your amphetamines and depressants into my pockets, except for the sedatives I forced the woman to swallow. My stash could come in handy later." Sylvia took a step backward and glanced at something resting below the cash register. "And I'm claiming Mr. Pickern's drugs and money while I'm at it. Yeah, I found them too in your hidey-hole. I'm sure it'll mean a bonus once I inform him of your demise and he gets the horse shipment you intercepted."

"And not the money, I suppose? Kindly skip to the end of the movie, all right?" The Terror took a step forward. "Stay here and let me get your gun before you talk me to death."

"I have no intention of doing that, boy." Sylvia swiftly pulled her other arm from behind her back. She carried something in her powerful grasp that reflected the meager light of the back office. "Look what else I found under your safe." A clear liquid swirled within a glass beaker, held inside by a black rubber stopper jammed tightly into the mouth of the vessel.

The Terror almost gasped upon seeing the flask. "Put that back. You don't know what it can do."

Sylvia laughed more loudly than she ever had in her life, due to the hyper-powered muscles in her diaphragm. When she stopped, she wiped a tear from the corner of her eye. "I read your dossier, Benton. I know what one whiff of the formic ether vapors did to you and the brat." The grin returned, twice as eerie and ten times as angry as she placed her thumb at the corner of the tightly packed rubber stopper. "It creates terrors."

"DON'T!" The Terror stepped forward; his hands outstretched in supplication.

"Don't what? *This?*" Sylvia flicked her thumb upward, sending the stopper flying into the fifth aisle at the far end of the store. "This isn't any weak sister formula you made up for your customers, is it? You're not about to share the good stuff you and the kid sampled, are you?"

"You're right." The Terror withdrew his hands. "My neighbors get a watered-down version of the ethers from the original formula, yes. That's so we don't have several dozen octogenarians running around with parahuman strength."

"I'm sure," Sylvia stated, her voice thick with disbelief. "You and your kid assistant, you're both strong enough to handle the extra power because of your youth, aren't you? Perhaps it's your gender." Sylvia lifted the beaker towards her lips, then paused with mock wide-eyed horror, "Or is it your race?"

The Terror froze. "Don't drink that!" His shout reverberated throughout the store. "There's a reason I only *inhaled* the formic ether."

"You knew you couldn't handle the power," Sylvia called out as she brought the glass to her lips.

"That's not it, you foolish cow!" Even with his unnatural speed, the Terror couldn't move quickly enough to stop the hit-woman from downing a healthy slug of the formula. Upon swallowing, Sylvia doubled over as she emitted the most terrifying retching noise any man ever heard. She shook violently as the Terror carefully pulled the vial from her weakened grip.

Sylvia trembled violently as she doubled over. Her unfocused eyes blinked back tears as she frantically tried to seize the wooden counter, but it seemed to dance just beyond her reach. Her eyes crossed and separated at random moments, one eye reflecting Sylvia's pain and shock, while the other narrowed in hateful fury.

The Terror leaped across the pharmacy, picked up the stopper, then pushed it firmly into the bottle before backing away from Sylvia.

"When mixing medicine," the Terror explained more like a pharmacist to his patient than a gloating adventurer while he slowly increased the distance between them, "one has to take into account how the formula will be affected by saliva, stomach acids, and a host of other physical factors. That's why I chose a formula that gave off a gaseous response for myself and Tim, and a far more diluted version to be ingested, to ease the effect on the user's body."

He placed the bottle on a sales shelf before kneeling beside Sylvia whose body practically folded in on itself, shaking like a tree branch in a high wind. "Let's get you some help."

Sylvia's response was to slam her forearm against the Terror's face with all her might. He barely saw it coming and never had enough time to go limp as he flew down the row. He smashed into and through a section of shelving in aisle two, shaken but otherwise unharmed.

The Terror pushed himself to a standing position, willing his muscles and mind to move more quickly. But Sylvia reached her feet first, so swiftly that the Terror barely registered the moves between her literally squatting on the tile floor and then standing at her full height. Sylvia turned her head so swiftly, the Terror could hear the air displaced by her small movement, sounding like a tiny thunderclap.

"HOW???" The Terror heard Sylvia's slight exhalation before the sound nearly caused his eardrums to bleed. He snuck a glance into his office but didn't see evidence of Jean Starr being there. His heart sank in fear for the woman.

"Take a deep breath, slowly. Everything will be all right. Just calm down." The Terror held out his hands to Sylvia, fingers spread wide. "I know, I know. It took Tim and me a bit of time to adjust to our new strength and abilities. Just calm down." Benton spoke with genuine human concern. "You already have some of the formula in your bloodstream. We don't know what a second dose will do to you. Let me help you."

Sylvia inhaled deeply, cautiously. She then pursed her lips and let her breath out slowly. She occasionally glanced at the Terror who stayed well beyond her reach as her movements grew slower and closer in relation to his own normal speed.

"I started to ask," Sylvia said slowly as if pacing herself, "how do you endure the pretense of normalcy when you have all this delicious power?"

The Terror said nothing. He recalled the government men who visited him inside his pharmacy; two men in black suits and a two-star general so well-connected that uttering his name out loud could get Bob Benton sent to a special Federal prison. The Terror possessed the strength of a titan, but felt himself cowed by their threats, knowing those men could carry out far worse punishments beyond his own fertile imagination.

A similar chill travelled through the Terror's spine as he listened to the beautiful assassin's snarling, "I could tear down this building and grind its stones to dust while shouting your true name loud enough that even the deaf could hear it. Then I would fold your white girlfriend in the back until she was all corners, laughing as every bone in her body snapped." Sylvia's chuckle grew in volume before she spoke again. "My last stop in town would be to retrieve my weapon, followed by pulling every muscle out of the Rowland woman's body while her brat watched."

Sylvia laughed so loudly, the Terror heard the new glass at the front of the pharmacy crack. "And the vilest thing I could do to you is allow you to live, knowing just how inferior you are, even with your damned strength."

For a moment, the Terror wished either Garret or even Tim stood beside him at this moment. Pushing his regrets and fear to the back of his mind, the Terror decided to live up to his name. He raised his fists and gritted his teeth. "Over my dead body."

Sylvia stopped laughing as she placed one hand on her chin, the other on the side of her skull. With a swift jerk to one side, she popped her neck, and the sound reminded the Terror of a rifle being fired.

"Truth be told," Sylvia said slowly, ominously, "that was my first choice for you too."

CHAPTER TWENTY-NINE

"You Won't Be Seeing Me Ever Again."

The Terror barely saw Sylvia Devereaux's fist. He barely had enough time to dodge the blow as he twisted his entire body instinctively. Sylvia's powerful punch carried her several feet past her opponent. Stumbling at first, Sylvia stiffened her knees and ankles, the force of which shattered her expensive boot heels against the tile flooring.

Sylvia whirled around, her eyes wide with amazement. She gasped like a bobby soxer meeting Frank Sinatra on her front porch. "How could you hide all this amazing power? It's intoxicating."

"It's dangerous, you fool," the Terror growled. "You think I didn't anticipate the possible effects of ingesting the formic compound?" The Terror fought the urge to shake his head in confusion. "Inhalation was the only safe means of intake. I knew this even before I found the key triggering ingredient."

"What the hell is so dangerous when you feel so alive?" Sylvia threw her arms out ahead of her. The motion propelled her towards the Terror, eliminating the distance that separated them in a heartbeat. Before Sylvia could strike again, the Terror wrapped his arms around her in a fierce bearhug that pinned her arms to her sides. "

With a little girl's high-pitched laugh, Sylvia gave the Terror a quick peck on his nose before flexing her arms. The man's locked fingers separated, his arms flew apart, and he fell backwards into another shelving unit. Bathroom tissue and paper napkins shot into the air to rain down upon the dark-clad hero.

"After I'm done with you," Sylvia stated, "I'm going to mail Garret Daniels back to his old precinct one tiny piece at a time." She ground the debris on the floor under her powerful feet, only to prove to herself that she could do it. "I'm going to tear down Raceway City to its foundations, just for fun, before I go back to

Chicago and do the same there."

Without a word, the Terror pushed himself away from the wreckage and slammed a fist into Sylvia's face. Although his parents raised a gentleman, he knew his only chance to survive the assassin's next attack might be to strike hard and fast before she could fully adapt to her powers. He slugged her in her gorgeous face a second time before planting his left fist deep into her flat stomach. The formic ethers did a human many favors but didn't render them impervious to pain or make their organs invulnerable. They could be knocked out or injured, although not as easily as normal humans.

Pain radiated along Sylvia's over-sensitized nerve endings. Explosions of light and color blotted out her vision as she felt an overwhelming amount of agony spread from her midsection. She knew she had to stand up, to defend herself against her attacker, to not let him win or take her in. But the ancient animal side of her brain screamed for relief and an instant end to the pain.

Again, and again, the Terror alternated between punches to Sylvia's stomach and backhanded slaps to her face. One of the killer's eyes closed as a dark purple welt formed under the right side of her cheek. She staggered under the weight of the Terror's super-powered punches, each one of which made him hate himself more and more. Each attack landed with the sound of a body striking concrete from a great height.

When the echoes of his grisly handiwork faded from inside the damaged pharmacy, the Terror stepped back to assess his victim. Sylvia swayed so far from one side to the other, the Terror felt sure his enemy would topple over. Tears rolled from Sylvia's still-open eye, and her arms dangled limp at her sides.

The Terror listened to Sylvia's heartbeat racing like Buddy Rich pounding his sticks against a share drum. She shuddered briefly before she launched herself at the Terror with the speed of a puma. Her fingers dug deep into the man's windpipe and only his grip on her wrists prevented his larynx from being crushed like an overripe grape.

Sylvia's bruises turned scarlet, then dull brown, before returning to their normal hue. The swelling under her eye diminished until the flesh flattened against her chiseled cheekbones. "I'll kill you," Sylvia growled, followed by a string of obscenities and racial epithets.

But as she vented her bigotry and anger at the Terror, her right hand flew up to her left breast and clutched her chest firmly as her eyes crossed in pain.

"N--no," the Terror managed to whisper. "You—your heart. Slow down. You might—"

"I might die? *I DON'T CARE!!!*" Sylvia shrieked through gritted teeth. "I'll gladly die and burn forever in Hell if I can watch your eyes bulge from your skull, Benton." The volume of Sylvia's heart valves slamming shut increased so much that the Terror believed he'd hear them even without his amazing senses.

The Terror ground his teeth as he rammed the inside of Sylvia's elbows with his fists, forcing the assassin to relinquish her grasp on his throat. He inhaled loudly, filling his lungs with sweet, sweet air. But even before he could completely inflate his lungs, Sylvia redoubled her violent efforts, and her hands drew closer to the Terror's windpipe once again. Wide-eyed and desperate, she pressed her thumbs and her advantage in one more fury-driven attack.

Sylvia howled like a banshee, her insane laughter filling the pharmacy as fireworks exploded silently in the Terror's gaze. Her shrieks resembled nothing human as she savored the imminent death of her prey. The Terror fought to live, to pull in one more lungful of life-giving air. However, darkness filled his field of vision, devouring the sight of the assassin's wounds returning as her sadistic leer transformed into absolute fright. The Terror blacked out, seeing Jean in his mind's eye for possibly the final time.

All Sylvia could hear was the sound of her heart until it seized up, pushed beyond even her own unnatural limits. Like any wild animal, Sylvia knew her time drew close to an end. She lifted the Terror by his throat and hurled him with all her might toward the sales counter, hoping the impact would snap his neck in her one desperate, final attempt at revenge.

But Sylvia didn't hear the man's body turn the wood and metal shelving into splinters and scrap iron upon impact. Instead, she instinctively clutched her heart again, her fingers burying themselves into her upper ribcage as if she could rip the agony from her chest in her powerful grasp. She held out her hand to the Terror in fearful supplication, unable to form the words, to implore Dr. Bob Benton to rise from the destruction and help her.

Sylvia Devereaux's eyes filled with tears as the only man who might save her lay unconscious, buried amidst the wood and metal that used to be his sales counter. Sylvia moved her head to see her enemy's face from behind the heavy metal cash register that rested on his chest. She dropped to her knees as darkness, regret, and pain claimed her. By the time she collapsed, face-first, on the linoleum, Sylvia Devereaux was already dead.

When the Terror awoke several minutes later, he ignored the pain of his injuries and slowly rose from what used to be several feet of quality shelf space. Packages that used to hold bandages and arm splints lay smashed on the floor. The Terror limped towards his attacker's unmoving form and listened intently. After hearing nothing for a minute, not even a faint breath, he limped back toward his office.

Jean Starr lay on the floor, unconscious on the far side of the room beside where the safe previously rested. Without its protective covering, Benton's secret hiding hole lay exposed. However, there was nothing there now to conceal, but an important life to possibly save.

The Terror painfully moved to his desk and opened a large drawer on the right-hand side. From there, he pulled out a well-worn medical bag and opened it quickly to find a vial of smelling salts. He unstopped the small tube and waved the open end under Jean's nostrils. She sat up, coughing, trying to fan away the unpleasant aroma.

Jean blinked her beautiful eyes rapidly, almost desperately. When her gaze came into focus, she saw a handsome Black man standing over her, a soft smile covering the lower part of his features. The florescent lights backlit the Terror, making it difficult for the woman to make out the masked man's exact features, as did the numerous cuts and bruises that covered his face, although they now began to heal as she watched.

The costumed hero reached down to wrap his gloved fingers around the ropes that bound Jean's arms and ankles. With the barest of effort, he snapped her bonds and carefully unwound them until Jean could regain full movement. She stretched out her legs and shifted position as the circulation in her extremities returned to normal.

"You're safe now," the Terror stated with conviction. Instinctively, he dropped the register of his voice into a lower, more commanding tone. "There's a telephone on the desk. Please call the police and don't leave or look outside this office until they arrive. It's...unpleasant out there. Tell the dispatcher that an ambulance will be needed." Despite the importance of his warning, the Terror couldn't help but smile as he took in the scent of Jean's perfume.

"Th-thank you," was all Jean could think of saying. She watched her rescuer rise to his feet, turn around, pull his shoulders back, and walk slowly toward the office door before she thought to ask, "Who are you?"

Part of Dr. Bob Benton stopped in the doorway of the business office. He weighed the option of turning around, smiling broadly, and revealing his civilian identity to this intelligent, vivacious woman. Then he spotted Sylvia's fallen body. He turned towards the limp, twisted corpse, and thought of the Rowland family. Despite their courage, their friendship with Bob Benton brought them a couple of years' worth of fear and uncertainty.

Tonight, however, ended with a closure of sorts.

Bob Benton didn't know all the answers to what plagued Raceway City, but he knew he could end one problem forever this day...and perhaps even more in the future.

"My name," he whispered, "is the Terror. You won't be seeing me ever again, Ma'am." He pondered his next words carefully before continuing, "You might want to forget I was even here in the first place."

The Terror left the office, pausing only to give Sylvia Devereaux's corpse one more glance. Then Jean Starr heard the bell over the front door ring once when it opened, and again when the Terror closed it behind him.

CHAPTER THIRTY

"Do Your Duty and Take Me In."

The Cobalt Scarab wanted to shake his head in the hopes of clearing it, but the torments in his skull hinted that something might fall out if he moved too quickly. Instead, he opened his eyes as his memory of Rodney Clark's attack returned.

He slowly turned his head from side to side, seeing nothing but metal cans and smelling little more than rotting food and numerous animals marking this territory as theirs. Moments like this didn't fill the Scarab with pride concerning his enhanced senses. He muttered as he sat up with his hand covering where he'd been shot, "For someone who can toss a Studebaker like a football, I sure hurt a hell of a lot. What was in that gun, anyway?" The Scarab watched his breath rise in the morning air.

The earliest rays of dawn shone above the apartment buildings and businesses in the east. Gaps between the clouds promised a brighter, if not warmer day. As the Scarab stretched his back muscles, he felt his vertebrae crack and endorphins flooding his bloodstream. He searched his memory for his most recent memory and came up with a bright light, the sound of a gunshot, and a noise like thunder.

Pulling his hood over the top of his head, the Scarab adjusted his scarlet goggles, and leaped upwards in the direction of Jean Starr's apartment. He pumped his legs rapidly and soon, the Scarab moved in defiance of gravity, curving his upward arc toward the fifth floor. He glanced inside the windows as he passed. The Scarab grimly thanked the fates that no one rose early on this Sunday morning, at least not before he concluded his business here.

And if that included a rematch with that rotten Rodney Clark, so much the better.

Once he reached Jean Starr's bedroom window, the Cobalt Scarab clamped his fingers around the concrete ledge and peered inside. His amazing eyesight amplified the light inside the room, revealing no signs of his conflict with Rodney Clark. The Scarab angled his head to peer past the bedroom door. Everything within his limited range of sight was immaculate. Even the sheets stretched across Jean's bed were military taut, as if someone could bounce a quarter off them.

The Scarab listened for any noises from inside the room but heard nothing. He glanced toward the east at the dissipating clouds and the first orange beams of sunlight before he released his grip on the ledge. A few kicks of his legs later, the Cobalt Scarab rose into the western sky.

Soon, the Cobalt Scarab located Bob Benton's apartment building. He angled his flight in a sharp plunge before he kicked upward at the last second, righting his body for a two-point landing. Once he set foot upon the roof with surprising stealth, Garret Daniels quickly stripped off his blue protective uniform and goggles, leaving on his red shoes, black slacks, and what used to be a white shirt. He wrapped his disguise in a bundle and dropped himself onto the fire escape one floor below. Daniels turned toward Benton's door and hoped his host forgot to lock it.

Daniels reached toward the handle when the sound of the locks disengaging from the other side reached his sensitive ears. The door swung inward swiftly. Bob Benton stood there; his eyes hollow. "Get inside," he commanded.

"I went to Jean Starr's place," Daniels stated as he entered the kitchen. "But she wasn't there."

"Yeah, I know." Benton stepped away from Daniels, buttoning up his white suit shirt. "She's safe." Benton stopped to look back over his shoulder. "But I killed that lady assassin."

Daniels nodded. "I find that hard to believe. I know you wouldn't do that deliberately. I'm sure you had no choice." He looked over to the foldout sofa and saw the Terror uniform, all neatly folded and resting on the seat.

"I should have looked for that other option. Instead, I pushed her into a heart attack after beating her like I'm a rabid animal." Benton tucked in his shirt tails. "I'm supposed to be a hero." As Benton straightened his clothing, he described everything that happened since he left Velma Rowland's home, up to the fracas in the pharmacy. "Whether she might have deserved it or not, I shouldn't push someone to their deaths."

"Push someone?" Daniels grabbed Benton's shoulder and pulled him around, so they stood face-to-face. "Listen, she chose her fate, not you. I'm a former cop, New York Police Department. Until I left the city, I made decisions every day that could determine if someone paid the ultimate price for their crimes or not. It went with the job, just like not knowing if I'd make it home that night."

Benton gave Daniels a weak smile. "Then perhaps I don't want this job anymore."

"I get it. When you choose to uphold the law, whether as a duly deputized officer or as a vigilante, your exposure to the criminal element changes you." Daniels' solemn expression gave way to visible sorrow. "The more I changed inside, it seemed the less the bad guys did. Eventually, I found people inside the Justice System who had no interest in enforcing the rules I needed to bring criminals to heel. That's when I became the Cobalt Scarab."

"So, you resigned from the Force?" Benton pulled his winter coat from the rack beside the front door.

"Not right away." Daniels stepped closer to Benton. "I tried to be a mystery man and a lawman at the same time. Soon, I had trouble reconciling and balancing the two roles." Daniels hid his smile behind a scarred hand. "Plus, I got really, really tired of being called a 'rookie cop' by the other guys."

"It all comes out now, huh?" Benton grinned as he slipped into his jacket. "I'm going to survey the damage to my shop." Daniels didn't hear the implied "*and check on Jean Starr,*" but he saw the intent in Benton's eyes. "Want to walk with me?"

"Sure." Daniels quickly rifled through his suitcase for a jacket to conceal his invulnerability to the weather. Once outside the apartment, Benton locked the door before handing the key to Daniels. "You can stay here if you want. I'm a couple months ahead on rent."

Daniels nodded as he dropped the key into his pants pocket. The two walked down the hallway, then the stairs, in silence until they reached the street.

Benton didn't even look at Daniels as he spoke. "I might have to turn myself in, Daniels. Thanks for being with me."

"Let's check your business first, okay?" Daniels placed his hand on Benton's shoulder in support. "We can always try to hide the body."

Benton pointed toward the corner and shook his head. "I don't think that'll be happening today, pal."

Daniels counted three police cars at the curb along with several other sedans parked along both sides of the street. He instinctively patted the place where his service revolver used to be and grimaced at its absence. "You should decide what you're going to do next, Benton, preferably before we go inside."

Upon reaching the front door, Benton pulled on the handle without hesitation as Daniels followed, his senses alert for any attack from all directions.

Inside the pharmacy, the first thing Bob Benton saw was a sheet draped over the body of Sylvia Devereaux. Brought to a halt by the grim reminder of his actions, Benton said a silent prayer for the woman, leaving the disposal of her immortal essence to the Great Unknowable.

"Are you Robert Benton?"

Benton looked up to see a burly man in a crumpled fedora and ill-kempt raincoat stepping over debris left from the earlier battle. He carried a notebook in one hand as well as a pencil behind his ear. From the puffiness of his eyes and a baked-in frown, Benton guessed this poor guy was pulled out of a sound sleep to come to the wrong side of Raceway City.

"Yes, sir. I'm Dr. Robert Benton." The pharmacist held out his hand to be shaken, but the detective dismissed the offering with visible disdain. "And you are?"

"Detective Barney Brickhouse, Raceway City P.D." He pulled out a leather wallet from his pocket, flipped it open to show his police identification, closed it once again a fraction of a second later, then dropped it back into his coat, all in one smooth, well-rehearsed action.

Brickhouse was a legend across Raceway City. Formerly from

Beantown, hence his nickname, the police detective often took on cases from the west side because he lived nearby, and he was good at solving crimes. He also riled his downtown superiors frequently, so they didn't mind waking him up early on a Sunday morning.

Obviously, Brickhouse made it clear he didn't consider personal relationships to be an important part of the gig, namely being civil to the criminal element, innocent civilians, or even his co-workers.

Rumors flew that Brickhouse was as clean as a cop could ever be and despite his age and the extra pounds around his beltline, he could outrun, outfight, and outshoot anyone on either side of the law. And now here was one of the best investigators the police had to offer in Benton's drug store, investigating a dead hitwoman in the middle of what had been a battle between parahumans.

"So, what happened here?"

Taking a deep breath, Benton prepared to spill his guts about Sylvia Devereaux gaining super strength from drinking his blood and the outrageous combat that occurred not once, but twice in this establishment. Then it dawned on Benton how implausible the story might sound to someone who didn't believe in parahuman beings.

Benton spoke slowly, carefully weighing his words. "My apartment is a few doors down from here. I woke up…" Benton hesitated, wrestling with his options before he continued, "…after hearing what sounded like explosions. So, I put on my clothing and came to investigate." Benton paused.

Brickhouse's eyes narrowed in suspicion. The detective studied Benton like he found the pharmacist clinging to the sole of his shoe before he jotted something in his notebook. "Found a car with Illinois plates outside with a bag of heroin in it." Brickhouse looked up. "There was a bunch of uppers and downers in a jar under the front seat. I assume they're yours?"

"I'll do a quick inventory, Detective, but they could very well be from this pharmacy. Who knows what she did before I found you and the other policeman in here." Benton tried to keep his tone even as he battled the urge to grimace. "I trust I can get my merchandise back if the quantities match?"

"Maybe." While he scribbled, Brickhouse asked, "So what's with the dame in back?"

"Dame?" Benton looked past the detective and fought the urge to smile when he saw Jean Starr at the rear of the store, speaking with another cop, this one in a patrolman's uniform. Her long blonde hair hung loose over her shoulders, and she shivered in the light blue blanket Benton kept in back with his First Aid kit for potential shock victims. With the iridescent lighting overhead, she was beautiful.

"No idea," Benton met the detective's eyes. Brickhouse looked at the pharmacist as if he could gaze into a suspect's thoughts. "Anyway, I was in my apartment, and I came down to see this? I just want to know who's going to pay for all this?"

"Mm-mm." Detective Brickhouse jotted another line onto the paper without moving his eyes from Benton. "This dame on the floor looks like she took a bit of a beating, Benton. But the shelves look like someone twice their size smacked into them. Any ideas?"

"I'm a pharmacist, not a detective." Benton immediately regretted his words as they came out of his mouth. "You think I'm some kind of superman or that I beat women?"

Detective Brickhouse grunted, a sound that compelled Benton to lay the rest of his cards on the table. "C'mon, Detective. If you think I did all this, if you think I busted up my own business, kidnapped Miss Starr, then murdered whoever's under that blanket, then do your duty and take me in." Benton held out his wrists. "Come on. Arrest me."

"I might just do that, pal." Detective Brickhouse reached into his pocket and Benton heard the sound of steel touching steel. He braced himself for the cop to handcuff him and end his career not just as Dr. Bob Benton, pharmacist, but also as the Terror.

"Not so fast, Detective."

All eyes turned towards the doorway.

CHAPTER THIRTY-ONE

"You Want the Blanket Back?"

Rodney Clark stood in the doorway of the pharmacy. His wide stance made it clear that no one would get past him to leave. He quickly surveyed the room, taking in who stood and where, except for the still form by where the magazine stand used to be. Clark appeared to be oddly uncurious about Sylvia Devereaux's corpse and the condition of the room they all stood in.

Bob Benton glanced at Detective "Boston" Brickhouse. Either Clark's lack of curiosity didn't set off the cop's alarms, or no one would do their pocketbook any good by playing poker against him.

Clark moved to one side and held the door open wide. A moment later, two ambulance attendants entered the room without any sense of urgency. Benton wondered why he didn't hear a siren to signal their approach before he recalled what part of Raceway City they were in. And who needed to rush when there's a corpse involved?

Benton told himself if he exited from this situation without penalty, he would definitely keep a closer eye on Rodney Clark, and not just for Jean Starr's sake, nor his own.

Benton repressed a sigh as the attendants loaded Sylvia Devereaux's covered body onto a stretcher. The senior man in white addressed the room as he pointed toward the corpse, "Whose blanket is this?"

Detective Brickhouse replied before Benton could open his mouth. "This guy's." He crooked his head in Benton's direction.

The attendant glanced at Benton. "You want the blanket back?"

"If I could." Benton surprised himself at the growl in his voice. He paused before saying, "Just leave it with Lost and Found and I'll pick it up later." He smiled insincerely. "Please?"

To Benton's surprise, the attendant smiled, nodded, then muttered something to his partner about setting the time of death. Seconds later, the ambulance men carried Devereaux's body into their vehicle. Everyone in the room maintained a respectful silence until the doors slammed shut and the ambulance drove away.

Rodney Clark cleared his throat and motioned for both policemen to join him in a far corner. As Brickhouse walked away from Benton, the pharmacist noticed a thoughtful Garret Daniels entering the building. Before he could ask why his ally what took so long to join him, Jean Starr exited the back office to join him.

Benton turned to face the woman as she pulled her coat shut without buttoning it. She cautiously stepped over the damaged goods and debris strewn over the linoleum floor. Benton couldn't help but smile with relief that she was safe.

Then from across the room, as if Daniels could read his mind, Benton's amplified hearing picked up his friend's whispered words, "I can read your expression. She wouldn't be alive if the Terror hadn't taken care of business. Keep that in mind next time you feel retirement coming on."

Benton ignored Daniels, as well as the comment about his vigilantism. Instead of debating the parahuman, Benton turned his full attention to Jean. "You okay, Miss Starr?"

"Yes, thank you." Jean smiled briefly before the corners of her mouth fell. "I don't mind telling you how scared I was when I was captured."

"I can only imagine." Benton replied.

"Can you?" Jean's neutral expression turned almost hateful. "I would be dead if it wasn't for that man in the black costume. Where were you? Why was that woman in *your* pharmacy?"

Benton took a step back, fumbling for an answer. His mind juggled his need to comfort Jean with the desire to maintain his dual identity or surrender to Detective Brickhouse for Sylvia Devereaux's death.

Ignoring Benton's visible confusion, Jean pressed her case. "You were in the same building and couldn't be bothered to check on your own business. Did you sleep through all the noise?" Jean turned away from the subject of her ire and blinked rapidly as she choked back tears of frustration. "That costumed man risked his life to save me." She paused as a single tear rolled down her cheek. "You're such a sweet man. Where the hell is your spine, Benton?"

Before Benton could formulate a reply, Rodney Clark seized a fistful of the pharmacist's sleeve and pulled him away from Jean. Clark leaned close to Benton's ear and whispered, "I think the lady's tired of your apelike eyes and your crude attentions. Better give her some room or you'll deal with me, something you'll never want to do, big boy."

His point made, Clark stepped back from Benton. He gave the pharmacist a hard clap on the shoulder before he announced, "The Raceway City Police have officially declared this case shut."

At the rear of the pharmacy, Brickhouse both averted his gaze from Benton's as he fished in his shirt pocket for a cigarette. Patrolman Fletcher stood beside the detective, gazing at his shoes with a hollow expression.

Benton turned to approach the policemen, but Garret Daniels placed a hand on Benton's shoulder. "I was eavesdropping on Clark and the men in blue over there," Daniels whispered low enough that he knew only Benton would hear him. "Things are moving fast in here. Don't react until it's all over."

"Sure, for now," Benton replied as he watched Jean Starr talk to Rodney Clark. She wrapped both hands around his arm and laid her head on his shoulder. Although Benton felt himself to be beyond any sort of schoolboy crush, the thought of Jean taking her comfort from that worm tore at his heart like no knife ever could.

Clark pulled Jean with him as he returned to talk with Detective Brickhouse and the officer accompanying him. He said to the senior cop. "I think you have something to announce."

The policeman looked nervously at his partner before he addressed his small audience. "No need for a statement right now, Benton. This looks like an open-and-shut case."

"Simple heart attack, right?" Clark asked, his eyes on Benton.

"Yeah, simple." A faint blush colored Detective Brickhouse's face. He turned towards Benton. "I might question you later, Doc, pending the coroner's report." His face went totally red when he realized how much louder he spoke than intended.

Benton opened his mouth to protest until he felt Daniels' grip on his arm. He turned to see the former cop narrow his eyes and shake his head once. With a soft sigh, Benton said, "Sure. Thanks."

Clark watched the proceedings like a stage director seeing his play running smoothly, without error, and with all the players knowing their lines. "One more thing." He smiled at the policemen. "Gentlemen, you still have an opening on the R.C.P.D., right?"

Detective Brickhouse looked at Clark as if he was trapped under a microscope. "You authorize the funds, Mr. Clark. You know we do."

"I think I can fill that position immediately." Clark turned to Daniels. "Report to Police Headquarters tomorrow morning, Mr. Daniels. I'm aware of your record and I think you'll be a fine addition to our police force." Clark sneered at Benton one last time. "Good luck cleaning this place up. Let's go, Jean."

Clark led Jean from the building. Instead of stepping over the cracked pieces of linoleum and chunks of wood, Clark simply kicked the debris out of the way without looking at it. The two policemen left on Clark's heels, leaving Benton and Daniels alone in the ruined pharmacy. The sound of distant church bells reached the men's ears as the sun emerged from behind the clouds to shine fully on the street.

"I didn't even fill out an application," Daniels muttered.

"Congratulations on the new job," Benton said softly before adding, "Rookie."

"Someone's read my government file," Daniels growled in a whisper as he tilted his head toward the departing Rodney Clark. "And yours too."

"I wouldn't doubt that. I'd love to get my hands on a copy." Benton looked at Daniels. "Clark doesn't seem to be aware of my dual identity, or else he's got the best deadpan since Buster Keaton."

But any further conversation paused when Benton yawned

loudly. At that moment, he realized how long he'd been awake and just how active he'd been during all that time, paranormal powers or otherwise.

"Let's head back to your place," Daniels said with surprising compassion. "With a few hours' sleep and a good lunch under our belts afterwards, we'll be in better shape to plan your next move back into civilian life."

Benton nodded and allowed himself to be led from the pharmacy to the front door of his apartment building, Benton said, "It's been one hell of a week, hasn't it?"

All Daniels could do was nod in agreement as he held the front door open for his new friend. He studied the length of the street in both directions. Only random piles of ice remained along the curbs and a fresh, warmer wind blew in from the southwest. Raceway City slowly awoke this Sunday morning, and the clouds overhead dissipated into nothingness.

Daniels grinned. "Yeah, definitely one hell of a week."

CHAPTER THIRTY-TWO

"Are You Still Our Protector?"

Bob Benton never could sleep past eight a.m. Even though he closed his business on Sunday out of respect for his neighbors, Benton always woke up just after seven-thirty in case someone needed an emergency prescription. Today was no exception.

While Benton appreciated honoring the Sabbath, he always found himself rising at the same time every Sunday without the intention of going to worship.

Although, Benton thought, *I've definitely earned it this week.*

Surrendering to the inevitable pull of responsibility as the clock hit eight, Benton slipped on some clothing and walked quietly into his living room where Garret Daniels slept on the sofa, not even bothering to pull out the concealed bed. Benton listened to his houseguest's even breathing and smiled. *So much for breakfast,* Benton thought as he hoped there might be an undamaged Valomilk Bar or Goo Goo Cluster to silence his growling stomach.

Benton held his shoes in one hand and jacket in the other as he left his apartment. He finished dressing before he reached the stairwell. A couple of minutes later, after he walked down the stairway at normal human speed, Benton stood on the street, enjoying the morning sunshine. A few cars passed him on the road. Several of the vehicles' occupants sounded their horns and waved at the young pharmacist. Benton grinned and returned their greetings enthusiastically.

As Benton approached his pharmacy, he noticed several trucks and sedans parked outside his establishment. Curiosity pulled him closer until he heard hammering and conversation from inside the business, past the newly replaced front windows and freshly repaired front door.

Dr. Benton walked through the entrance of his pharmacy, unable to believe his eyes. A half dozen men picked up the larger pieces of debris and carried them through the back door where Benton saw the tail end of a pickup truck. Ladies from the church down the street gathered up damaged goods from the floor, assessing each item to verify its potential shelf-worthiness while Tim Rowland and Davie Clanton swept the floor in the ladies' wake.

A quick look around the room left Benton silently wondering, *"Where's the safe? And the ethic formula?"*

Mrs. Cavanaugh poured coffee for a couple of the workers with her usual contented smile as Ellie Clanton spoke into the telephone by the cash register. Benton picked up the words, "We can always use another set of hands. Thank you, Bettie," before the older woman hung up the receiver.

"About time you woke up." Velma Rowland entered through the back door of the building. She wore a work shirt with overalls and Benton thought she was the most beautiful thing he'd seen outside of a Hollywood film. She removed her canvas gloves as she crossed the room.

Benton watched everyone stop their labors to turn their attention toward him. All he could think to say was, "What's all this?"

Ellie Clanton called out from the rear of the business, "You do so much for us every day, Doctor Benton. When Velma told us this morning you needed help, we decided to do something good for you."

Velma stood by Tim, her arm around his shoulders. "Stop gaping, Dr. Benton, while I explain."

"I may or may not have left the house a couple of hours ago," Tim volunteered. "Just to, um, get some fresh air after being under house arrest." He nodded in his mother's direction as she delivered an elbow to his ribs that he didn't feel.

"Fresh air." Benton smirked. "Uh-huh."

Tim refused to look at his mother's grin. "And I'm not admitting to anything, you know, but it's possible I came here…" The boy's voice trailed off as he searched for the right words. He still winced when he twisted his midsection, but Tim's injuries didn't appear to be as painful as they were a few hours ago when he last saw his mentor.

Velma continued. "Tim snuck out of the house, as usual." She turned her most motherly glare towards her son who averted his gaze and pretended to inspect his sweeping. "Tim poked his nose in here, hoping to find you, and saw the…mess, probably caused by some hoodlum from out of town."

Benton marveled at the ease at which Tim's mother lied to cover her boy's clandestine activities, just in case someone overheard their conversation.

"Yeah, a hoodlum." Benton noted the quiver in Tim's voice and wished he could have spared the boy the sight of Sylvia Devereaux's fallen body. "You must have just missed me and Garret."

Tim nodded. "But I took care of that big thing in the middle of the floor." Tim pointed to the indentation in the floor where Benton's office safe landed. "Plus, there was some stuff on the shelf, something in a bottle, that I put back in its place."

Benton nodded and smiled, relieved that the chemical that gave him and the young man their paranormal powers was safely concealed again.

"So, my boy came home and told me what he saw." Tim didn't resist when Velma wrapped her arms around him protectively. "I phoned the police anonymously." Velma grinned. "I also might have placed some other calls to meet up here this morning to help you out." She smiled warmly. "It's our way of saying thank you, thank you for protecting all of us in your own special ways."

Benton nodded at the added meaning behind Velma's words. He turned his gaze to the cleaned floors, the new windowpanes, and the smiles of his neighbors as they watched Benton struggle with his emotions. He could fold a trunk lid with his bare hands and punch his way out of a railroad car, but at this moment, Benton proved helpless to stop the tears of gratitude from rolling down his cheeks. He closed his eyes, speechless and aware of Velma and Tim's embrace, followed by the applause of his extended family, his neighborhood, and his friends.

The applause ended when Ellie Clanton called out, "Okay, that's enough mush. I'm making another pot of coffee and I expect this place cleaned up and done by the time I start pouring."

"You heard her, friends." Velma clapped her hands three times, and everyone returned to their labors. "We might still have time to get cleaned up before church." Velma stepped closer to Benton, speaking in conversational tones, "Mrs. Cavanaugh called some people. You know how she is. The floor and the shelves will be fixed by the end of the week, so it looks like you'll need to take some time off."

"After this week, I can use it." Benton sighed. "Thank you, Velma." He leaned closer to whisper, "How much did Tim see in here?"

Velma pushed her hands into her overall pockets. "More than I wanted. But he's a strong kid."

Benton chuckled. "He should be. He gets that from you."

"Maybe," Velma admitted. Then she leaned closer to Benton and whispered, "The police already took that…woman…out of here."

Benton squeezed Velma's hand firmly. She smiled and squeezed back. "So, Bob…are you still our protector? You going to help us…stay safe?"

"I'll have to restock once the shelves are back up," Benton said, "but yes, I will."

Velma narrowed her eyes. "That's not exactly what I meant."

Benton looked around the room to make sure they weren't being overheard. "Something's rotten in Raceway City. Not just how we, as a community are forced to live, but the city as a whole." Benton paused as he noticed Tim listening from across the room. "I guess the Terror is back on the job." Benton smiled at Tim. "Excuse me. the Terror Twins."

Tim poured some condensed milk into a small pitcher with the biggest grin his mother ever saw her son give when it wasn't Christmas.

"Who wants some muffins?" Garret Daniels carried two large boxes from a local bakery into the room. Despite a few quizzical stares, Daniels moved to the back of the room, making certain to say hello to everyone he passed and introducing himself.

Tim barely restrained his parahuman speed to help Daniels with his load. The smell of warm muffins and doughnuts filled the area. "So, who's open at this hour on this side of town?"

"No one nearby." Daniels winked. "I know a place on the south side." He looked up at Benton and Velma. "I woke up when you left this morning, Bob, and I decided to follow you. I saw these good people working up an appetite and figured I could do my part." A grin brightened the ex-policeman's face. "I practically…flew to get these here."

With a grin and a shake of his head, Benton said, "Thank you, Garret."

"I've got a place cleared off for you." Tim indicated a clean patch of sales counter near Benton's office. "Let's dig in."

Benton smiled as Velma went back to her labors. He could only watch with awe as his friends came together for him and his heart swelled with love. Despite the odds against him, both as a healer and as a vigilante, Dr. Bob Benton looked forward to bringing comfort to the afflicted, while the Terror happily anticipated the misery he intended to bring to the appropriate parties.

However, any tactical plans vanished as Benton's stomach rumbled audibly. Daniels called out, "Hey, Bob. I can hear your belly all the way over here."

Surrounded by friendly laughter, Bob Benton allowed himself to become vulnerable to the sirens' lure of warm muffins and coffee. As he took a sip of the strongest coffee he ever enjoyed, he reminded himself, *This is why I will do what I do until the Terror is no longer needed.*

* * * * *

"Okay, I might have overreacted," Garret Daniels confessed to the person on the other end of the telephone line later that morning. "Call it my usual Irish nature." He focused his enhanced hearing in all directions, hoping not to hear Benton's footsteps approaching the apartment. With any luck the pharmacist would still be straightening up his shelves or spending a quiet morning with the Rowlands.

"Sometimes, you need to get these feelings out of your system," the voice stated with a surprising amount of sympathy. "Water under the bridge, I assure you." After a pregnant pause, the voice continued, "Let's keep our mutual pathways as dry as can be, shall we?"

"I will do my best." *But I promise nothing,* Daniels thought, *until I can bring you and your organization down. Maybe then I'll be out from under your thumb.* "Any further instructions?"

"No. I'll let you know. Enjoy your day." Then the line went dead in Daniels' hand.

* * * * *

Across town in his study, several minutes later, Ben Pickern watched his housekeeper pour his fourth cup of coffee. Pickern nodded his gratitude as best he could while he pinned the telephone receiver between his chin and shoulder.

"Yes, sir." Pickern no longer attempted to conceal his impatience to be off the phone. "My contacts in the Coroner's Office called me and Sylvia Devereaux's dossiers are now in my possession. Again." He took a quick sip of his dark, heated brew as the housekeeper left the room. "One of my cops found that bitch's roadster and brought her belongings to me. I'll drop them off at your place later today."

"Good." Pickern heard a gentle sip on the other end of the line. No doubt, the other man started his day with some fresh joe also. "I understand there's some collateral damage downtown and on the west side. I don't think anyone needs to hear much about that, do you?"

"Agreed. I own a substantial piece of the newspaper and the radio stations in a twenty-five-mile radius of Raceway City. If anyone wants to talk about the attack on the mayor's mansion, all they'll know is a gas line ruptured upstairs and no one was injured."

Pickern pulled the collar of his bathrobe closed. "As for the west side, no one cares what happens there unless they live there, believe me. But I'll keep an eye on them. I've got the mayor by the purse strings, and he owns the rest of the city movers and shakers. Between the two of us, there's nothing to worry about, sir."

Tiring of the conversation, Pickern pulled a silver flask from his bathrobe pocket. As the man on the other end of the line continued to share his suggestions for moving forward, the mobster unscrewed the cap and poured a measure of Irish whiskey into his coffee. Pickern swirled the cup until the man stopped talking.

Following a deep swallow from the China cup, Pickern said, "I think you'll be glad I'm in Raceway City. I promise not to let you down. Give my best to the President and Eleanor, if you would." Pickern's smile turned into a full grin. "Goodbye, Colonel."

* * * * *

Dr. Elmer Bancroft didn't get along with very many people. In his fifties and still unmarried, Bancroft contented himself with working alone in the City Morgue and listening to the radio in his solitary evenings.

Bancroft wanted to pursue his interest in anatomy in college, how the amazing machine known as the human body worked. His single mother raised him to enjoy his own company and he found even as an adult, he preferred solitude over the inevitable, distasteful interactions with other people. He could stand them long enough to conduct business, but down here, Bancroft found the chill of the autopsy room comforting when filled with classical music and freshly brewed Earl Gray.

As Dr. Bancroft's tea seeped beside the telephone, he wheeled the equipment cart to its place alongside the surgical table. The weekend attendant did his usual careful job of preparing the body for its autopsy, including the deceased's name and vitals written neatly on the report that rested beside the victim's head. Bancroft pulled down the bloodied cover that lay over the young woman's body to expose her head and torso. He decided to forego the radio for now and carefully turned on the wire recorder, ready to speak into the microphone overhead.

"The subject is female, probably early thirties, approximately 5 foot, seven inches, black hair." He paused to survey Sylvia Devereaux's nude body. "Quite attractive. Beginning the initial incision at the axilla." Bancroft preferred the scientific name for the body part over its more common name, "armpit."

Bancroft rested the scalpel against Sylvia Devereaux's stiff, icy flesh before sliding the blade through her skin and downward towards her sternum. He learned in medical school not to press down on the blade but allow its sharpness to do all the work. The scalpel buried itself in the woman's flesh, but no blood emerged from the wound.

As Bancroft opened his mouth to relate his initial findings, Sylvia reached up and gripped the doctor's throat with the speed of a cobra.

The scalpel struck the floor, clattering as it rolled under the table. Bancroft tried to draw in a breath, to scream for help. His final thought, before passing out, was to wish he had a friend to help him right now.

Sylvia released the coroner's throat and smiled as she watched his limp body drop to the floor. She chuckled as his chest rose and fell while the bruises around his throat immediately turned dark. She listened intently to verify no one would come to investigate the clatter before kneeling to strip Bancroft's outer garments.

As she slid into the medical examiner's clothing, Sylvia saw her flesh knit rapidly. If she was surprised, it didn't show on her face. By the time she stepped into the man's too-large shoes, Sylvia was completely healed of the coroner's damage to her body.

Minutes later, Sylvia stepped outside the morgue unsteadily. She wrapped Bancroft's lab coat around her much smaller body as a defense against the cold she could no longer feel. She stumbled to the only vehicle in the parking lot, a used black Marmon 16, and less than a minute later, the automobile screeched onto the street.

The assassin muttered to herself in a vocabulary that only her damaged brain could decipher. She gritted her teeth as she attempted to recall how to pilot the vehicle within the confines of her lane. Something deep in her damaged psyche told her to not draw attention to herself and chastised herself for leaving the coroner alive.

But she knew she needed to hide, to gather her resources and heal as she muttered again and again with growing hatred, "Tuh-rurr...tehrr...terruh...terror...terror..."

THE END

THANK YOU
FOR READING THIS BOOK!

We at Rising Tide Publications sincerely hope you enjoyed this book. Everyone involved in the production of this edition is proud of our work, and we put a lot of that into what you now hold in your hands.

It's our sincerest hope that you'll enjoy reading this story again and again. We also hope you'll mention your enjoyment of the book on social media and share it with your friends.

And if you like what you just read, Brian K. Morris has writing in many anthologies, as well as novels and non-fiction books. We hope you'll check out his other works, available where you purchased this.

Also, we have a major favor to ask…

Reviews help our work gain attention from the buying public and on social media. It's also the toughest thing for us to get from our readers.

If you would take just a couple of minutes, please go to Amazon.com, Goodreads, or whatever platform from which you purchased this book. Then please leave us an **honest review**.

That review doesn't have to be detailed. Just that you read the book, what you did or didn't enjoy about it, and whether you'd recommend the book to others. Simple, huh?

And it helps us so much.

Sincerest thanks from **Rising Tide Publications**

ABOUT THE AUTHOR

BRIAN K. MORRIS is a freelance hybrid author/editor, independent publisher, "award-winning" playwright, Facebook-famous YouTuber, and former mortician's assistant.

His work has appeared in publications from Stormgate Press, Stone Door Studios, Pro Se Press, Flinch Books, Crazy 8 Books, Becky Books, BEN Books, Hogan's Alley, TwoMorrows Publishing, GDC Publishing, BiMor Comics, and Lion's Share Press, as well as his own Rising Tide Publications and Freelance Words imprints.

The winner of the 2022 Pulp Factory Award for Best Short Story ("Snow Ambition," BEN Books), he also once received an award for not murdering a stage director with his bare hands.

In addition to being a prolific writer, Brian often broadcasts on YouTube and Tik Tok. He is also a frequent convention guest and lecturer on writing, publishing, and overall creativity.

An Illinois native, Brian lives in Central Indiana with his wife, Cookie, who is also a freelance editor and book designer, along with no children, no pets, and too many comic books.

For more information on what keeps Brian busy, but rarely out of trouble, please sign up for his free insider information email at www.RisingTide.pub and check out his twice-weekly blog, "Every Blog Deserves a Name," exclusively for his Patreon subscribers at www.Patreon.com/briankmorris

ABOUT THE ILLUSTRATOR

JEFFREY RAY HAYES is a freelance illustrator and graphic designer living in the Austin metro area of Central Texas. He began his career doing pen and ink art and magazine layout work for Austin-based tabletop gaming companies. Jeff has also worked as a commercial artist and display designer for a Texas-based grocery company in the 1980s until he made a career change, serving for 30 years as a police officer until his retirement in 2019 at the rank of assistant police chief. During that time, he never stopped working as a freelance artist and formed Plasmafire Graphics, LLC.

Jeff has worked in the art department on several indie television / web-based productions and indie films in the United States and United Kingdom, creating promotional materials and key art for entertainment industry marketing. Today, his primary focus is on cover illustration and graphic design for small-press publishers, indie authors and game designers. Recent recognitions include the Spring 2022 RED (Reims Excellence Director) Movie Award for Best Film Poster (*Yorktown: A Time to Heal)* and the 2023 Pulp Factory Award for Best Pulp Cover (*Tim Bruckner's Major Marjorie*).

"I've had the pleasure to work with many talented authors, publishers, directors, and producers. I value my working relationships and the many collaborative opportunities. I enjoy trying to interpret the characters, locations, plots, and ideas that producers, directors, and writers have etched in their mind's eye. I love the collaborative process and watching their faces light up when I have successfully captured that image in an illustration. I find just as much enjoyment when fans of a particular book, television or film get excited about seeing their heroes, or villains in some cases, come to life visually." – Jeff Hayes

Website – www.plasmafiregraphics.com
Facebook – www.facebook.com/plasmafiregraphics
E-mail – jeffrey.hayes@plasmafiregraphics.com

Thanks to our PATREON patrons!

Patreon is a subscription service where you can support your favorite creators directly with an affordable monthly stipend.

As one of Brian's patrons, you can read his irreverent and informative twice-weekly blog, "*Every Blog Deserves a Name*" and know that you are directly supporting the work of The Rising Tide. You may also find your name in a future publication, just like the fine folks below.

These amazing patrons helped make this book possible:

Keisha Acuff	**Jeffrey Hayes**
Kellie Austin	**Wanda Helm**
Trish Bengston	**Molly Helpingstine**
Rick Bradley	**Cindy Koepp**
Morgan Straughan Comnick	**Grant Lankard**
Dan Dougherty	**Ken Leinarr**
Angi Dudas	**John B. Pyka**
Teresa Dunn	**Brian Rodman**
Amy Hale	**Damion R. Waldbrunn**
Clyde Hall	**Rick Welchans**
Eric S. Hawkins	And **Renmeleon**

Hall of Fame: **Brian Hawkins**

For more information, go to **www.Patreon.com/briankmorris**